What the critics are saying...

"*Bloodstone* is absolutely riveting! Ms. Vremont's story has all the elements of a wonderful story: mystery, magic, suspense, hot sex, love and an amazing plot. I could not put this book down! ... Pick this one up if you enjoy a well-written and extremely hot read." ~ *Jacque, Fallen Angel Reviews (November 2004)*

"Ann Vremont creates a world of dark magic and evil sorcerers, who would change the world, as we know it. This is a story about the power of love and its never-ending battle over evil. I became totally immersed in the pages of this book. Ann Vremont is an author to watch for and I'll be looking for more of her books in the future. I recommend this book highly to those with a love for romance with a slightly dark side." ~ *Diane Tugman, The Romance Studio (September 2004)*

"*Calabi Chronicles: Bloodstone* is a paranormal novel that will keep you guessing to find out what will happen next. ... The love scenes in this story are sizzling, spicy, and passionately HOT! All in all, I found *Calabi Chronicles: Bloodstone* to be an amazing story ....." ~ *Susan Holly, Just Erotic Romance Reviews (September 2004)*

"The *Calabi Chronicles: Bloodstone* was erotically delicious. Ms. Vremont was able to weave a tale that ensnared this reader from beginning to end. ...This is a fantastic read for those who enjoy romance with paranormal elements." ~ *Dianne Nogueras, eCataRomance (October 2004)*

Bloodstone
Calabi Chronicles

Ann Vremont

CALABI CHRONICLES: BLOODSTONE
An Ellora's Cave Publication, April 2005

Ellora's Cave Publishing, Inc.
1337 Commerce Drive, Suite #13
Stow, Ohio 44224

ISBN #1419951823

CALABI CHRONICLES: BLOODSTONE
Copyright © 2004 Ann Vremont
Other available formats: ISBN MS Reader (LIT), Adobe (PDF),
Rocketbook (RB), Mobipocket (PRC) & HTML

Edited by: *Mary Moran*
Cover art by: *Syneca*

Warning:

The following material contains graphic sexual content meant for mature readers. *Calabi Chronicles: Bloodstone* has been rated *E-rotic* by a minimum of three independent reviewers.

Ellora's Cave Publishing offers three levels of Romantica™ reading entertainment: S (S-ensuous), E (E-rotic), and X (X-treme).

S-*ensuous* love scenes are explicit and leave nothing to the imagination.

E-*rotic* love scenes are explicit, leave nothing to the imagination, and are high in volume per the overall word count. In addition, some E-rated titles might contain fantasy material that some readers find objectionable, such as bondage, submission, same sex encounters, forced seductions, etc. E-rated titles are the most graphic titles we carry; it is common, for instance, for an author to use words such as "fucking", "cock", "pussy", etc., within their work of literature.

X-*treme* titles differ from E-rated titles only in plot premise and storyline execution. Unlike E-rated titles, stories designated with the letter X tend to contain controversial subject matter not for the faint of heart.

Also by Ann Vremont:

Adonis 5000

Bloodstone
Calabi Chronicles

Author's Note

Ceremonial invocations in "Book 3: New Blood" were inspired by the "Song of Amergin" as translated by Robert Graves in his classic study of the divine feminine "The White Goddess: a historical grammar of poetic myth" (Faber & Faber, London (1948)).

Dedication

I have said elsewhere that I tried to write Cenn and Kean as men I could lose heart and soul to but that can never really be. Two thieves laid claim long ago and this book is dedicated to them — Terry and Jared, husband and son.

With thanks to…

Mary and Sue-Ellen for the extra depth they demanded; Chere for her time spent on earlier versions; Syneca for the gorgeous cover; and to the readers who are as touched by Aideen's story as I am.

Prologue

Danu was falling through space and time, racing light and winning. The Calabi, the invisible center of being, was before her, yawning wide, ready to swallow her whole. Her flesh began to tingle and then burn. The heat stripped her of all corporeality, leaving only the white brilliance of her soul. Myr hurtled behind her, picking up speed. The unnecessary layers of his humanity were more easily peeled away as the swirling red center beneath welcomed him home.

Joy convulsed through Danu and she straightened her spirit like a diver on a high cliff. She felt the heated mass parting, accepting her, transforming her in its search for balance. And then the shrieking began. She tried to stop her ears against the ethereal wailing, but she had no hands or ears anymore. Plugging her ears would have been useless, anyway. The shrieking was a part of her now.

Myr was there, his essence swimming around and through hers, comforting her in this new environment suddenly grown hostile. *Imbalance*, the voices cried. *A soul too pure, a love divine.* Something had to be pushed out or the center would not hold. Myr's swimming turned to a spiral, the spiral to a whirlpool. Down the funnel, molten creation poured, distilled to a single fat drop a kilometer wide and a hair's width in depth. As it fell, it folded itself once, twice, a hundred times more. Myr sped after it, his supernatural vision scanning the dimensions, searching for a soul to catch the drop. *There!* He saw the woman sitting in the crowded room, humming to herself in irritation. An angry buzz, yes, but the voice was pure, as was its owner's soul. Her attention was fastened on a crate. Her will was set—she would make the crate hers. Without a body to breathe, he blew on the still falling drop. It cooled to a hard, brilliant red. He plucked the woman from where she sat, holding her no more than a heartbeat while he placed the stone in her hands.

Then, as if she were a toy that had fallen into disfavor, he tore the woman in half, flinging the empty-handed portion back down to the crowded room, leaving her less than herself. The other half he let drop, down through the dimensions. A portal opened at the broken doll's feet. As the last of her disappeared, Myr erased the opening and drew a circle of fire in the air.

So it begins...

Book 1: The Book of Cenn

Chapter One

Aideen swore lightly under her breath as she hefted the wooden auction crate from the back of her truck and onto a small hand truck. Some idiot had parked a rental car in the space behind her shop, forcing her to park at the end of the alley. Worse yet, her half-ass assistant, Ricky, wasn't answering the shop's phone, leaving her with the sticky choice of leaving the crate unattended a few feet from a busy Dublin street or lifting it onto the hand truck herself.

Oomph! God was it heavy. Her knees popped as she bent down and placed the crate on the steel lip of the dolly, the swift downward motion pushing air between the wooden slats and treating Aideen to the smell of old packing straw and even older leather.

Books. A small thrill traveled up her spine and reached around to caress her nipples. *Old books.*

The books had better be very old indeed, she told herself as she pushed the hand truck up the alley. The crate, its contents unknown, had set her back several thousand at the auction. But Aideen had arrived late, thanks to Ricky and a convoy of Sunday drivers, and all the other items being sold off from Michael Meyrick's estate were gone.

Meyrick... A second tingle covered her, pricking her flesh and raising the soft blonde hair on her arms. The faux Wiccans that wound their way into her shop would drool over anything associated with the man and provide her a tidy return on today's investment. While alive, rumors had clung to the name Michael Meyrick. He was, according to some, an Arch-druid. Most any consumer of the weekly tabloids considered him a psychic extraordinaire who had scried his way to the remains of a millionaire's missing son and, eventually, the murderer. He was, Aideen acknowledged, a first-rate collector of the arcane.

Which is why, she thought as she unlocked the back door to her shop, *I'm going to kick that little rat bastard in the balls for making me late!*

Ricky heard the jingle of bells as Aideen entered and poked his head around the door to the storeroom. "Hey, back already?" He grinned at Aideen, the movement breaking the harsh point of his goateed chin. Like the mass of hair that hung to his shoulders, the sliver of beard was curly and dyed a perfect Goth black. He tucked a lock of hair behind his ear to reveal a silver earring.

"That's new?" Aideen's voice lost its usual melody and took on the tone of an inquisitor. *If that little punk left the shop...*

"Christ, Aideen," Ricky complained. "How about telling me it looks good, or something?"

He flashed her one of his trademarked wicked grins and started to step into the storeroom but she held one hand up. Those pale blue eyes and tinted lips might play well with the girls at the pubs and some of the less artful customers who ventured into her shop, but Aideen was immune. "I've told you a dozen times not to leave the store. I wasn't even gone for three hours!"

Another wave of irritation flooded her as she thought of the frantic race to Meyrick's spooky little manor in Drogheda after she had been forced to cover a private viewing for clients that Ricky had agreed to show. He had sauntered in an hour late, interrupting her sales pitch and then acting the expert on a Dalyell text. Apparently, as the dangly bit of silver attested, he had already spent the commission that he anticipated Aideen would pay him. *He'll be lucky if he doesn't leave here with a slip for the job commission.*

"Don't sweat it, boss." A silvery set of chimes announced a customer at the front door and Ricky half-turned from Aideen to nod at the newcomer. "Brenna did it in the store while you were gone."

"This isn't a beauty salon," Aideen said and grabbed a crowbar from her workbench.

"It was dead quiet—like it always is." Ricky offered the excuse as he impatiently nodded a second time at the customer before letting the door swing shut behind him and returning to the storefront.

Aideen glanced at the clock radio on the workbench. It was almost closing time. In half an hour, she could say good-bye to Ricky for the evening. *Or forever*, she thought and slapped the top of the little clock radio, music pouring from it at her touch.

As she worked the last nail from the crate's top, Aideen racked her brain to remember why she had hired the little shit in the first place. The effort evoked a memory of his tight ass in equally tight black jeans and a warm flush heated her thighs, reminding her that she had not been entirely immune in the beginning. Undersexed for far too long, she had immediately dumped the résumé of an Irish history major into the trash when Ricky had turned in his application.

Pushing back the first layer of packing straw, Aideen banished the image from her mind and pulled out a large lump of moth-eaten black velvet. The heaviness of the cloth washed away the small wave of disappointment that had threatened and replaced it with curiosity. Something was wrapped inside, its weight promising some small icon or stone. Slowly, she pulled back the moldy layers of velvet to uncover a dark red stone slightly smaller than her fist but as heavy as if it were lead. She held the stone up to the storeroom's light to reveal a small glimmer of transparency. The stone was smooth but misshapen and, as her fingers enveloped it, she found it perfectly fit her closed hand.

"All locked up," Ricky said as he swaggered into the storeroom and slid one leg over the stool next to her. Her fingers curled more tightly around the stone and she brought it to her chest. "Now, about that sale this morning..." he started.

"You mean this afternoon," she snapped the words at him, her chin in an angled downward tilt so that she could still glare at him while she pushed through the second layer of straw, the hand holding the stone still clutched to her breast. "And if you're thinking about asking me for a commission, you'd better bite your tongue!"

He stuck his tongue out at her, a small silver rod bouncing along its tip. "I'd rather have you bite it," he purred as he tried to run a hand along her sleeve.

"There'll be none of that," Aideen reminded him. "And no commission, either."

Ricky's lips pushed forward in a pout and he pulled at some of the packing straw that Aideen had exposed. "Well, can I at least look through this with you?"

"It isn't Christmas and I'm not Santa," she answered, her body stiffening as he reached for her closed hand.

"What's that?"

"Just go on with you," she said, pushing him toward the door. Aideen had never had the slightest hint that Ricky stole from her, but the idea of showing the stone to him panicked her.

His pout grew fuller but he allowed her to lead him to the door. "Maybe Tuesday?" he asked hopefully.

"Maybe," she offered, knowing already that she would never let him see the stone.

"Or later tonight?" The occasional hunger that lit Ricky's eyes when he looked at her was shining bright.

"Come back tonight and I promise that I'll fire you," Aideen said and pushed him out the door. In one quick sweep, she rotated the two locks and threaded the safety chain on the door before crossing the storeroom and double-checking that he had properly locked the front door.

Still holding the stone in one hand, she opened the register's cash drawer, saw how little was there, and decided it wasn't worth putting her small treasure down to record the cash and checks. She would perform that task before the store opened Tuesday. Back in the storeroom, she held the stone to the light again before removing the last of the straw from the crate.

A small wrinkle of disappointment furrowed her brow. At the bottom, in a large flat square, was a single mass of bundled black velvet. The smell of leather and aged paper still greeted her, but not in the quantity she had expected as she had hauled the heavy crate, first onto her truck and then into her shop. *Still*, she thought, the stone growing warm in her hand, *it's not a total loss.*

Snapping a latex glove on one hand, Aideen leaned into the crate to remove the promised book. In a slow tease, she stripped the rotting fabric from the book, small sections of the leather covering revealed with each bit of cloth she peeled away. At last, the cover of the book lay naked before her, black marks burned into the deep red leather. Her eyes, long familiar with the old glyphs, touched the embedded images in a slow caress as her mind raced ahead to reach a translation. *The Book of Cenn Cruach.*

Crom, she thought, pulling the god's name from her memory. A sense of foreboding pricked her scalp as she opened the book to the first page — she had either purchased a very good forgery or a priceless manuscript. A sheaf of paper, of modern commercial quality and folded several times over, slipped from the book and onto the surface of the workbench. Placing the stone on the tabletop, Aideen unfolded the piece of paper. Jumbled sentences mixed with snippets of clarity were scrawled in the folded sections. Diagrams with descriptions of chemical compounds crowded the edges.

Putting the paper to one side, Aideen grabbed a black smock from a peg by the door and returned to the book, her ungloved hand absently picking the stone back up. Delicately thumbing the first page over, she began reading the second page. Expecting the book itself to be written in Latin and to begin with the long, sonorous invocation common to the priestly texts that served as the primary records of early Irish history, Aideen was surprised to see the glyphs that covered the front continue on, page after page. She let out a deep breath and turned back to the first page of text before fumbling around for a notepad and pen. It was, she told herself as she scribbled the translation to the first line of the second page, going to be a long night.

Chapter Two

"Tonight I invoked the Bloodstone. Called to it. Demanded that it recognize me as its master and reveal its location. But another holds sway over its power. I have seen her, a sorceress, robed in black, waves of sunlight rippling over her shoulders and back. Moss green eyes she turns on me as she looks up from her magic tomes, one hand holding the sacred stone."

Aideen's hand began to shake as she finished translating the paragraph. She was some twenty pages into the book, the first sections carefully annotated by a long dead hand with spells and ingredients. She was sure, by now, that the writer truly was long dead. The syntax of an ancient people filled the pages, the flow of the words too beautiful, the knowledge displayed too perfect, for even the most uncommon forger. Glancing up at the sheet of paper, she nodded once. Meyrick, too, had been convinced of the book's authenticity. His excited, if sometimes inaccurate, translations served as a testimony to his belief that he had made a great discovery.

And now, the manuscript's first mention of the Bloodstone. Aideen's gaze focused on Meyrick's sheet of notes. "The Bloodstone, sacred heart of Crom, granting power of life and death, of victory over time, to he who wields it."

Her fingers, half numb from the death grip with which she held the stone, twitched slightly as she read Meyrick's words again. Was this the stone? Did he really think in the days leading up to his death—for the notes were dated—that he had, at last, both the stone and the book that would reveal its secrets?

Aideen returned to translating the text. The ancient writer repeated his attempts to locate the Bloodstone, the duration and danger of his rituals increasing. On the night of the full moon, he went so far as to reveal his true name, Cenn Cruach, in the invocation ceremony. Aideen raised a brow in academic appreciation of the elaborate ritual he described and at the power required to both reveal and conceal one's true name.

Aideen glanced at the clock radio; it was near midnight. She flipped to the next page, her vision blurring as she began to write.

"Again, the Bloodstone mocks my call but I understand the nature of my error. It is she who must be made to answer my call, to feel the force of my powers. I will rest until the new moon, preparing to call this witch to me, to place her and the stone at my command."

"Rest." The word was like a warm salve to Aideen's cramped hands and complaining shoulders. She blinked, her dry, scratchy eyes filled with tears and she put the pen down to rub them. Tomorrow was Monday, the store's regular non-business day. She could afford a few hours of sleep and still have the book's contents translated before the store opened for business on Tuesday. *Hell*, she thought, sliding the stool back from the table, *I can have it translated and have excerpts posted on the website as teasers before the store opens.*

A greedy thrill ran through Aideen as she carefully wrapped clean muslin around the book. With the book safely covered, she removed the latex glove and pulled a torn vinyl couch from the storeroom's only unshelved wall. A rich pattern of wood paneling lay against the wall, the individual pieces running in seemingly haphazard geometric designs. Her fingers expertly slid along the deep grooves of one panel piece until she heard the soft click of a spring lock. Aideen removed the panel to expose a cylindrical wall safe approximately a half meter in diameter. She had a floor safe, as well, but it primarily served as a decoy, holding only a few thousand in currency and medium-range trinkets.

Packing the safe's contents to one side, Aideen put the book inside. Sliding the panel back on and repositioning the couch, she pulled two ragged blankets from a storeroom shelf. She placed one over the couch's shredded vinyl surface and folded the other into a pillow. Then she lay down, pulling the edges of the first blanket over her and drifting into sleep, the stone centered against her chest.

Even as she slept, the stone and the words that Cenn Cruach had written over a millennium ago crowded Aideen's thoughts. She had the sense of watching over him as he performed a scrying ritual, his head, crowned in a mass of blue-black curls, bowed as he stared intently into a shallow silver bowl filled with inky black water.

The same dark hair shadowed his cheeks and chin. Just below, at his neck, his robes parted in a deep V to reveal a chest that was hairless and intricately tattooed. She tried to pick out the symbols that covered him, but in the low light of her sleep, the patterns ran together and traveled inexorably down the smooth skin until her attention reached his navel. From there, a thin line of blue-black hair disappeared into the thick robes.

Aideen moaned lightly in her sleep and he raised his head, granite blue eyes flecked with black staring up at where she hovered in her dream. His eyes widened in recognition and his lips, flushed a deep red, opened to form a single word translated across time. *You.*

Aideen woke with a start, the beat of her heart traveling through the stone to pound against her palm. The pressure in her chest grew and she realized that she was holding her breath. Letting it out, she drew deep calming breaths and relaxed her hand. When she was sure that she could stand, she got up and pulled the couch from the wall, once again releasing the hidden panel and pulling the book from the safe. Heart still pounding, she sat down at the workbench and continued her translation.

"The ritual is complete and all I have for my efforts is a tantalizing glimpse of the witch. Soft petal pink lips in a delicious part, the verdant eyes half-concealed behind lids heavy with sensual delight. Even now, I feel myself growing stiff as I think of her and the sweet torment that I would visit upon her for denying me what is mine."

Aideen closed her eyes, the image of his intense blue stare causing the pressure that had remained lodged in her chest to reach down and squeeze at her thighs. She could feel his mouth pressing against her breasts as it formed the accusatory word of recognition. Her nipples grew hard and she ran a distracted hand over them to brush the sensation away. She thought of a second book concealed in the wall safe. Pocket-sized and covered in a cheap black vinyl, the pages filled with her father's minute handwriting.

No. Aideen shook her head as if the violence of the motion could cast away what she was considering. Memories of childhood participation in her father's ceremonies surfaced. His zealous devotion to the Ancient Rede, the hours spent in meditation to the goddess. The unyielding requests for blood and his cold indifference to her after she had relinquished her sacred virginity to the neighborhood rebel at the age of seventeen.

She had performed her first scrying ceremony at the age of five, her mother already a year in the grave. Her father, Gerald, had woken her from a deep slumber and half-led, half-dragged her to his study. There, where only candlelight — shadows dancing — illuminated the room, he had explained to her the preparations that preceded his waking her. As sleep sought to claim Aideen, her child's head drooping with fatigue, he had roughly tapped the underside of her chin. Then he made her stand in front of a scrying bowl and poked, prodded and cajoled her until she sang the odd rhymes her mother had taught her. With Aideen's song complete, he had been rewarded, she tortured, with nightmare images that played along the water's surface.

Aideen blinked that long ago night and its illusions away. Her mind, once again filled with Cenn, his exposed chest and stomach rippled with muscles, and the thin ladder of black hair that promised a tangled garden of delight. Unaware of her movements, Aideen walked over to the wall safe and pulled out the little black book. She flipped through it until she found a description of a scrying ceremony. She glanced at the small calendar on the wall behind the clock radio and frowned to see that the moon was not in its most favorable phase. Her father, meticulous in all things, would have waited, his curiosity — and the image of Cenn — postponed until the most opportune time.

There is a rare power in you, Aideen, and you have squandered it on that boy. Gerald's admonishments filled her head. She pushed them aside and grabbed a flashlight. In the showroom, she went to the display of dried herbs from which she pulled small bags of rose, hyssop, jasmine and sea salt. She tossed the little bags into a silver bowl she had grabbed from the locked display case next to the register and returned to the storeroom, hoping none of the garda on patrol had noticed her flashlight bouncing around the store.

Her father's book called for a weeklong fermentation of the ingredients. His obsessive precision irritated Aideen and she merrily dumped the ingredients into the bowl and mixed them together with the plastic spoon she had pulled from Ricky's coffee cup. Rummaging through Ricky's locker, she found the incense he burned, ostensibly for "mood", but really to hide the smell of the pot he smoked when she was away from the store.

Aideen lit the incense and several of the candles kept in the storeroom for those days when Dublin's spring storms knocked the power out. With the other lights off, she slipped the smock off and began to undress, the damp spot between her legs growing wetter as her bra came off and the cold air licked at her nipples.

She held the Bloodstone in her left hand while she coaxed the smoke from the incense to pool over the bowl. The words she had chanted as a five-year-old child returned to her and spilled forth with the melody of her matured voice.

Over hyssop, rose and jasmine,
Over the very sea, I scry.
Reveal to me, eternal eye,
The truth I seek but do not ken.

Slowly the smoke swirled into a vision of the man in her dreams. His robes were gone as he stood before the same scrying bowl that she had seen before. The tattoos that adorned his chest crawled along his back. That broad expanse was filled with the endless weaving of roots from the Tree of Life, blue vines unfurling over his thickly muscled thighs. For a second time that night, a mesmerized moan escaped Aideen's mouth as she saw Cenn's cock, stiff and straight, rising from the black mass of curls. She willed him to raise his head from the bowl. *Look at me, Cenn Cruach, I command you.*

Aideen gasped when he heard and obeyed, the blue eyes piercing her as he issued his own command. *Come to me, witch. It is I who commands you.*

Aideen collapsed against the stool, the sudden movement of her body dispelling the eddy of smoke that lay atop the bowl. With unsteady hands, she reached down and pulled the smock from the floor. She put it on and fumbled with the tie as the thickness of the air around her threatened to send her crashing to the floor.

She pinched out the candles and incense and put them on the floor, along with the bowl. The Bloodstone still in her hand, she turned the lights back on and returned to the book.

"Exhausted, I swore I would not seek the sorceress again until I had further rested, but her body calls to me. And so I dared to summon her again tonight. Ah, sweet temptation. She drives all thought of the Bloodstone from my mind although she holds it to her as she dares to command me. She stood before a silver bowl, smoke dancing against her pale white skin. Pink nipples erect and begging to be suckled. A golden triangle pointing down to paradise. My tongue grows thick at the thought of tasting the sweet nectar that flows from between her legs. I swear I will have her and the stone."

A swoon threatened Aideen and she took a step back from the book. With the book in hand, she moved to the couch and tentatively turned the page.

Nothing! She flipped the remaining pages, each one revealing aged white vellum devoid of content. In desperation, she tossed the book onto the couch and grabbed Meyrick's notes from the workbench. She folded and unfolded the scrap of paper as she read Meyrick's insane babbling. In slow motion, she felt her body slide to the floor, the Bloodstone still clutched to her chest. *This cannot be the end!* her mind screamed as she passed into darkness.

Chapter Three

Aideen woke halfway through Monday. The clock and her stomach told her it was late afternoon. Asleep on the floor through the remainder of the night, she had never released the stone. But the constant contact with the Bloodstone had rewarded her with its eternal secrets, shown her the key to obtaining her deepest desire.

Rising from the linoleum, she walked to the couch on stiff legs. She picked the book up and placed it in the wall safe, reluctantly setting the stone beside it for safekeeping. After she re-secured the panel and pushed the couch back in place, she went into the shop's small bathroom and relieved the pressure that had built in her bladder as she slept on the cold floor. Finished, she splashed water on her face and patted it dry with paper towels. In the storeroom, she retrieved her clothing from the floor and dressed before leaving the store to grab a bite to eat and pick up a few supplies that she would need for the night ahead.

When Aideen returned to the store, she placed a shopping bag in the bathroom and plopped a second one on the workbench before setting an alarm and stretching out on the couch for a light nap. When the buzzer roused her at eight, she was dreaming of Cenn. She could still feel the rough caress of his hands on her breasts and the tickle of his coarse facial hair against her thighs. She cupped her breasts and gave them a gentle squeeze as the last of the delirious sensations he had aroused ebbed from her body.

The clock radio, still bleating at her, drove Aideen from the couch. She viciously switched the alarm off and grabbed the smock from its peg by the door. In the bathroom, she filled the sink with water and measured more dried herbs into it before she stripped. She dipped her long, blonde hair into the water and then whipped it back, rubbing the water that dripped from her head into her cheeks before grabbing another handful and cleaning her arms. She looked in the mirror, her gaze skipping a half-finished tattoo, and watched her nipples grow hard as she massaged the water onto her breasts in slow circles. Her hands traveled over her stomach, a smile curling her lips as she parted her labia and scooped another handful of water, stroking the smooth skin until it was squeaky clean and her clit was a rigid nub of live wires. With the same slow, sensual caress, she cleaned her legs and feet and then squeezed the last of the water from her hair. The floor was a jumble of wet clothes and puddled water and she shrugged at the mess. If she was still in the shop when the sun rose tomorrow, she would deal with it then.

Concealing her naked body with the smock, she crossed the showroom floor and disappeared into the storeroom. She refreshed the water in the scrying bowl and added new dried flowers and sea salt. She removed the smock and rubbed rose oil over her breasts and thighs. The clock radio flashed 9:30 at her and she hurried to the wall safe, emptying all its contents except for the stack of cash she kept for extra special purchases. She put the safe's contents on the workbench before she strapped on a stylish velvet hip pack that she had purchased earlier in the day. She had no way of knowing whether the pack would survive the trip, but she put Cenn's book and her father's inside. She spilled the contents of a cheap velveteen pouch into her palm, a glittering of ceremonial jewels peeked at her before she scooped them back into the pouch and then into the hip pack.

Remaining on the workbench were the Bloodstone and a *scian d'scairt*, a ceremonial dagger so named from its placement into the diaphragm of the person being sacrificed before the priest would slice an opening in the victim's gut to allow the entrails to be pulled from the body and read by the priest. With the scrying bowl in the center and surrounded by incense and candles, Aideen picked the Bloodstone up with her left hand and the *scian* with her right. With the flat of the knife, she shepherded the smoke over the bowl as her chant slowly built in volume.

Cenn's naked form smoothed across the water as he summoned her in return. A slow fire lit in her stomach. Its warmth slowly coiled between her legs as she watched Cenn masturbate above his scrying bowl, his seed spilling onto the surface and forming small pearls before sinking. Aideen brought her left hand, still gripping the Bloodstone, over her bowl and raised the *scian* to her arm. Beginning at one edge of her wrist, she sliced a thin gash to the other side, her blood dyeing the water a dark crimson.

She continued to chant, the gentle stream flowing from her wrist building to a flood of red that obliterated Cenn's image and threatened to overfill the bowl. Aideen stumbled over the words as the candles blew out and she was wrapped in darkness.

Chapter Four

"You have answered my call in the flesh, witch," Cenn said as he pulled Aideen into a kneeling position before him. His voice was filled with a warm pleasure that rippled through her and cleared the red haze that clouded Aideen's mind. "And brought the Bloodstone with you, I see."

Naked but for the hip pack, and shivering, she swayed into contact with him. Her forehead rested against the sharp angle of his hip, her blonde hair intertwined with his blue-black pubic hair. The blood on her wrist was congealing to a slow ooze and she struggled to lift her hand.

Running a hand through her hair, Cenn pulled her head back until her moss green eyes met the depthless blue of his gaze. Bending slightly, he brought her right arm up and pulled the *scian* from her hand, tossing it across the room.

"Who are you, sorceress?" Cenn demanded. His hand still forced her head back, her lips centimeters from his cock, which slowly bobbed to life. The tangy smell of the semen he had produced during the ritual bit into her taste buds and she groaned lightly.

"No sorceress am I," Aideen said, offering both the Bloodstone and her body to him.

Cenn's grip relaxed and he shifted hands, cupping her head close to him while his other hand curled around the stone. Aideen nestled her face against his stomach, his scent filling her lungs and forcing her eyes closed in sleepy satisfaction. Aroused, his cock grew rigid, its stiff mass pressing against her cheek.

Cenn tossed the Bloodstone onto a nearby pallet and gently tipped Aideen's head back. He ran a finger over her lips and her tongue darted out, gracing the tip with a slow lick before closing around it in a kiss. A shudder passed over his body and his cock pulsed forward in search of her seductive mouth.

"What are you then, if not a sorceress?" he asked, his words slurred as he gazed into her eyes.

"Yours," Aideen answered, her hand traveling up the inside of his leg to lightly stroke his thigh. "To do with as you will."

Cenn dropped down to both knees and pulled Aideen to him. Fear that he would send her away twisted through her stomach and she pressed a kiss against the hollow of his throat with trembling lips. Holding her left wrist up, Cenn squeezed until the blood flowed fresh. His own wrist bore a fresh cut and he pulled at the scab then joined their wrists, which he locked between their bodies. Aideen felt the sweet press of his cock against her mound and she parted her legs, throwing her head back as he slid into her.

"Open your eyes," Cenn commanded and she did. His gaze held hers as the long strokes of his cock pushed her mind over the edge of ecstasy. "On your word," he said, his breath torn from him in ragged gasps as he struggled to hold himself in. "Say that you are mine."

Aideen tried to peer past the deep blue of his eyes, past the hint of desperation and dark secrets that clouded his soul. Cenn's blood mingled with her own and she knew that, whatever there was to discover, she would stay with him, her body and soul at his command. "Yes," she moaned, pressing her mouth against his as her body jerked in wild release. "I am yours, forever."

Book 2: Sorcerer's Apprentice

Chapter One

Cenn looked at the sleeping form of the witch. Her long frame was stretched across his mattress, a heavy woolen blanket hiding the soft curves his hands had explored a few hours before. Her long blonde hair was partially fanned across her face and he gently pushed the hair back.

He glanced at her face to see if she was awake and was instantly lost in contemplation of her exquisite features. Taking in the heavy fringe of her eyelashes, the full, pink pout of her mouth, he felt his erection begin to return. By the gods, he wasn't sure what he had done to have this creature beside him, pledged to him for eternity, but he knew he would already do anything to keep her.

His fingertips outlined the perfect shell of her ear and caressed the curve of her neck before stopping at the incomplete image of a firedrake just below her collarbone. It was a powerful symbol, only half done and stretched as if she had been marked with it quite young. His confusion seemed to reach the witch in her sleep, her muscles tensing beneath his touch.

The woman stirred, turned until she was on her back. The movement pulled the blanket down far enough to expose one breast. The coarse rub of the wool over the sensitive nipple brought it to a hard, pink point. Cenn cupped the breast, pulled the nipple taut before covering it with his mouth. She moaned in her sleep and brought her hand up to caress his cheek. Her willingness to receive him even in sleep sent another arc of need through his body. Yet, his own instant readiness to possess the witch distressed him and he rose from the mattress.

Cenn's gaze caught the black velvet pouch she had worn slung around her hip and he let his hands play over it. The ends of the odd buckling material that she had called "plastic" had fused in her journey to him, as had the "zipper" made from the same material. He had cut the hip pack from her body before claiming her a second time, but its contents were still unknown. Curiosity pricked his mind as he wondered what other marvels the mistress of the sacred Bloodstone had brought with her.

Memories of the witch's more evident gifts urged him to return to her sleeping form and awaken her with the gentle teasing of his swollen tip against her silken pink clit. He tried to content himself with watching her, instead. She reached along the mattress, her mouth parting in a sultry sigh as she searched for his warmth. One of her shapely arms curled around his pillow and his chest tightened as he remembered the firm grip of her hand on his cock, the energetic pumping while she laved her tongue along the tip with her own sex pressed heatedly against his hungry mouth.

"Ah, witch," Cenn moaned and quietly returned to the bed. "How is it that you can cast spells even as you sleep?"

Crawling onto the mattress, Cenn rested his upper body between the small valley formed by her canted hip and outstretched leg. He eased the blanket over her hips and his gazed raked the exposed flesh. Her cunt was still flushed from their earlier passion, still glistened with his seed and her own wet nectar. Cenn thumbed the spongy exterior of her vagina, slipped the honey-slick pad over her rosy nub. Again, she moaned in her sleep and lifted her ass to meet his probing tongue. He massaged her clit, rolled it between thumb and forefinger as her body fully awakened to his touch.

She reached down, stroked the dark crown of hair and absently murmured his name. "Cenn."

"Crom." His voice was rough when he corrected her and his hands stopped the delicious rub against her labial lips.

"Crom," she agreed, breathless in her desire for him to continue his caresses. She could see caution darkening his gaze and she turned on the mattress until they were face to face. Her lips whispered a kiss across his mouth as she voiced her apology.

"Perhaps you should tell me, witch, what you are called and how you came to know my true name."

"I am Aideen," she answered too quickly. Fear pricked along her skin at the mention of her name. She tried to shake the feeling, told herself it was silly to think someone could hold power over a person through a name. Still something coiled around her, wrapped her in a cold embrace. Cenn's eyes casually flicked over her and the sensation disappeared as immediately as it had arisen.

"And how is that you know my name?" His voice bordered on disinterest but Aideen saw the slow, rhythmic tensing at the corner of his jaw.

Her hand moved to her hip until she remembered how he had cut the hip bag from her body. An erotic thrill passed over her at the memory of the heated look his eyes had held as he slowly pulled the blade against the bag's belt. The motion was joined by his cock, swollen with his desire, sliding into her. Thrusting until he was fully embedded in her clenching cunt, Cenn cut the last of the belt with a rough flick of his wrist. Visions of the night just shared brought a flush to Aideen's breasts, hardened her nipples to sharp points that ached for his mouth. But although his gaze caressed her body, his hands remained at his sides.

"My name?" he inquired again. Menace tinged his words and Aideen's breathing hitched uncertainly as she scanned the room for her pouch. When Aideen's gaze fell on the velvet hip pack, Cenn bounded from the mattress. He scooped the pouch up, his hand reaching for the *scian* that rested on a table next to him. The finesse that had marked his earlier use of the dagger was gone as he inserted the blade and ripped through the fabric.

The contents spilled onto the table and his hand immediately wrapped around the age-worn diary. His dark gaze jumped from the book to Aideen. He flipped through the pages, looked at the characters drawn by his own hand. He crossed the room to stand in front of her. He was still naked, but the erection was gone. The observation produced a wistful hunger in Aideen and she reached out to stroke his thigh. She saw the slightest contraction of the muscle along his perineum. Otherwise, she might as well have been stroking steel, he held himself so tightly in defiance of the pleasure her touch offered him.

"Where did you get this?" he demanded.

"I bought it." The words came out in a stutter and she pulled back, only to have him grab her upper arm and force her forward.

"What thief—what spy sold this to you!" He tightened his grip on Aideen's arm. Her small squeak of alarm shamed both of them and he released her, stepped back from the bed and demanded again. "From whom did you buy it, witch? Tell me."

"From a dead man!" Her voice grew strained as she answered him and the last restraints holding her temper in check began to snap.

The dark arch of his brow rose higher. "By your hand?"

Aideen searched his tone and stance for some suggestion that the question was meant to mock her. Cenn appeared serious, terribly so, and she stumbled over her response. "I cannot imagine killing someone for a book and an unknown stone."

At the mention of the Bloodstone, Cenn's gaze became hooded and darted to the heavy wooden chest in which he had locked the magical stone after their first round of lovemaking. "I can."

The words were cold enough to freeze Aideen's blood and she edged away from him until her back pressed against an icy stone wall. A greater chill spread across her body and she wrapped the blanket around her while she watched Cenn walk to the room's small fireplace. He pulled the screen from the hearth and began feeding the pages of his diary to the greedy flames. The crackle of the fire danced along with the sharp rip of the pages. Aideen pulled her knees to her chest and hugged her legs. When the leather covering touched the fire, she buried her nose beneath the blanket.

With the last of the diary reduced to smoke and ashes, Cenn returned to the table. The long, firm fingers that had teased her body to unimaginable heights quickly sorted through the rest of the hip pack's contents. Pouring the ceremonial stones onto the table, he cast her a guarded look but said nothing until he picked up the small vinyl-covered memo book that contained her father's spells and rituals.

"What is this?" he asked and held it forward for Aideen to see. "These scratches — do they have meaning?"

Aideen nodded and wrapped her arms more tightly around her legs. "Notes made by my father."

"On magic?" He eyed her again as if assessing anew the threat she presented to him.

"Yes."

"So, you are the daughter of a sorcerer, if not a sorceress, yourself," Cenn said and turned back to the table to sweep the gemstones into their cheap velveteen bag.

Aideen suppressed a laugh at the idea of anyone calling her father a sorcerer. She pictured Gerald as he had been before his death — dry as the herbs that hung in his garage. He was nothing like the smoldering, dark mage before her. Aideen's body shuddered with another chill and she wondered what Cenn had planned for her now that she had answered his summons and brought the Bloodstone with her. As if reading her thoughts, he spun around, his cock slowly bobbing to life as his long stride brought him back to the bed. His fingers curled protectively around the velveteen pouch and its semiprecious contents while he reached with his other hand to stroke her cheek.

"You are pledged to me, witch," he said, his voice low and smoky.

"Not if you continue calling me that," Aideen warned him. Her traitorous cheek flushed at the gentle caress of his finger along her jaw-line but she somehow managed to keep her voice level. "My name is Aideen."

"You cannot go by that name beyond these doors," Cenn advised her softly. He caught the withdrawal in her eyes and cupped the back of her head, tilting it until she was forced to look into his eyes. "You are light and delicate, Aideen...like a butterfly floating on a warm breeze. I will call you Etain."

Aideen nodded her consent. She closed her eyes against the desire to rest her face against his flat stomach, to breathe in the strong masculine scent that hid just beyond her senses.

Cenn had no desire to rest. He raised his hand, drew her attention to the small bag. "As you are pledged to me, Etain, I will provide for you." He gave the bag a small shake and she could hear the light clink of the faceted stones. "But these...these are no longer yours."

His voice caught on the announcement and he turned quickly from her. Speechless, Aideen watched him snatch up a lightweight pair of doeskin pants from the floor and step into them. The dark fabric instantly molded itself to his lean, muscular thighs. He topped the pants with an unbleached linen shirt and a coarse, half-length woolen cloak dyed a dark crimson before pulling on leather boots that rode high on his calves.

"Get some more sleep," Cenn advised her, his gaze taking in her pale features and the dark circles under her eyes. "I will return with food and clothing."

Her body still reeling from the light caress along her cheek and the gentle cupping of her head, Aideen watched him leave. Mourning filled her as the last of him vanished from her field of vision and the door swung closed.

The unmistakable slow turn of a key in the lock brought Aideen back to herself. With the blanket wrapped around her, she walked to the door and tried to pry it open with her fingers. She bent down and eyed the lock, expecting and finding it to be of the simplest construction. The keyhole was nearly two centimeters wide and she looked around the room for the *scian*. The slim-bladed dagger was on the table. Her gaze moved from the table to the bed, then down to her body that still was covered by no more than the blanket.

"Fuck it," she whispered and returned to the bed to unwillingly heed Cenn's advice.

Chapter Two

Cenn stood alongside the mattress where Aideen still slept. He carried with him a tray lightly loaded with meat, bread and cheese. He leaned to look at her and the plate slid forward on the tray until he had to catch the plate and its contents before they had a chance to spill on her. Despite his sharp intake of breath at the near accident, her body remained still and he wondered whether she feigned sleep.

Aideen. The word never left his lips but it was enough to make her open her eyes and look at him. A fragment of the dream he had shaken her from lingered in the air, teased its way up from the mattress to his cock. Cenn tightened his grip on the tray and forced himself to turn from her. Each footstep from the bed to the table measured an eternity. His arms ached from the light load and he dropped the tray onto the table with a small thud. He tried to calm his breathing, to count away his desire for her, but the rapid pumping of oxygen through his lungs, like the heavy throb of blood through his cock, was too much and he found himself turning back to her. *How am I to control the Bloodstone*, he asked himself, *if I cannot control my lust for its mistress?*

"Eat." Cenn spat the word out. His attention was not so focused on the soft rise of her breasts that he failed to notice the quick ignition of fury in her mossy green eyes or the angry twist that turned her soft mouth into a kissable challenge. *By the gods, even her anger undoes me.*

"I do not like being locked in a room," Aideen said. She had moved into an upright position and her shoulders were pressed against the cold stone of the wall. One hand lightly held the blanket across her breasts. Her gaze swept over his body, saw the solid outline of his erection against the doeskin pants. "Regardless of the jailor," she added, her tone softening at the edges.

"For your protection, I assure you," Cenn said and moved back to the bed. The robe he had been wearing when she summoned him in the scrying glass lay on the floor next to the bed and he picked it up, offering it to her. "Now eat while I summon a bath for you."

He saw her attention flick to the table but she didn't move from the bed.

"I said—"

"Aideen." Cenn said her name softly but the effect on her body was visible. She was pinned to the wall as if held by unseen hands. With his voice, Cenn kept her suspended. "You must learn to obey me."

Aideen's gaze grew wide and her voice shook from strain as she fought against the invisible force that held her. "Whatever put that ridiculous idea in your head?"

"Again, woman, you are pledged to me." His voice rose at the end and he pulled the blanket from her. Another swell of desire threatened his body and the mental strength he exerted in holding her to the wall lessened. "After a proper joining ceremony tomorrow, I will accept no disobedience from you," he finished, the words forced through tight lips that yearned to tease the pink nipples he had just exposed.

"Joining ceremony?" Aideen asked. Her voice grew alarmed and her whole body strained forward. "Are you insane?" She bit out a laugh with her question. "Do you mean marriage? Matrimony?"

"Matrimonium." His tongue pushed forward, eager to expel the Roman word from his mouth. "Yes, if you would call it that."

"I am not marrying you, or joining with you, or whatever you want to call it," Aideen protested.

Cenn's gaze traveled over her flushed breasts to the small triangle of gold nestled between her legs. "You already have joined with me," he reminded her.

His cock, swelling to larger proportions, urged him to refresh her memory with more than words, to leave her shuddering in ecstasy beneath him as she had been the evening before. He knelt beside her on one knee. His hands hovered over her skin, a centimeter of air, thick with their heat, parted his flesh from hers.

"Aideen," he whispered and ran small circles in the air above her skin. "I know a woman of your beauty could do better in wealth and in rank than to join with me." His thumbs pinched the air and Aideen groaned, her body jerking forward as he teased her nipples without touching them. "But not in power," he cautioned.

His hands moved to the space above the triangle of hair. The air beneath his palms vibrated and parted the already glistening lips of her pussy. Her hips thrust forward while his mind still sought to keep her ground against the wall. The pink clit, exposed, trembled. His tongue ached to taste it and darted up to lick his own upper lip.

"God, no," Aideen moaned. She could feel the muscles of her pussy begin to contract as his mind stroked her closer to orgasm. *Sweet Jesus*, she wondered as the tension throbbed against and inside her, *how can it be this good without his touching me?*

"Cenn. No." The words broke from her and she clamped down on the climax that threatened to send her mindlessly wrapping her limbs around him, pledging again that she was his as long as he would not stop touching her.

With the utterance of his name, Aideen slumped from the wall. Her body shook and she weakly reached out to grab the robe he had offered her earlier. As she wrapped it around her shoulders, she raised her chin and looked directly at him. His eyes were wide, disbelieving that she had wanted to or could stop him. Still shaking, her thighs quivering in revolt, Aideen stumbled from the bed and made her way to the table where she managed to slide onto a chair before she slid onto the floor.

Aideen heard the soft slap of his leather boots as he moved to stand behind her. His hands curled around the top of the chair in which she sat. The center of her shoulders ached with the knowledge that his cock was on the other side of the wooden chair, that the thick shaft pulsed with the need to be buried inside her. Again, she had to force down the orgasm that waited to wash over her.

"I do not need magic to make you join with me, Aideen," he threatened softly. "I am the law here and I will enforce your pledge tomorrow evening." He moved to her side and gently forced her chin up until their gazes were locked. "My people have had little to joy over, Aideen, and I would give them something to celebrate. Do not engage in a battle you cannot win and deprive both them and yourself."

Aideen blinked back a tear at the pain she heard in his voice. Pretending to focus on the meal before her, she turned away from him and his depthless blue eyes that were flaked with hard obsidian. She wanted to scream at him, yell obscenities, tell him in a way that left no doubt that there was no way in hell she was going to marry him. But her mouth wouldn't shape the words. Her hands were unwilling to curl into fists and pound the table. She could not raise her foot to stamp her denial against the floor. Her whole body had betrayed her.

When at last, a tear did slip past her defenses to slide down her cheek, Cenn put his hand on her shoulder. The tip of his finger caressed her neck, lingered over her partial tattoo, as he bent to murmur his assurances to her. "Do not be so sad, little sorceress," he said. He took the lobe of her ear between his lips in a soft kiss and released it. "I will not let it be without pleasure for you if you will but open yourself to me."

Chapter Three

Pleasure. The word sounded empty in Aideen's mind as she smoothed a misshapen bar of soap over her arm. In Dublin, standing over the workbench in the storeroom of her little eclectic antiques store and watching Cenn in her scrying bowl, pleasure at his hands was all that she had wanted.

All that I thought I wanted, she corrected herself. The soap stung her eyes as she wiped more tears away. The chill of the room corrupted the bathwater and Aideen quickly finished scrubbing herself clean. A coarse towel was draped over the back of a nearby chair and she dried herself and put on Cenn's robe. Its owner had gone in search of clothing.

Aideen was pulling the chair over to the fireplace when she heard a tentative knock at the door. Irritation at the false formality stung her cheeks and she ignored the sound. When the second knock went unanswered, she heard the scrape of a key inside the door's lock followed by the brush of the wood against the stone floor.

"Still pouting, I see," Cenn said and sat at her feet. "A waste of such a pretty mouth."

Aideen glared at him and he let his gaze drop to the stack of folded clothing on his lap. He lifted them up, his hands hovering above her knees and she couldn't tell whether it was with genuine or mock reverence he made the offering. She took the pile and pulled out a long shift made of lightweight wool that had been dyed an earthy brown. An unbleached linen under-tunic was folded beneath it. Her father had dragged Aideen to a sufficient number of historical society meetings for her to know that the under-tunic should be worn with the chiton. But looking at the two garments, she wasn't sure how they should be fastened together.

"There are no women in the cashel of your rank, Aideen," Cenn began hesitantly. "There is a cloth merchant who comes by occasionally and a fair in a month if things do not..."

His voice trailed off and she looked at him. The realization that there was a certain thinness to everything around her struck Aideen for the first time. Even Cenn, with his larger-than-life physique, appeared worn. She looked at the fireplace and noted that, stacked among the small logs and branches, were bits of recycled wood.

"These are fine," she assured him and her hand darted out to thumb his shoulder in a brief caress. "I just do not know how they go together."

Cenn looked at Aideen, saw that she was telling the truth and rose from the hearth, pulling her up with him as he stood. His mouth twisted into a wicked grin and he ordered her to disrobe. She hesitated and he took the chiton and tunic from her. Casually tossing the garments on the chair, he reached to remove the robe. His hands each held an inside edge of the robe in a manner that threatened to sweep the fabric back over her shoulders. She put her hands over his to stop him.

"Just tell me how they go together," Aideen protested.

"Just where do you come from, sorceress?" he asked and tightened his grip on the robe until Aideen was standing on the tip of her toes, her body pressed against his.

"*Baile Átha Cliath*," Aideen answered, providing the older name for the Dublin area. Her hands moved with his as he pulled the robe open to expose her upper chest and breasts.

He pressed his thumb against the faded image of her firedrake. "How did you come by this?"

A snarl twitched along her upper lip as she answered. "My father thought to put it on me."

"You did not wish it?" His question, a disconcerted sigh, hung between them.

Aideen glanced down at Cenn's hands, as tattooed as the rest of his body. She shook her head. "No, I did not."

Cenn noted the growing distance in her gaze and tried to soften her mood. "So it often is between parent and child." He pulled the robe's edges further apart. "Still, *Baile Átha Cliath* is a considerable distance for any sorcerer and you did it outside a cromlech." The flecks of obsidian pooled and darkened his gaze. "And you did this under your own power?"

A flurry of thoughts passed through Aideen's mind. Her father's words came unbidden as they always did: *There is a power within you Aideen...* She dispersed the bodiless voice with an angry twitch of her head. *Surely*, she thought, *it is the Bloodstone.*

Cenn released the robe's collar and let his hand travel down to her breast. He teased the nipple in a protracted pinch until Aideen tipped her head back and parted her lips. His teeth grazed along the lower half of her mouth and sucked the bottom lip. His fingers released the nipple only to make her gasp a second later as he pulled the sharp peak taut. She could feel herself growing wet, the walls of her vagina coating themselves in anticipation of the long strokes she hoped he would soon be delivering.

The robe began a slow slide down her body. Cenn's mouth trailed behind the fabric and covered her with sharp kisses. His tongue played at her navel while he urged her legs further apart. "Will you not tell me," he said and paused to ease his fingers into her cunt, "how you crossed this distance on your own?"

His tongue played along her clit and Aideen twined her fingers through his hair. She pressed his mouth more firmly to her, relishing the rough brush of his facial hair against her labial lips. Cenn moved to withdraw and she gave him a short, visceral growl. "Finish it," she warned and looked down into the dark blue eyes. "There is time for your questions later."

Hunger—hot, erotic—flashed across his face and in his gaze. He pressed against her legs with his elbows until her legs were forced into a wide stance that wrapped the walls of her cunt around his probing fingers in a tight grip. His tongue laved the lobes of her pussy, pulled greedily at her clit like a wild beast that had been caged too long without food or water. He sucked, pumped and nibbled at her, her body rocking against him as the tension coiled inside her to the point that she was curled over him, riding his mouth to orgasm.

When she would have pulled away from him, he held her tighter, sent her crashing against another wave of pleasure that threatened to rob her of her sight. He stood in one swift motion, his hand staying between her lower lips to guide his cock into her with the same quick, single action. Aideen wrapped herself around him and he lifted her, impaling her with his shaft as he carried her to the mattress. He towered over her, still forcing her legs apart as he took slow strokes, teasing the exterior of her cunt with the tip before driving it into her. His nipples had hardened into dark pebbles and she trailed her nails down his chest. Cenn wedged himself into her, his hands curling under her ass and around her hips to pull her closer, to pump her in quick thrusts that had her raising her body from the bed and flinging it back down as another orgasm tore through her and left a trail of tingling flesh from her face to her toes.

"Now, witch," he said. His seed erupted inside her in a hot burst and he collapsed against her. "I am finished." He panted the words against her neck, the brusqueness eased with tender kisses. "Tell me how you came to Kenmare."

"The Bloodstone," Aideen answered. Sleep tugged at the corners of her words and she snuggled against him. Her hands traveled over his chest, followed the outline of a stag near his heart. The animal reared its legs against—or in cooperation with, she could not tell—a firedrake. But for its blue coloring and wholeness, it matched her own. Frowning, she wrapped her arms around his neck. "It told me how to find you."

Cenn released Aideen long enough to grab the blanket and pull it over them before returning to embrace her. "The Bloodstone is said to be capable of many things," Cenn said before finishing with a short snort, "but no one has ever claimed that it can talk."

"In my dreams," Aideen explained. Irritation quivered along the length of her nose and he kissed its tip. "At least it seemed that way," she finished with a heavy yawn.

"But without a portal and at such a distance?" His voice remained alert, with no sign of fatigue as he traced slow circles along her bottom.

Distance? She tried to wrap her mind around the relevance of his question but couldn't. The distance she had traveled paled in comparison to the other half of the journey—the chasm of more than a thousand years.

"Tired," Aideen mumbled and burrowed further beneath the blanket.

"Fair enough, little sorceress," Cenn said and pillowed her head against his chest. "There will be time for answers after the ceremony tomorrow."

Chapter Four

Aideen woke to find Cenn hunched over the room's small table. He had a string of leather that he was weaving through a cut circle of similar hide. He was chanting quietly as he did so, but the room was heavy with his words. The language, foreign to her, cautioned silence. Confused that the Bloodstone didn't ease the translation as it had with Cenn's more ancient dialect, Aideen concentrated. No meaning revealed itself and she tried to roll the tension from her face and shoulders. She let the words wander through her mind until she understood that she was listening to the fifth language, the language the druids had learned from the Celtic sorcerers that preceded them. Just as easily, she understood the spell he was pouring into the small pouch that he was making. A spell to bind and protect and yet conceal the magic of the pouch and what it was to hold — the complexity astounded her.

When she saw what the pouch was to hold, a possessive flare shot through her body. The Bloodstone sat on the table half a meter from where Cenn's hands moved rhythmically to complete the pouch. A slight shift of Cenn's body told Aideen that he was aware of her presence as he moved to block her view of the stone. She fought the urge to rise, to remind him that it was she who had brought the Bloodstone to this room, to this time and place.

Cenn stood and placed the stone in the center of the cut circle. He repeated the chant as he cinched the leather lacing tight. He tied the ends together and lifted the pouch and strings into the air.

"Come," he commanded Aideen.

Aideen pushed the blankets aside. The cold air licked at her bare flesh and made her ache for the stone's warmth and that of the man holding it before her. Cenn slipped the leather string over her neck and the pouch comfortably wedged itself between her breasts. He pressed his palm against the pouch and a hot burst of energy enveloped them. His fingertips brushed lightly against her nipples before he pulled her to him and rewarded her obedience with a slow kiss of tangled tongues and bruised lips.

"You are mistress of the Bloodstone, Aideen," he whispered against her ear. "It will have no other…nor will I."

Emotions unknown flooded her, squeezed at her chest until her knees began to buckle and Cenn was forced to lift and carry her back to the bed.

"You must learn to control your power, little sorceress," Cenn said. His lips and tongue teased her breasts between his words, pulling her back from the confused whirlwind of her thoughts. "I cannot have my enemies learn of my two newest and best allies."

"I told you, I am no sorceress." Her hands stroked the thick black hair that crowned his head. Her arms stretched to maintain contact as his kisses descended to cover her stomach.

"With or without the stone, magic spills from you, Aideen," Cenn said. He moved back up the bed to plant a kiss on each temple. "So, if, as you claim, you are not a practitioner of the arts, you should apprentice yourself to one."

"And do you know of anyone looking for an apprentice?" Aideen teasingly asked even as she began to squirm beneath the expert rub of his hands over her body.

"Think not that I would let another have you, Aideen, even as an apprentice," he growled against her ear.

"Think not that I would take another," she echoed.

Cenn rolled on top of her. The warm press of his erect cock pushed against her stomach and she inched further up the bed until she could wrap her legs around him and invite him to enter her. "Nay, temptress," he said and kissed her before he left their bed. "There are preparations for the joining ceremony that I still must make." He leaned over for an instant to cup her breast and indulge in a soft, sucking kiss of her nipple. "I will enjoy you more fully this evening—once we truly are bonded forever."

Aideen snuggled beneath the blankets and watched him dress for the day. When he was fully clothed, he returned to the bed and caressed her cheek. "I will send breakfast and bathwater up, and a maid to dress you for the ceremony." Worry momentarily clouded his features and he held her chin between his thumb and index finger. "Remember, you are Etain," he cautioned. "The maid will address you as such."

Aideen nodded her understanding and watched him go. A maid came up a short time later. She carried a tray with some cheese and bread, a small bowl of blueberries and a cup of milk.

Remembering the prior evening's meal, Aideen gave a small frown. "Not much variety, I see."

The maid didn't respond and Aideen looked at her. The girl's face was pinched and she kept her gaze focused on the floor. She held her hands behind her back but

Aideen could tell that the girl was worriedly wringing her hands. Clothes, too wide for her thin frame, hung from the girl's shoulders.

"Sit down," Aideen suggested and pushed the chair next to her away from the table. The girl's gaze darted to Aideen and then back to the floor.

"I would like you to sit down," Aideen repeated. She broke off a piece of bread and cheese and put them on a piece of cloth. Grabbing an empty wooden cup, she poured half the cup of milk into it. "Please."

The girl glanced nervously at the closed door before she allowed her gaze to meet Aideen's. "I cannot," she said. "I...I have to get your bathwater."

"Will a few minutes of sitting with me matter?" Aideen asked and reached up to gently squeeze the girl's shoulder. The Bloodstone grew warm against the leather pouch that held it and Aideen was overwhelmed by a stabbing pain that twisted its way through her stomach. The girl was half-starved.

"Please, I know no one here beyond..." on the verge of saying Cenn's name, Aideen stopped herself. She drew a deep breath, released it, and pushed the chair a little further from the table. "I know no one here beyond Lord Crom."

The girl glanced once more at the door before sitting down in the chair. She sat as if made of stone and Aideen pushed the food and milk closer to her.

"It is not customary to eat alone where I come from," Aideen said. Immediately, Aideen wished she could swallow the words back but the girl's state of hunger overwhelmed any curiosity she might have about Aideen's home. After she watched the girl swallow a few bites,

Aideen risked asking her a question. "I have not seen the sky in days...how is the weather?"

Confusion clouded the girl's gaze and she stopped eating to stare at Aideen. "Why would you expect any change since your arrival, lady?"

Aideen wondered how many questions she could risk asking the girl and what small lies Aideen could tell to cover her own truth. "It is just that I come from a distance and am not familiar with your weather this season."

"There are no seasons in Kenmare now, lady." A small shudder passed over the girl as she answered. "When it should be spring or summer, blackness covers the sky all but a few hours a day and the sun cannot pierce the gray fog that weighs heavy in the air regardless of the hour."

"For how long has this gone on?" Aideen asked.

The girl shot Aideen another confused look before gulping down the last of the cheese. "I would say you come from a very great distance, indeed, lady," the girl began, "if you do not know. But we have had no news of the other provinces, so I should not be surprised that you have had no news of us."

"How long?" Aideen repeated her question.

"Two winters?" the girl ventured. "It has become hard, indeed, to tell sunset from sunrise or when the moon has shown us all her faces."

"And the cause?"

Here, the girl's expression closed in on itself and she gave an emphatic, negative shake of her head. "I must be getting your bathwater, lady," the girl said and backed quickly from the room.

Aideen did not press the girl further when she returned with the water and helped her put on a bleached silk chiton. She would, Aideen decided, ask Cenn tonight after their joining ceremony. He had his own questions that he wished to ask about the Bloodstone and it was only fair, she mused, that he answer a few of her questions.

Chapter Five

Aideen stepped into the stone circle. Even in the fog-shrouded daylight, she knew the circle well and its familiarity wrapped her in a cold embrace. Had Cenn not told her earlier that she was in Kenmare, she would have known the location as soon as she saw the dolmen and its ring of companions. She had accompanied her father on visits to every Irish circle still distinguishable as such. Prepubescent, clothed in a light cotton shift, moonlight falling on her shivering flesh, she had been placed on Kenmare's center boulder, a burial capstone, as a participant in one of her father's ceremonies. She shuddered as she remembered how her father would raise his arms in offering, his sleeves falling back to reveal inked images identical in theme to those covering Cenn.

"What worries you, my lady?" Cenn whispered against her ear as he pulled her to him and led her to the center stone.

"Memories," she answered and forced a smile. "Nothing more."

Cenn hesitated to accept her answer and she forced the smile wider. His gaze continued to question her and she looked away from him to the group of people within the circle's stone boundary. Except for the maid who had led her to the ceremony, the same maid that had brought her food and dressed her, Aideen had seen none of Cenn's people. They looked at her now. Their expressions revealed nothing, but the clothing and the tired way their skin hung from them told her that Kenmare was suffering from some blight. She looked back at Cenn. Was this why he had made such a desperate search for the Bloodstone? Or was it his lust for the stone that had reduced his people to poverty?

His gaze sharpened as if she had asked him the question directly. "Just memories...my lady?" he asked.

Aideen nodded and he gently urged her closer to the center stone. A middle-aged man in white robes too close to those her father had worn joined them on the other side of the dolmen. A finely wrought chalice of gold stood empty beside a silver dagger. Watching the man's hands gesture above the cup, a hollow feeling began to build in Aideen's stomach and she leaned against Cenn for support. Her vision narrowed and the man's voice came to her as if she were listening from the bottom of a drowning pool. The cold crept closer to her, threatened to consume her but for the Bloodstone's warm press between her breasts.

"Etain!" Cenn's voice, low and urgent, reached her and she looked at him, forgetting for a moment that he had given her the name.

Cenn motioned her hand forward and she felt a new heat as the priest's dagger sliced across her palm. Cenn's hand held hers and she saw that he, too, was bleeding, their blood joining in the cup. She had time to think that this was no simple handfasting ceremony before the cup was placed against her lips and she was required to drink. Aideen swayed wildly backward and Cenn caught her. His arm encircled her waist, steadying her with its firm presence.

The priest carried the cup, still holding Cenn and Aideen's blood, to an old woman standing in front of the circle's entry stone. He handed the cup to her, watched her take a shallow drink and then bowed to her before handing the cup to the man on her left. A decade's worth of medical warnings on contact with another's blood went squirming their way through Aideen's head as she saw the cup's journey come full circle. The priest returned to the altar and took his own mouthful of the congealing liquid.

As silently as they had watched the ceremony and taken their turn drinking from the cup, the small group bowed and faded into the fog. With the audience gone, the priest shot a sharp glance at Aideen before addressing Cenn. "No good will come of this," the man said, his gaze raking over Aideen's shivering body.

"Not now, Dhonn." Cenn's voice was reverent but tired.

"How many more days shall I wait?" the man asked. "How many more days are you to spend locked in your room, rutting with this wench you now call wife while the darkness holds sway?"

Cenn drew Aideen closer to him and answered the man, his voice etched with the threat of violence. "There have been no raids, no visits these past few days—"

"Because the darkness is gathering itself and its minions, this is but the calm before the storm!" Dhonn protested. He gestured wildly at Aideen. "Do not let this creature weaken you, Crom. I beg you!"

The wound in Aideen's hand began to throb. Its ache pulsed through her and she felt the Bloodstone drum a sympathetic beat. Dhonn's gaze darted to her chest and Aideen brought a protective hand up to cover the spot where the pouch rested against her skin.

"You should have spent these days of calm searching for the Heart of the Stag," Dhonn protested. "Women are weak, their flesh too easily cut, their minds awash in illogic and too easily confused. Better you had fucked some serving girl and kicked her down the stairs the next morning. At least you would be closer to finding the sacred stone."

"Teacher, you press your privilege too far," Cenn growled in warning.

The Bloodstone's beat against her chest became violently erratic as it echoed the anger building in Aideen. Her hands clenched into small fists, the pressure forcing new blood from the wound. But Dhonn ranted on, oblivious to the triple danger he now faced.

"The Stag will be our salvation, our Savior, but how are we to find his heart if you are busy bedding this miserable cunt?"

A blow, unseen, knocked Dhonn to the ground. Aideen felt Cenn stiffen next to her in surprise. His glance darted to her then to the unconscious form sprawled at their feet. His mouth was just beginning to form a question when Dhonn moaned softly in pain.

Cenn knelt beside the priest. "Teacher, forgive me, I did not mean to harm you."

The lie flowed smoothly from Cenn's lips and Aideen had to hide her own surprise. Cenn had warned her that his enemies could not know of her power. Was Dhonn, then, Cenn's enemy? She felt another ball of anger begin to build and quashed the emotion. The priest certainly was her enemy, she thought as she looked at the angry flush that covered his face and the baleful glare he directed at her.

"No," Dhonn said and dipped his head in apology. "As you said, it was the wrong time." With Cenn's help, he rose and brushed the dirt from his robes. His gaze searched the darkening sky and he turned, motioning for Cenn and Aideen to follow him. "Come, they will be waiting in the hall and we cannot be caught out in the dark."

Chapter Six

A fire lit one end of the hall and the solemn crowd from the ceremony lined the tables next to it, silently vying with one another for the place closest to the rare blaze. Spreading from the tables by the fire were smaller groups of lesser nobles and household servants. Dim torches added to the light from the hearth.

Cenn escorted Aideen to the head table. A heavy otter skin cloak was draped across the back of one chair and he pulled it around her shoulders before he sat down. Dhonn, she noticed, sat directly to the left of Cenn's elbow. Cenn clapped his hands and called for music and warm mead. Two young men dressed in worn doeskin carried a harp into the center. A middle-aged woman followed behind them with a stool. As she sat the stool down and began to play, a serving girl brought food and drink to Cenn and Aideen. Aideen's stomach gave a delighted gurgle when a plate of freshly cooked meat surrounded by baby potatoes and carrots was placed in front of her. She looked around the hall to see surprise registering on the faces of the guests as similar dishes were presented to them.

"From whence came these provisions?" Dhonn asked. Caution mixed with suspicion cloaked his voice and his gaze drifted between Cenn and Aideen.

"From traders." Cenn's response was brusque, warning the priest to leave off with any further questions.

"With what in trade?" Dhonn asked, either unaware of Cenn's tone or unwilling to heed it.

"My freedom," Cenn answered. A smile played at the corner of his mouth and he shot a warm glance at Aideen.

The glance didn't go unnoticed by the priest and his gaze settled on Aideen and narrowed into thin beams of hatred that pricked at her skin and made the Bloodstone grow hot once again.

"The dowry the wench came with could have been put to better use," Dhonn grunted even as he gnawed at a piece of rib.

"Better use than feeding the hungry?" Cenn asked. A look of incredulity settled over his features and he stared at the priest. But the man was impervious to the questioning gaze.

"Informants, spies, assistance in finding the heart of the Stag or gleaning information on the forces that are amassing beyond the veil of fog," Dhonn rambled on. "This will but last a few days."

Aideen saw Cenn bite back a response. True, in her times, the ceremonial stones Cenn had taken from her were semiprecious or of a mass-market quality. Amethyst, opal, jade, emerald, sapphire, ruby—the stones could be purchased over the Internet or at a local jeweler or department store. But the stones were faceted beyond a skill level she could imagine Cenn's artisans to be capable of and some might be rare for the times in which she now found herself. Having the stones to barter with had been her whole reason in bringing them. One stone, she would expect, might be worth a month's rations for the cashel's inhabitants.

Cenn could not completely hold back a response and he turned to Dhonn. His arm rested on the back of the priest's chair and his heavy hand encircled the back of the man's neck. "I have paid informants, sent spies," Cenn spoke, the words tight and clipped. "And such fees brought me no closer to possessing the Bloodstone than when we first set out to find it."

"Patience," Dhonn clucked. "Have I not—"

Cenn rose from his chair, cutting Dhonn short. He offered Aideen his hand and motioned to a servant to gather up their plates. Cenn handed Aideen a cup and raised his own to the guests. "I bid you all a good meal and a good evening," he said and took a long drink of mead. "But my wife and I retire to more fully satisfy our appetites."

A blush heated Aideen's cheeks and spread to flush her face and throat as a chorus of *huzzahs* erupted from the guests. Once they were clear of the hall, he swept Aideen up into his arms and bounded up the steps. The maid, plates and cups bouncing against the tray, had to run furiously behind him to keep pace. Cenn already had placed Aideen on the mattress when the girl dropped the tray on the table and bolted from the room.

"What do you think she was afraid of seeing?" Cenn teased.

His fingers plucked at the chiton's side ties. After he had the ties unknotted, he lifted the shift over Aideen's head. He kissed her eyelids closed and brushed his lips across her mouth before lingering at the hollow of her neck. While Cenn nuzzled her neck, his hands worked her nipples into hard tips until her body strained against his from the need he was creating inside her. His mouth latched onto her nipple—his lips pinched the sensitive peak. His hands massaged their way down her sides, over her hips, and he clasped her ass, kneading the muscles while his thumbs traced hard circles against the entrance to her vagina. His mouth fastened on her clit, sucking, sucking while his thumbs entered her pussy to fuck her to her first climax.

"By the gods, woman," Cenn groaned and flipped her onto her stomach. "You have a body and soul meant for loving."

Aideen felt Cenn's cock, blood-thickened, stretch her walls wide and plunge into her in one sharp thrust. He eased out slowly and made shallow, gyrating thrusts against the spongy entrance. His fingers slipped beneath her and parted her labial lips to find the hard little nub that his mouth had just pleasured. He pulled it, stroked it until her wild bucking buried his cock inside her. Cenn pushed her forward, his hands gripping her ass and hips, and began to ride her in long strokes. He could feel her cunt contracting around his cock as her orgasm peaked. Aideen's body writhed along the mattress as she gave up all pretext of control and let her body and his cock take command of her mind.

Even after another climax claimed her, Cenn held his own pleasure in check. His hands roamed her body in appreciation. His lips and tongue teased her a hundred different ways but he denied his own release. Aideen twisted beneath him then forced him onto his back.

"My turn," she said, her tongue licking the lobe of his ear.

His hands moved to stop her and she shook her head. She looked around the room, saw the robe with its sash on the floor beside the mattress. Freeing the sash from the robe, she rolled him onto his side and tied his hands behind his back. She brought his legs up and out so that they formed a sideways diamond. Holding his feet in position with one hand, she began to stroke his cock with the other. While she stroked, her tongue ran the length of his erection, beginning below his balls at the smooth tissue of his perineum and ending with a flick at the mushrooming tip. She pressed his feet closer to his body until his heels were wedged against his ass, exerting pressure on the heavily muscled hole. She covered his cock with her mouth. Her lips, wet with saliva, contracted against the shaft, swept up and down its length, the tip pressing against the back of her throat as Cenn surrendered, his seed rushing hot against her throat. She felt the walls of her cunt squeeze and her own climax thundered through her.

While he still trembled and jerked beneath her, Aideen's mouth released his cock. She turned abruptly, and slid onto his shaft in one fluid motion. With deep, rocking motions, she held him inside her. His cries of pleasure joined the rhythm of the rocking. Pressing his heels against the opening to his ass while her cunt, fluttering in waves of climax, swallowed his cock, Aideen rode him to their mutual oblivion.

Chapter Seven

"Dhonn is your enemy?" Aideen inquired gently the next morning as they lay recuperating from a long night of lovemaking.

"He is my teacher," Cenn corrected her. "Or was. I am apprentice no more...have not been for over ten years."

"And yet you did not tell him that the Bloodstone is in your possession or admit the source of the power that knocked him to the ground last night?" Aideen continued.

"What logic does that make?" Cenn asked.

His words reminded her of Dhonn's and Aideen let off lightly stroking the dark ladder of hair that ran down from Cenn's navel to mix with the black curls that tangled against his shaft. She returned her hand to her hip. "Ah, I forgot, Dhonn was your teacher and so you have been taught that women are *awash in illogic*," she said with no hint of play.

Cenn paused as if to consider her statement then noticed the cold anger building in Aideen. Contrition furrowed his brow and he pulled her to him. "That is not it," he explained. "It is just that friend or foe can betray a secret."

"He does not feel like a friend to me," Aideen said. Cenn was massaging the small of her back and she brushed his hand away in irritation.

"He spent far too much time among the Romans," Cenn said and tried to roll her onto her back but she pushed him away. "He has too great a love of their philosophers and mathematicians, their logicians, their Socrates and Aristotle, to be content with the company of a woman."

Aideen bit back a snicker at what she thought was the true cause of Dhonn's disenchantment with women. "So, you do think we are illogical."

"Women are," Cenn began, choosing his words as carefully as any newly married man could, "without instruction in such matters."

Aideen sat up and began to scan the room for the *brandub* board she had seen earlier. She spotted it lying on the wooden chest wedged into the corner. She crossed the room naked, but for the Bloodstone and its pouch, and scooped up the board and its pieces. In the center, she put the king-piece and its four knights then she arranged her eight opposing pieces. While Cenn watched her, his dark gaze quiet, she made her opening move.

"What is your point, my lady?" Cenn asked, his voice a soft caress of reconciliation as he moved one of his knights.

"That Dhonn is wrong and that I do not merely *feel* that he is a danger to you." Aideen moved a second piece and blocked two of his knights. She saw by the sharp knit of his brow that his attention had become split between her arguments and her board strategy.

"And you have proof, having been absent from this room no more than a few hours total?" He moved another knight forward, saw his error and winced as Aideen removed one of his pieces from the board.

"I have a set of objective observations that make the possibility more likely than not," Aideen began, her pieces pressing in on the king. "And something that, by your own beliefs, you cannot deny."

"Which is?" His lips were pressed into a thin line of concentration, making the question sound like a single-word statement of *witches*.

Aideen smiled and removed another of his pieces from the board. *Witches*, indeed. "The Bloodstone," she answered simply and made his king retreat further from the center.

His interest redirected, Cenn lifted the *brandub* board from the mattress and placed it on the floor. "You have proven you are most capable at a game of strategy," he agreed. Cenn reached up and trapped the pouch that rested between her breasts. He pulled the string tie over her head and removed the Bloodstone.

"And the stone speaks to you," he added before dropping the stone back in the pouch and returning it to her. "What then," he asked, "do you advise?"

Aideen began to speak but a sharp knock at the door interrupted her. Cenn gave a dismissive shake of his head and waved the interruption away but the knock sounded again, harder and more urgent.

"Crom, it is unforgivable for me to intrude," Dhonn's voice came from the other side of the heavy wooden door. "And yet, I must..."

"Cover yourself," Cenn said, his lips once again set into a thin line. "It will only take a few seconds to send him away."

Cenn tossed on his robe and lifted the latch on the door. He opened the door a crack, just enough for one eye to pass over the priest in an irritated glare. Dhonn pushed impatiently at the door and Aideen hurriedly fastened the ties to her gown. Cenn's strength was too much for Dhonn and the priest resorted to his persuasive powers.

"Do not be so quick to shut me out," Dhonn warned. "I know why you no longer seek the Bloodstone."

Cenn hesitated just long enough for Dhonn to give a hard shove against the door and push his way into the room. Dhonn pointed a shaking finger at Aideen, his voice trembling as he levied his accusation. "You no longer seek the stone because you have it, and it is this witch who brought it to you."

Dhonn lunged at Aideen and Cenn jumped forward to intercept him. Both men fell to the floor as a protective burst of energy erupted from the Bloodstone. Cenn sat up, blood dripping from his nose. Dhonn crept toward the mattress, one hand still reaching out for Aideen. Cenn flung the priest back onto the floor and straddled him, his thumbs pressing against Dhonn's Adam's apple.

"The enemy has sent her, can you not see this?" Dhonn pleaded. "She has used the stone against you."

"Against you," Cenn corrected but Aideen did not miss the backward glance of suspicion he gave her. "The enemy would not give me the Bloodstone, the very weapon with which I will defeat this army of fog and darkness."

"Ah," Dhonn crowed. "The enemy is smarter than we can know. He has sent the greatest of gifts, our Savior, the Heart of the Stag, but wrapped it in the worst of evil—a woman. She will use the stone at this close distance to destroy you!"

"That is not true!" Cenn yelled and his thumbs pressed more persuasively against Dhonn's throat. "You have gone mad, my friend."

"Can you command the stone?" Dhonn screamed the question. Dhonn saw the confusion that filled Cenn's second backward glance at Aideen and he pressed his point. "It is as I suspected, then. You cannot." Foam began to fleck Dhonn's lips as his argument grew more venomous. "Kill the woman," he urged, "and the stone will be yours to command!"

Shock filled Cenn's gaze and he loosened his stranglehold on Dhonn's neck. Aideen scrambled backward off the mattress and desperately looked around the room for a weapon within her reach.

"Why do you hesitate?" Dhonn begged, his screams bringing the guards crashing through the bedroom door. "There are plenty of whores for you to bed. Kill this one, and you will have the power to be king!"

"Take him," Cenn ordered the guards, his voice rough with emotion. "He does not leave his rooms, is that understood?"

Once Dhonn, hurling curses at them, had been dragged from the room by two guards, Cenn closed the door and looked at Aideen. Her back was pressed to the wall. Her gaze, wide and fearful, jumped around the room, measuring and then discarding the value of each object as a weapon. Mindful of the stone's power, he approached her carefully. He held his hands in front of him, the palms open, but she still shook as he touched her.

"Shh," he coaxed and pulled her to him. "I would never hurt you and, even if you do not believe me, the stone does."

Aideen realized he was right. The stone did not burn her flesh in warning as it did in Dhonn's presence. Rather, it emitted calming waves of warmth. She relaxed against him and brought her hand up to caress the blood smear across his cheek. "I am sorry—" she began but he placed a fingertip against her lips and then kissed her.

"Bad aim, that is all," he said and wrapped her more tightly in his embrace. "You sought to protect yourself from a madman... I got in the way."

Aideen nodded and wiped a tear from her cheek. Her breathing hitched then released in a ragged sob. "What he said..." she started and then trailed off. Dhonn had said too many terrible things for her to focus on just one.

"He has gone mad," Cenn reassured her. "We have been fighting this unseen evil for so long, none harder than Dhonn. He was the first to recognize it, the one who started me on my search for the Bloodstone. The fight has, at last, consumed him."

A warning premonition pricked the back of Aideen's neck and resonated across her body. She looked at Cenn, saw the fatigue that weighed him down and decided not to press her feelings about Dhonn at the moment. He had just placed his mentor under house arrest. Surely she could allow Cenn a few hours rest before she asked him to consider whether the priest had orchestrated the menace from the very beginning.

"What is it, love?" Cenn asked as he saw the doubt that still lingered in her gaze.

His body sagged against hers and Aideen guided him back onto the mattress. She smoothed a fingertip over his brow and across each eyelid. Her chest rested against his to allow the Bloodstone's calming effect to ease the tension from his mind and body. She didn't answer him, choosing, instead, to massage his temples until his curiosity surrendered to fatigue.

Chapter Eight

Aideen drifted off to sleep next to Cenn. Her dreams were troubled by shadowy figures that crawled and grunted at the edge of perception. She recognized the scene from the scrying ceremony her father had made her perform and yet there was the taint of premonition in what revealed itself. Black metal encased disfigured bodies and she saw the occasional dark flash of an unsheathed sword. Screams filled the air and a path of chaos stretched all around, strewn with the bodies of women and children who could not outrun their doom. Instinctively, she reached out to Cenn in her sleep but found only empty air and blankets still bearing traces of his body heat. She opened her eyes to see him stepping into his leather boots.

She sat up and reached for her clothing. "What is it?" she asked.

"Raids," he answered. "More than half a dozen in the last few hours."

"Was anyone—" she began but he cut her short with an ominous look that told her she would rather not hear the answer. The heat of the Bloodstone bore against her chest like acid on sheet metal. Again, she heard screams, but this time it was the wailing of women greeting the dead and dying that Cenn's soldiers had carted from the surrounding settlements.

"I must leave you for a short time, Aideen," Cenn said as he slipped his cloak on. "A counterattack must be coordinated, we have to flush these demons from the darkness." His gaze fell on the Bloodstone's pouch and his expression hardened. "When I get back, we must talk..." he faltered as he contemplated what he was about to ask of a woman. "I would not ask you..."

"You do not need to ask me," Aideen assured him. "I could not bear for you to go without me."

Cenn embraced Aideen and covered her mouth in a kiss that promised to remain with her for an eternity. When he finally broke from her, he swore a quick return. Aideen put the bar on the door after he left and rummaged through his clothing for pants and sturdier footwear. She could ride a horse but she had no intention of doing so in a chiton. All the pants were overlarge and trying to cinch them with a sash did no good. In frustration, she put the woolen dress back on and sat in front of the fire. Another premonitory prickling of the scalp, this time of Cenn injured, his blood mixing with the muddy soil of the marsh, seized her and she fell to the floor.

When she recovered from her faint, Aideen grabbed a cloak and left the room. She half-expected to see a guard outside the door but no one was there. She followed the winding staircase down to where it split into two separate staircases. One would lead her toward the hall, the other, according to the maid who had escorted her to the ceremony, to the kitchens. She started down the stairs to the kitchens and was met by the same maid.

"My lady," the girl gasped as she encountered Aideen on the narrow steps. "I was coming up to see if you needed anything."

"I do," Aideen answered and took the girl by the elbow. "I..." she paused when she realized she did not know the girl's name. "What is your name?"

"Niamh," the maid said. Her answer matched the low tones with which Aideen had asked the question. "Is something the matter?"

"I need a book," Aideen answered. Niamh provided her with a blank stare and Aideen searched her mind for an explanation. She mimicked leafing through the pages of a book. "Sheets of blank lambskin with leather binding," she said. The image of Cenn's book filled her mind and she pulled Niamh closer until her lips were pressed against the girl's ears. "But red leather."

Something familiar gleamed in the girl's eyes. "Is it a secret?"

"Yes," Aideen answered and clutched at the sleeve of Niamh's dress. "Please, do you know where I can find such a book?"

Niamh looked up and down the staircase before she nodded her head slowly. "I do, my lady, but I am not supposed to go to that part of the cashel," she whispered. "No one is."

Despite the girl's air of reluctance, Aideen knew Niamh would not refuse her. "But it is the prohibition of Lord Crom that stays you?" Aideen asked. Niamh answered with a slow, affirmative nod of her head. Encouraged, Aideen pressed on. "But I am his wife. He does not intend, I assure you, to deny me access."

A conspiratorial smile played at the corners of Niamh's mouth and she took a step back down the staircase. Aideen hesitated but the girl motioned her to follow. As they reached the bottom of the steps, Niamh flattened her body against the staircase wall and stopped. She inched her head around the corner and made sure that the short bridge of kitchen floor between their staircase and the opposing one was not being observed.

"Run!" Niamh whispered urgently and bounded across the floor and up the other set of stairs.

Aideen dashed across the opening and silently raced up the staircase to reach Niamh. The staircase split, one branch climbing higher, the other descending into darkness. Niamh took the path to the right, leading Aideen deeper into the cashel's bowels. With the cashel's scarcity of wood, Aideen was surprised to see the occasional torches that lit their way, offering welcomed patches of light between stretches of inky black. When they reached the last of the torches, Niamh took it from its sconce and grabbed Aideen's hand.

"This way, Lady."

The passage that Niamh led Aideen down ended in a stone wall.

"What is the meaning of this, Niamh?" Aideen asked. "I do not have time for tricks."

"Patience, my lady," Niamh said and handed the torch to Aideen. "A wall is not always a wall."

"No, sometimes it is a banana," Aideen nervously quipped as she watched Niamh shove against the door with all her weight. The Bloodstone's heat, already at the point of being unbearable, seemed to burn more fiercely against her skin.

Niamh responded with a confused frown and an impatient jerk of her head in the direction of the wall. "Help me push, my lady."

Aideen added her weight to Niamh's efforts and they were able to coax the wall forward a fraction less than a half-meter. Niamh took the torch and slid through the narrow opening first. Feeling the darkness pressing in on her, Aideen quickly followed behind the maid. Once past the wall, she found Niamh standing in the middle of a chamber. The light from the torch coldly glittered in the girl's dark eyes.

"Niamh," she said, her voice growing alarmed. "How is it that you know about this passage?"

"I showed it to her."

The voice that answered was followed quickly by the sound of a sharp blow to the back of Aideen's head. She stumbled forward an instant before falling to the ground. There was a vicious pull against her throat as the pouch was ripped from her neck. Sidestepping Aideen's outstretched arms, her attacker took the torch from Niamh and bent down. Dhonn's face, contorted in triumph, shifted in and out of focus.

Dhonn looked up at his newest protégé and smiled. "How did you get her down here so quickly?"

"She was desperate to find some bound lambskin," Niamh answered dully. "It was easy, really."

"You...you are supposed..." Aideen struggled to find the words but her brain seemed to be pounding against the back of her skull. Warm blood oozed through her hair and she stopped straining to look at Dhonn. She rested her head against the cool flagstone, the torch's feeble light all but gone from her dimming vision.

"I am supposed to be in my rooms," Dhonn agreed. "Guarded night and day." He gestured in the direction of the small passage Niamh and Aideen had created. "One of many, my dear chit."

"Tell me." Aideen's words, muffled by her impending unconsciousness, were lost against the stone floor.

Dhonn bent closer to her and cocked an ear in her direction. "What was that?"

Aideen's fingers inched across the floor but he caught her intent and raised the pouch above his head.

"No, Lady," Dhonn laughed as he waved the pouch in the air. "I cannot risk your touching the Bloodstone, can I?"

Aideen pulled in a deep breath of air and forced the partial accusation past her lips. "From the beginning…"

Dhonn smiled down at Aideen. That he was supremely confident in his victory was evident in his voice when he answered her. "Yes, Etain, from the beginning. I have plotted to take first the seat of power Crom holds and then to spread my glory and rule throughout the five provinces, and I have an army of demons with which to conquer. Yes, from the beginning I have planned this, and here we are, very near to the end."

"No," she said and struggled to rise.

"You sound so sure," Dhonn mused and forced her back down with a rough push against the middle of her back. "Why is that?"

"I know something you do not."

"You know several somethings that I do not know," he grunted and stood. "But I intend to pull them from you one way or another, starting with Crom's true name."

Dhonn placed the Bloodstone's pouch around his neck and handed the torch to Niamh. From his pocket, he pulled an umbrella-shaped dagger. Aideen noticed with detached appreciation that the center blade was surrounded by three hinged blades that pointed toward the knife's hilt. To make sure she understood the dagger's purpose, Dhonn unfolded the three secondary blades and made a withdrawing motion.

"A rather pleasant toy," he said. "Provided you are on the right end of the blade."

Fear pushed aside the pain that threatened to wrap Aideen in darkness. Her pupils dilated until no trace of the mossy green irises remained. In the dim light, she tried to focus on the pouch and calculated her chances of success should she make a desperate grab at it. Dhonn backed away from her. His hand clutched at his chest and she could see smoke rising from the fabric of his overshirt. In the distance, she could hear someone calling her name. But the voice was too far. She didn't dare shift her attention from the stone.

Dhonn slapped at his chest with his free hand. His own pupils widened in fear as he heard the voice and recognized its owner. Light filled the room as men pushed the stone inward and entered the hidden chamber. Aideen realized the voice that called her name belonged to Cenn. Her gaze broke from the Bloodstone's pouch just in time to see the forward thrust of Dhonn's arm as he stabbed the vicious dagger into Cenn's chest. A spell, ancient and terrible, parted the flesh, pushed past the ribcage and buried the blade in Cenn's heart. The words were cast in reverse as he pulled his arm back, Cenn's heart trapped in the vicious dagger's claw.

"No!"

The scream that ripped from Aideen's throat carried a maelstrom of liquid fire with it. Dhonn's flesh ignited at her cry and he fell to the floor to quell the flames even as the heat peeled the skin from his face. The heat evaporated the leather pouch that hung from his neck and Aideen reached through the fire engulfing him to snatch the

Bloodstone. New energy and purpose pulsed through her at the stone's touch. Her hand began to glow bright red, like when she would hold a powerful flashlight to it as a child. The stone whispered its true name to her in a long forgotten language. It was the Stag's Heart, grantor of life and death, keeper of eternity.

With the power of the stone pounding in her hand, she turned to Cenn's fallen form. She could read his final feelings on the death mask into which his face had frozen. Determination, surprise, regret, all spoke to her in an equal voice. She knelt down, her hand delving into his parted chest. She reached the hollow where his heart should have been beating and she released the Bloodstone. Cenn's flesh grabbed at her hand as the Bloodstone began to close the wound. The stone encased itself in new tissue and tapped its steady rhythm against the broken ribs and rent muscle. Slowly, the blue pallor of death receded from him and he drew a choking breath of air into his lungs.

The men who had rushed into the room with him backed slowly from their revived leader. The word *unnatural* mingled interchangeably with *miracle* as they looked to one another for confirmation of what had just happened.

"Aideen?" The words came out in a harsh croak. One hand fluttered against his chest and he looked at her.

"Rest," she coaxed. "I will get some men to carry you to our rooms."

"I cannot. I must prepare the soldiers," he argued and struggled to sit up. He saw that she didn't understand and he grabbed her by the shoulders. "Do you not hear them?" he asked frantically. "The drums…listen to them beating!"

"It is just the Bloodstone, no more than that," she tried to assure him. "You must learn its rhythm."

"No," he protested with a vigorous shake of his head. "They are beating...the war drums are beating. It has begun."

Chapter Nine

The war drums were beating. Their heavy menace pounded through the air for seven days. The noise was incessant, the drummers untiring. Search parties went out but the sound seemed to come from every quarter of the earth. The enemy's location went undiscovered and the cashel's occupants were left with the grim realization that the enemy sought first to destroy their spirit and weaken their minds before it turned its attention to their flesh.

During the week, Cenn spent most of his time in a makeshift war room planning for the cashel's defenses. When Aideen was able to coax him back to their room, he was forced to sit down at the table with a new red leather-bound diary.

"Woman," he said, irritation oozing from every pore. "There are better things to be doing with our time alone. The drums could stop at any moment."

Aideen put her hand to his chest where the Bloodstone's rhythm had become Cenn's own heartbeat. She closed her eyes and listened with her mind. She shook her head. "Not yet. They will not stop yet and no attack will come until after there is silence," she assured him. "And you are almost to the end."

"I do not remember what comes next," he said.

As she had done several times during the week, Aideen moved behind him. Her stomach pressed against his back and her arms rested over his shoulders so that her hands covered the center of his chest. "Listen to the stone," she commanded. "It remembers everything."

Cenn blinked against the memory then began to write the closing paragraph of his diary.

Exhausted, I swore I would not seek the sorceress again until I had further rested, but her body calls to me. And so I dared to summon her again tonight. Ah, sweet temptation. She drives all thought of the Bloodstone from my mind although she holds it to her as she dares to command me. She stood before a silver bowl, smoke dancing against her pale white skin. Pink nipples erect and begging to be suckled. A golden triangle pointing down to paradise. My tongue grows thick at the thought of tasting the sweet nectar that flows from between her legs. I swear I will have her and the stone.

"I still do not understand how you came by my diary or the condition to which it had degenerated in the space of a few days or why I must recreate it," he said, repeating the question he had asked her more than a dozen times since the drums began.

As she had on the other occasions, she hesitated while she considered how much, if anything, she could tell him. She understood the paradox of the diary that had helped bring her to Cenn having been destroyed. She knew, too, his fate and her own. Both were approaching with a dismaying speed, Cenn's slightly faster than her own. Her hand moved from his body to briefly caress her stomach. The fate of the child after her time in Kenmare ended remained unclear, but she would have nine months to plan for its care and to plan for the day the Bloodstone would return to her. Already, she was filling the pages of her own diary, a book of magic and ceremony to protect her descendants through the centuries until the circle was complete.

"You said that we are bound for eternity," she answered once again. "This will make it so."

"That is not enough of an answer, Aideen," he said and turned to her. He pulled her onto his lap and hugged her to him. "Why does the stone not speak to me as it spoke to you? Why does it only offer you mumbled half-answers?"

Aideen shrugged her shoulders and buried her face against his chest. Half of what she wrote in her own diary made no sense to her, her hand guided by another. Pushing despair aside, she breathed in the intoxicating odor of wool and heather and his distinct masculinity. "Perhaps because answers will not help against the inevitable."

She felt him tense beneath her and she cupped his face, covered it with calming kisses. "Do not worry, love, the power the Bloodstone has granted you will carry the battle. Do not doubt this."

Cenn responded with a worried grin that turned suggestive. He pointed to the diary on the center of the table. "The book is complete, woman," he said and redirected his outstretched finger toward the mattress. "Now, do you not think that I deserve a reward for my efforts?"

Cenn carried Aideen to the bed. With reverent fingers, they undressed one another. Their bodies twined together in a slow, luxurious series of caresses, thrusts and kisses. No haste corrupted their love and they touched one another as if all of time extended before them. When at last they surrendered to sleep, they did so in one another's arms. And sometime in the middle of the night, as Fate — her heart flooded with regret — looked down on the lovers, the drums stopped beating.

Book 3: New Blood

Chapter One

Aideen opened her eyes to find herself in the small storeroom of her antiques shop. Images of the Bloodstone's vision still flitted before her and she flung the stone from her. *Not images*, she told herself and looked at the diary on the worktable, *hallucinations. Like the mold in King Tut's tomb that killed everyone.*

Still, Aideen could not escape what she had witnessed through the night. She saw herself sitting in the cashel's hall. The sun, so long absent from Kenmare, poured brightly through the shuttered windows. The doors were thrown open and the men streamed in, bodies on litters trailing behind them instead of the fog that had so often insinuated itself in their footsteps. She felt her heart breaking as one of the litters was placed before her. Aideen had known that the Bloodstone would abandon Cenn once victory was assured but the horror of its infidelity came crashing down on her as she saw the headless body. She put her hand on his chest and felt that the Bloodstone, too, was at rest. She looked around and observed that no bodies of the enemy had been dragged into the hall. Those soldiers who had survived the battle shuddered and jerked as they described otherworldly warriors that had vanished or self-destructed in the returning daylight.

"No, no, no, no, no," Aideen yelled in the storeroom. She crawled into one corner, closed her eyes, and pressed her hands to her ears in a futile attempt to stop sights and sounds that existed only in her mind. "A dream. Just a dream. Snap out of it, Aideen. Goddamn it, snap out of it!"

Slowly, the vision's intensity faded until she was able to block it completely. She looked around the storeroom and remembered the mess she had left in the bathroom the night before. She glanced at the clock and saw that the store would open in less than an hour.

"Fuck," she swore and grabbed the smock. She unhooked the hip pack and stuffed the Bloodstone, diary, and jewels back into the secret safe before she dashed through the storefront to the bathroom where her clothes still waited in a semi-dry heap on the floor.

Dressed in the damp clothes, she stepped into the storefront just in time to hear someone knocking at the glass door. It was a young man, slightly older than her, his expression bathed in impatience. Her gaze lingered on him just long enough to take in the impeccable black hair and the expensive tailored suit with its tucks and darts that hinted at a powerful swimmer's body — broad-shouldered and thin waisted. Visions of Cenn still plagued her and the man's visual perfection barely registered.

"Half an hour still," she yelled through the glass and pointed to the clock on the wall.

The rapping became more insistent and he mouthed the word "now".

Aideen waved him off and went back into the storeroom. She looked at the worn vinyl couch against the wall safe and smiled. Hell, she didn't need to open the store any time soon. The suit out front could knock all day. She would schedule an appointment with her insurer for an appraisal of the book this afternoon. Its sale could, quite possibly, eliminate the financial need for her to ever open the shop again. She reached for her address book, her hand hesitating on the drawer pull.

"Don't be stupid, Aideen, girl," she chided herself. "It's nothing but a moldy old book that's given you a bad dream." Still, she couldn't bring herself to open the drawer and retrieve the insurer's phone number.

The shop's phone, ringing from the storefront, stopped her internal debate, effectively wiping away the money signs that were dancing lewdly in front of her. Avoiding any eye contact with the man who was still outside her store, she picked up the phone and gave a brusque greeting. "Dublin Arcanum."

"Miss Godwin, open the door."

It was a man's voice on the other end. The words were lightly accented with a southeastern lilt and Aideen slowly turned to look at the man standing on the other side of the shop's glass door. He held a cell phone to his ear and the impatience that had colored his cheeks was tinged an angrier red.

"Why would I do that, Mister..." She let the question fade and stepped over to the glass. Her gaze moved over him in quick appraisal. With the distance between them bridged, she could see that his eyes were a dark gray that matched his designer clothes and his black hair flashed blue when the light hit it. She tried to remember if she had seen him at an estate sale, perhaps even Sunday's sale. She examined his face more closely, becoming lost in the sensuous mouth and cloud-gray eyes. She blinked, breaking the spell.

"Toland," the man answered. "You'll do it because you have stolen property in your shop."

"I'm afraid I have no idea what you're talking about Mr. Toland," she said, but her concern betrayed her and she glanced back at the storeroom door.

His gaze followed hers to the door and he flashed a predatory smile. "I believe you do know what I'm talking about—your purchase from the Meyrick estate."

"As you said, I have *purchased* something from the Meyrick estate." She stepped forward, steeling herself against the magic of his dangerous smile and mysterious gaze. "That's the opposite of stealing."

"I understand your position, Miss Godwin—"

"Aideen," she interrupted. Her hand hovered next to the deadbolt and he glanced down, a hungry anticipation flashing across his features before Aideen took a nervous step away from the door.

"Aideen," he agreed hurriedly, his hand touching the glass in an effort to summon her back. "As I said, I understand your position, but the property you purchased was stolen from my ancestral lands nine years ago."

"Where?" she asked and returned to the glass. *The eyes, there's something about his eyes,* she thought as she searched his expression for any sign of deception.

"Kenmare," he answered. "Please, let me in so we can discuss this privately."

"Who are you?" she asked. His identity flitted at the periphery of understanding and she quickly jerked her head to the side in an attempt to catch a glimpse of his shadow self. The ghost of a dream flickered across the man's features but she shattered the image with a sharp puff of air. *Just a dream,* she reminded herself.

"I told you, Miss Godwin," he said and his suave voice once again grew irritated at the confusion and resistance he saw in her. "My name is Toland, Kean Toland. And what you purchased from the auction was stolen from my ancestors' graves."

The small hairs along the back of her neck became prickled and she nervously rubbed them down. She shook her head at him and tried to turn but his presence commanded that she stay. She gave him a hard, appraising look but found no solution that would calm the vortex of questions that vied for her attention. *Kean, Ancient, Cenn...*

"Aideen, open the door."

"No," she half-stated, half-pleaded. "This is something for our solicitors to resolve."

Kean pressed against the glass, every fiber of his body ordering her to open the door. "Aideen, you have no idea of the power of those items that waits to be unleashed or the forces that seek it. Forces that will stop at nothing."

"No." This time her voice was firm when she denied him.

"Please!" He banged his entreaty against the glass. "You're in danger, Aideen."

"The only danger I see, Mister Toland, is from you," Aideen responded and turned abruptly from him. She replaced the phone on its receiver and walked on shaking legs back into the storeroom. With the storeroom door shut, she collapsed against the workbench, her body trembling. *Only a dream*, she told herself over and over. *Only a dream.*

Chapter Two

Kean paced in front of the Dublin Arcanum as Aideen disappeared into the storeroom. He glanced at his watch and then slammed an open palm against the door's metal frame. There was little chance she would open the store now that he had frightened her and, surely, Donald Meyrick would know by now to whom his uncle's estate had sold the Bloodstone. It would not be long before one of Meyrick's henchmen, or even the man himself, showed up to forcibly take the stone from her.

"Dammit!" he shouted and hit the door's frame a second time. He'd nearly had her. Standing there—her pale, luminous face almost pressed against the glass, her green-eyed gaze captured by his words—she had almost opened the door. But something had risen up in her, breaking the spell he was weaving with his words and motions.

Looking up and down the street at the unopened shops, he shook his head. No, she hadn't broken the spell, he just hadn't cast it well enough. Whatever Gerald had been grooming his daughter to become, she was just a shopkeeper now. And he was just a man whose heart she had carelessly and unknowingly scarred a decade ago. Still, when she had stared straight into him with her sharp gaze, he was sure she had read his soul. He ran a hand roughly across his chin while he surveyed the street one last time. A certain ease settled over him, calming his frenetic heartbeat as he realized what he had to do next.

Aideen may have turned her back on her birthright, but he couldn't leave her as an innocent pawn in Meyrick's dangerous game.

Kean quick-stepped to his car, a sleek, black Jaguar XK8, turning off his alarm system and unlocking the door as he did so. Inside the vehicle, he opened the glove box and pulled out a Desert Eagle handgun. Its titanium body threw off a silver glare in the early morning light and he shoved it beneath his jacket, fastening the holster clip to his belt. Kean put the Jag in reverse and pulled from the parking space in a wide arc. Turning left onto a side street, he found the alley that ran behind the row of shops that held Aideen's. At the alley's mouth was a small white truck with the store's name on it. He drove past it and parked at the end of the alley on the far side of a dumpster. Getting out of the car, he reached under the seat, from where he pulled a slim leather case. There was an electronic blip as he reactivated the car's security system and then he spun around, scanning for any shop owners on the way into their stores.

Satisfied that no one had seen him, he walked to the alley door marked *Dublin Arcanum*. Taking a deep breath, Kean unzipped the case and pulled a set of lock picks from it. *Ah, Gerald*, he sighed. *Forgive me, old friend, but I'm about to scare the hell out of your daughter.*

Kean cupped his palm against the metal door and listened. A muted scraping noise, like something being dragged across a cement floor, reached him. He slipped the first pick in and hoped the noise would disguise the sound of the lock's tumbler falling into place. The deadbolt slid back and he heard a sharp cry followed by more scraping, louder than before. For an instant, he thought of shooting the second lock off but slid the pick into it, no longer concerned with working quietly. The lock sprang open and he crashed against the door, a slim chain breaking from the pressure.

Aideen was running for the storeroom door when he stumbled in front of her. Her eyes went wide, darting in the direction of the open door and then behind him. She hesitated half a second too long and Kean was upon her. He clamped one hand over her mouth and wrestled her to the floor. With his foot, he reached out and kicked the door shut.

He pinned Aideen's arms to her sides with his legs, her smaller frame buried beneath his. Kean shifted his weight onto his heels and felt her relieved intake of breath. Fear dilated her pupils and his cheeks reddened in shame.

"Miss Godwin," he started hesitantly. "Aideen, I'm going to take my hand away from your mouth."

He started to remove his hand but forced it back over her lips as she drew a heavy breath. Kean rotated his wrist until he could read the dial of his watch. There were only a few minutes until her store was supposed to open. He needed to get the stone and get out of there. With his free hand, he reached under his jacket and pulled out the handgun. He rested it alongside his thigh and gave her a hard stare. She blinked at him, her eyes starting to water. Slowly, he removed his hand from her mouth and coiled her long blonde hair around his fist. He rose, gently pulling her with him to the door. He reset the top and bottom lock and then let his gaze sweep the small storeroom. His heart rate spiked as he noticed a cheap vinyl couch a few centimeters from an elaborately paneled wall. That couch, he smiled, had been the scraping sound. She hadn't finished replacing it before she bolted for the storeroom door.

His grip still tight in Aideen's hair, he guided her to the couch. "Pull it out," he commanded. She resisted and he raised his arm until she was standing on her tiptoes. "Pull it out, Aideen."

"Shit," he swore under his breath when she still refused to move. Reholstering his pistol, he kept her pulled taut at arm's length and dragged the couch from the wall. He looked at the seemingly random geometric shapes that paneled the wall. Turning to her, he caught a smirk lurking in her green eyes. The smirk faltered as he smiled back at her. "Your father built this panel for you, didn't he, Aideen?"

When she didn't answer, he rotated his belt until the gun was centered at his back. Then he grasped the coil of blonde hair with his left hand and forced her to her knees. He bent down beside her, his right hand exploring the deep grooves of the panel. His smile grew more carnivorous as he fingered the trigger to the panel's spring lock and the covering fell back to reveal a wall safe.

"What's the combination, Aideen?" he asked.

"Go find a corner to bugger yourself in," Aideen suggested, her green gaze growing heated. "And how do you know my father?"

Before Kean could answer, there was a soft thud against the door to the alley. Kean's hand leapt to Aideen's mouth and he pressed his weight against her, pinning her to the wall. The door handle jiggled and she struggled against him. Close-mouthed, she screamed and he bumped her roughly, forcing the air from her lungs. "Shut up," he hissed. "Or you're signing the death warrant of whomever is on the other side of that door."

Aideen stiffened and went silent. From the alleyway, she could hear her assistant Ricky yelling for her to come and open the door. *Fuck*, she swore silently. *Why did the little shit have to be on time today?*

"Good," Kean said as he felt her relax against him. "I just want the stone and the book and then I'll…" He paused, realizing he wouldn't be able to leave the store without Aideen. She knew his name and face and Donald Meyrick might torture her for pure sport. But how, he wondered, was he going to get her to the Jag and back to Kenmare? The hair on the back of Kean's neck rose to sharp points and he released Aideen, his gaze going to the door. There was a dull pop and the sound of something heavy falling against the door.

"Meyrick!" The word erupted from him in an involuntary whisper. He pulled the gun from its holster and thumbed the safety off. He glanced at Aideen and saw her shocked surprise that he had threatened her with the pistol's safety on. There was the scrape of metal in the door's top lock and Kean stood up. Positioning himself between Aideen and the alley door, he turned his back to her and aimed the gun at the door. "Open the goddamn safe, Aideen," he pleaded.

Aideen's hands flew to the safe's combination lock. The numbers passed in a blur as she spun the dial. The last number in place, she heard the safe's lock slide open just as the deadbolt to the alley door slid back. There was the sound of something, Ricky she guessed in a ragged breath, being dragged away from the doorstep and then the scrape of metal in the bottom lock. She reached into the safe and pulled the diary and stone from it, clutching them to her chest as she stood. She had the sudden image of a man on the other side of the door. Pale, white-haired, he was nearly albino in appearance except for his ice-blue eyes. At his feet, Ricky, his skin drained of color, blood seeping from the back of his neck, wore a death mask of surprise.

"Stay behind me," Kean cautioned as he moved across the room, keeping the gun leveled at the alley door. They reached the storeroom door and he stopped her. "Check the front," he whispered.

"It's clear," she said without looking. The Bloodstone propelled her forward and she grabbed Kean's arm and pulled him into the showroom as the man in the alley finally managed to pick the bottom lock. She raced across the room and threw the bolt back on the front door. The door's silver chimes joined the heavy discharge of Kean's gun ringing in her ears.

Kean turned and pushed Aideen the rest of the way through the shop's front door and onto the sidewalk. Grabbing her elbow, he broke into a sprint, his nervous gaze returning to the door of her shop. A small alley shot off to their left and he pulled her into it, his head popping around the corner to see if they were being pursued. Kean's grip tightened on her arm and they ran to the end of the side alley. They emerged into the alley behind Aideen's shop, some twenty feet from the dumpster that hid his Jaguar. He pulled his car keys from his pocket and deactivated the alarm system.

"Get into the car," he said, walking backwards. His gaze flicked between the side alley and the back door to Aideen's shop.

Forcing herself not to look back down the alley at Ricky's inert body, Aideen obeyed him. She opened the driver's side door and slid over the gearbox. One hand still clutching the stone and book, she pulled the seatbelt across her chest. Kean climbed in after her, lightly tossing the pistol to his left hand as he placed the key in the ignition.

"Get down," he said and switched the gun back to his right hand.

Rolling down the window, Kean stuck the gun out and glanced back down the alleyway. But no one was following them. "I didn't kill him," he said, his voice heavy with doubt.

Aideen closed her eyes and saw the man wrapping his tie around his thigh, the leg dragging behind him as he returned to the alley door. His gun was raised to chest level, a cold, murderous gleam in his eye. "No, now go!" she yelled.

Chapter Three

They headed west out of Dublin, in the direction of Enfield. Kean checked the rearview mirror so often, Aideen worried they would hit one of the slower moving cars in front of them. When she wasn't closing her eyes in anticipation of such an event, she was watching Kean. The gun, its safety back on, nestled between his muscled thighs, his left hand resting lightly at the bottom of the steering wheel, two centimeters above the pistol's grip. When they passed the exit for Laragh, the traffic thinned and she saw the tension ease from his body.

"Where is it you think you're taking me?" she asked.

Kean's gaze tripped over her, the stone and book she still pressed against her chest and a mild look of surprise registered on his face. A wave of irritation crashed against her as she realized he'd forgotten about her. She still wasn't sure whether he had saved her life or merely kidnapped her to preserve the stone and diary. Her grip on the objects tightened and Kean returned his attention to the road.

"Where?" Aideen repeated the question.

"He's seen me," he muttered, more to himself than to her. "I can't take you to Kenmare now." He looked at the road signs, searching for a solution. "I have a place along Galway Bay."

Cold fingers pressed against Aideen's flesh, prickling the skin and making the small hairs on her arms bristle. If he knew her father, there was only one place he could be taking her. "Not to Árainn," she said, her words stilted. "Not to Inish Oirr."

Kean's lips pressed into a thin pucker and he took a deep, bracing breath but didn't answer Aideen. She looked down at the diary she held, the *Book of Cenn Cruach*, and the Bloodstone. The diary's contents were indelibly imprinted upon her memory. She looked at Kean, weighing her options. He wouldn't risk losing the diary, couldn't know that neither would she. The muscles along his jaw-line were working furiously as he tried to drive without glancing in her direction. In his agitation, he brought both hands high up on the steering wheel.

"Well then," Aideen said and quickly slipped the stone between her thighs and rolled down her window.

Her right arm across her chest, she held the diary out the window. The Jaguar jerked to the right and Kean cursed her softly. His hand shot out to pull the book back inside, but he froze as he felt the soft slide of her palm across his thigh and heard the metallic click of her thumbing the pistol's safety off.

"The diary, the stone, or your balls. Which is more important to you, Kean?" she asked, her voice barely audible over the purr of the Jaguar's engine.

Kean calmly returned his hands to the steering wheel and signaled to traffic that he was pulling off to the side of the road. For a long moment, he watched the other cars passing and then he turned his darkening gray gaze on her. He shifted in his seat until he was looking directly into her eyes and his groin was pressed flat against the pistol's barrel. "Yes, Aideen, to Árainn," he said.

Aideen answered his challenge by nudging the barrel forward. She saw the barest twitch of his mouth but he otherwise remained impassive. "I'm not going to Árainn," she said. "You're taking me to the nearest police station."

"Once I know the stone and diary are secure," he replied, his voice low and cold. "I'll take you wherever the hell you want, Aideen."

"They're mine," she said. Aideen's grip on the pistol tightened and her hand began to shake.

Kean put his hand over hers and clicked the safety back to its *on* position. "We both know you wouldn't kill for the stone, Aideen."

Aideen was struck by the sudden image of her dream from the night before. Cenn interrogating her, demanding to know how she came to possess his diary. His grip, tight on her arm, commanding her to tell him from whom she had received it. At her answer of a dead man, he queried whether it was by her own hand. She had chafed at that and replied she couldn't imagine killing someone over a book and unknown stone. That was when his gaze had become hooded and she had realized another's death was but a small obstacle to him in his pursuit of the stone.

Aideen looked at Kean. His gaze was hooded, his cheeks flushed and his breathing shallow. The eyes were off, she thought, as she looked at the storm brewing in them, but otherwise Kean and the dream lover who had haunted last night's sleep were identical. She felt moisture pool between her legs even as her heart constricted at the memory of some vague tragedy. She forced the flash of recognition away — the dream would fade in time and she couldn't let it influence her reaction to her kidnapper.

"You know me now?" he asked, his eyes unreadable. He didn't wait for her to answer but continued. "I was surprised when I didn't recognize you immediately in the store. But it's been ten years since I last looked at a picture of you."

She shook her head, denying what he was saying. "I don't know you. We haven't met...we haven't met."

"Perhaps that was an error, but your father thought it best," he answered, a wry frown suggesting he was only humoring her. He took the gun from her and put it back in its holster. Then, without warning, he reached between her legs and took the Bloodstone.

As unexpected as his action was, Aideen still had to suppress a moan at the brief touch of his hand against her mound. She forced her gaze out the window and tried to school her features to match the cold, stone mask Kean wore. *No, not a mask*, she corrected herself. She thought of the gray eyes, now as flat as unpolished granite. *That is his nature.*

"How did you know my father?" Aideen asked once she was sure her voice wouldn't tremble. She still didn't dare look at him. Her nipples had hardened to harsh, painful peaks and her skin felt like it had been coated with acid.

"He was my master." He saw her confused frown reflected in the Jaguar's window. "I was his apprentice in...in the ancient way," he explained.

Aideen bit back a sharp laugh, surprised by the bitterness that suddenly welled inside her. No wonder the man had been insane enough to kidnap her and displayed no fear when she held the pistol to his balls. She gave a short, hard shake of her head as if, by doing so, she could dispel the nonsense surrounding her.

"You've had the Bloodstone since Sunday and still you scoff at the idea?" he asked.

"Mold," she whispered. She heard his soft chuckle and turned to glare at him. "Mold," she repeated and jabbed a finger at the diary. "You. That ghost in the alley. You've all been infected. Some parasite eating away at your brain cells."

Unwanted and uninvited, the memory of the scrying ceremony she had performed surfaced. That she had gone so far as to cast a spell shamed her and she blinked against the memory. But the image remained of Cenn, so many centuries ago, standing in front of his own scrying bowl, his robes on the floor and his cock, stiff, proud, rising from the mass of blue-black curls like a directional rod homing in on her. Unable to stop herself, her gaze darted to Kean's lap. His own excitement was evident and her tongue darted from her mouth to appreciatively wet her upper lip.

"Mold?" he asked, his tone mocking her. His thigh muscles contracted, his cock bobbing beneath his trousers.

"Yes," she insisted. "And I demand you take me to a hospital."

Kean's hand snaked out and captured hers. He dragged her to him, forcing her palm open, and she closed her eyes as she struggled against him. Her palm came into contact with something warm, smooth. Thick, the object filled her hand and tapped out a steady pulse against her skin. She opened her eyes to find that she held the Bloodstone.

"You were born...no," he corrected himself. "You were bred to possess the Bloodstone, Aideen. We both were." She tried to drop the stone but he held her hand captive and forced it more tightly around the stone. "Don't tell me you're indifferent to its vibrations."

Aideen tried to avoid his gaze. She couldn't. A part of her tried to force the lie past her lips that she felt nothing. The part of her that was still nine years old, stretched out on a dolmen, the cold stone penetrating the thin white shift. Her father was there, hovering above her, a dagger in one hand, a cup of wine in the other. He would pass the knife above her head and force some wine down her throat before passing the blade over her lower torso and pouring the wine from the cup to stain her gown and panties red. With every new ceremony, each pass of the knife, she trembled in fear that, this time, the knife would find her flesh, would penetrate her stomach and carve out her womb.

"Aideen?" His hand moved to rest along the back of her neck, his heat penetrating her skin and promising peace if she would but yield to him.

"I'm not going to Inish Oirr," she persisted. Its rhythm equally unrelenting, the stone told her she would, indeed, go.

Kean massaged the back of Aideen's neck and leaned closer to her until his lips whispered against her ear. "Aideen, whatever you're afraid of in Inish Oirr, I guarantee it's not as bad as Donald Meyrick."

Meyrick. The name echoed through her, producing a small shudder that would have made her laugh only a few days ago. Michael Meyrick, reported seer extraordinaire, was dead—or, at least, dead enough to require an estate sale and a published obituary. *Who, then, was Donald?*

"Michael's heir?" she asked.

Kean turned back to the steering wheel and put the car in drive. "In more ways than one, so it seems." Checking his side mirror, Kean merged back onto the road. "Look," he said, his sharp glance taking in her pinched features and tired eyes. "We're still a good hundred and seventy kilometers from where we can catch a boat out to the island. Why don't you rest?"

Aideen, her expression wary for an instant, watched him driving. Questions bounced through her mind but the Jaguar's smooth hum quieted them and she soon fell asleep.

Chapter Four

Kean stopped for petrol half an hour from Galway. While an attendant filled the tank, Kean stepped from the Jaguar and walked to the trunk. Keeping his attention focused on the front seat, acutely aware of the slightest motion of Aideen's blonde head, he pulled a blanket from the back. For reasons he didn't know and couldn't guess, her clothes had been partially damp when he took her from her little Dublin store and, even with the car's heat turned on high, Aideen was shivering in her sleep.

He handed his credit card to the station attendant, who ducked inside to run it through the machine. While he waited, Kean spread the blanket over Aideen's sleeping form. Her body uncurled in a sigh and he had to force his hands back onto the steering wheel, cursing the slowness with which the attendant was handling the transaction. He snapped in irritation at the young man when the card was returned. The sound disturbed Aideen and she turned to her side, drawing in to herself once again and creating gaps where the blanket covered her. Kean reached over and tucked the blanket underneath her. He caught the faint scent of fresh flowers and cupped her face before he could stop himself.

Kean jerked his hand away and slammed the Jaguar into drive, nervously glancing down at Aideen to see if he had woken her. She continued sleeping and he relaxed a little while he silently berated himself. It was of no use, he assured himself, becoming attached to her, desiring her as he had a decade ago when, in all her freshness and purity, she had been promised to him. No, he was merely trying to keep Gerald's daughter safe and prevent Donald Meyrick from using her to control the Bloodstone. For she was the Bloodstone's mistress, he acknowledged, more so than he would ever be its master. The sacred stone, exposed to the world at auction, had somehow found its way into her hands.

The Bloodstone. His gaze jerked down to where it lay curled in her hand, pressed between her breasts. But the stone couldn't hold his attention. The cold had teased her nipples to hard pebbles and Kean felt the car slowly veering to the side of the road. He shook his head violently to clear the image clouding his mind. But his fingertips still tingled with the imagined touch of her, his tongue felt the velvet brush of her nipples. *Goddess*, he wondered, how was he going to control himself alone with her on Árainn, on the island, cut off from his staff or anyone in the temple that he could pass Aideen's care and safety off to.

Aideen stretched and emitted a soft, cramped groan. Again, the blanket slipped from her, only this time, Kean didn't move to cover her. From the corner of his eye, he saw the pert thrust of her breasts beneath her blouse and her hand brushed over one straining peak as she sought to wrap herself in a warm hug. Keeping his eyes locked on the road ahead of him, Kean's grip on the steering wheel tightened until his knuckles whitened. No, his soul confessed. Even if he could hand her care off to another, he had no intention of letting her out of his sight.

* * * * *

Aideen woke at the sound of the Jag's tires pulling onto a gravel driveway. At the end of the drive, she saw the bay and a small building attached to a pier. The lonely air of the building and the grounds around it told her it hadn't been used recently. "Where are we?" she asked while she brought her seat back to an upright position.

"Boathouse," Kean answered, his voice tight. He punched a button on the Jag's console and what had looked like a windowless wall slid open to reveal the interior of a garage. He pulled in and hit the button again, plunging them in darkness. He turned on the interior dome light and the car's headlights before opening the driver's side door. "Stay here a sec."

Kean popped the trunk and Aideen could hear him rummaging around in its contents. He dropped an overnight bag on the driver's seat and put the diary inside it. He reached out to her for the stone and she reluctantly handed it over to him. She moved to open her door and found that he had parked too closely to the wall.

"Climb over," he suggested.

Her legs, cramped from the long ride, protested and she found herself stuck in a rather uncomfortable position above the center console. Her palms behind her, pressed flat on the driver's seat, her bottom on the console, she tried to push with her legs but couldn't. She heard Kean's irritated growl and then he tucked his arms under her breasts and hauled her into a standing position. He slowed right before she would have touched the cement slab and she felt the slow glide of his cock against her backside as he gently stood her on her feet.

"The space is a little tight," he said, the words clipped short. "You'll have to press against the wall and feel for a door about four feet down."

The space was indeed tight and Aideen could feel the thick swell of his erection pushing against her jeans as he pivoted to close the door. Her knees went weak and started to buckle but there was no room in which to fall. She began a slow accordion fold to the floor but he hoisted her up with one arm, his hand cupped along the underside of one breast. She suppressed a moan and the desire to arch against his utilitarian embrace. She reached out and grabbed the Jag's roof with one hand and the wall with the other to steady herself.

"My legs are still asleep," she grumbled and tried to pull away from him.

"You'll be able to stretch them out on the boat." Instead of releasing her, Kean pulled Aideen closer to him. Again, he caught the scent of fresh flowers and he pressed his face to her soft, blonde hair.

"You can let go of me now," Aideen said, nearly strangling on the words as they came out. Something warned her that, if he didn't release her soon, she would be crawling all over him.

"Sorry." The word came out in a mumble and was followed by the hesitant withdrawal of his hand. He took a deep breath and let it out slowly, hoping she wouldn't hear. He needn't have worried; she was already feeling her way toward the door that led to the docked boat.

"How many locks on this door?" she complained. The first two bolts shot back and she pushed at the door, but it wouldn't budge.

"Here, hold this." Kean handed the travel bag to her. He bent down, his shoulder brushing her hip, and released a third lock. "Umm…you're going to have to…" he paused.

"What?"

He could feel the impatient tap of her foot against the cement slab and he groaned. "Move...somehow," he said. "There's a top lock and I can't get up from this position."

Aideen turned slightly to the right and found Kean's face pressed against her stomach. She didn't know whether to curse his height or be thankful he wasn't half a dozen centimeters shorter. Aideen fought to catch her breath as her womb contracted in answer.

Kean's voice was muffled against her body as he suggested that their current position wasn't working. *It's working for me,* Aideen sighed inwardly and pressed her back flat against the door. The minute change in position was enough to allow him to slowly climb to a standing position. He used Aideen's hips and then her shoulders to steady himself as he rose, the flat of his cheek offering her breast the briefest caress.

"One more lock." He reached above them to the top of the doorframe. The swell of his erection thickened against Aideen and, this time, she couldn't resist nudging him with her body. She closed her eyes, glad that Kean had turned the car's lights off and he couldn't see the emotions warring across her face. He slipped his free arm around her waist and pulled her to him. "It's going to open all of a sudden," he warned. "Better brace yourself."

The bolt clicked back and their combined weight sent them crashing to the boat dock's wooden flooring. The impact knocked the wind from Aideen and Kean had to scramble after the travel bag before it fell into the water. With the bag secured, he sat with his head between his legs and Aideen heard the soft hiccup of a laugh.

"Really," he promised. "On the average day, I'm much smoother than this." Standing, he tossed the bag into the boat and helped Aideen to her feet. "There's a flotation bag under the bench," Kean said as he helped her into the boat. "Put the travel bag inside while I slip the moorings off."

Aideen secured the bag and then shrugged her way into a lifejacket. Kean boarded the boat and handed her a push pole. They both pushed until they cleared the boathouse. Waving off the lifejacket Aideen offered him, Kean started the boat's engine and checked the gauges.

"Not too much longer," he smiled cheerfully as the boat headed out into Galway Bay.

Aideen nodded and tried to return the smile despite the tightening knot in her stomach. She tried to remember the last time she had stepped foot on one of Árainn's islands. Well over a decade ago, she recalled. It was when she was sixteen, the summer before she lost her virginity, and it would be the last ceremony of her father's in which she participated. On the return trip, storm waves rocked the ferry and turned her gut into a clenching ball of protest. Gerald had hinted that her participation in the ceremonies would soon change. The idea had sent her racing to the ferry's railing to spill the remains of her breakfast over its rusted sides. From that point on, she had fasted, feigned illness, pulled every stunt she could think of to avoid any more trips with her father. And, just before their annual trip to Inish Oirr was due to roll around, she offered up her virginity to the neighborhood bad boy on what she thought were her own terms.

Aideen remembered the soul-withering look her father had given her upon learning of the loss and wiped a tear from her cheek. She glanced at Kean, but his attention was focused on the approaching shoreline. She wondered if he had been there, at her father's ceremonies, one of the faces behind the many masks. Only a few years older than her, he would have been barely out of his teens. Aideen felt another tear at the edge of her eyelid threatening to spill. She swiped it away and set her face to the wind.

Kean turned to her and gestured toward an outcropping of rocks. "We'll make land just beyond those."

Aideen arched one blonde brow at him. She saw nothing more than a sheer cliff of limestone beyond the rocks. She ran her hands over the lifejacket's buckles and jerked the straps tighter.

Kean looked down at her testing the lifejacket and a frown marred his chiseled features. "There's a cave, with moorings and steps up to a safe house," he explained. "And a barred gate to make sure we're the only ones using it."

She gave him a small salute and gripped the edge of her seat as the cliffs loomed closer. The island, she knew, had cliffs three hundred feet above the water and she was briefly grateful that she only had about ten stories of cliff to climb. And no luggage, she thought. He could damn well carry the travel bag and be thankful that she wasn't asking him to carry her. The absence of luggage reminded Aideen that she was still wearing yesterday's clothes and she dipped her head and took a discreet whiff. Only the salt spray from the surrounding water was noticeable.

"I hope this safe house has a shower," she said as Kean pulled the boat alongside heavy cast iron bars set into the mouth of a limestone cave. "And some fresh clothes." He frowned at her again just as her stomach growled. "And some food," she added. She took the push pole from Kean and helped him guide the boat into the small cave.

"Food, shower," he grunted and jumped from the boat. Aideen handed him a heavy length of rope and his gaze swept over her smaller form. "We'll find something for you to wear while your clothes are cleaned."

Kean hopped back into the boat and grabbed the travel bag and a flashlight. He placed them on the deck and, without warning, put his hands on Aideen's hips and lifted her to the deck as well. She turned, ready to offer him a hand. He was staring at her in the cave's low light. A lock of his blue-black hair had fallen across his face, further shadowing his features, but she still could see the speculative sparkle in his gray eyes. He took her hand and stepped lightly onto the deck.

"The steps?" she said, her hand still trapped in his.

His hand fell back to his side and he bent to pick up the bag and flashlight. He flicked the switch on and let the beam of light play against the back of the cave. Aideen saw the steps. They were carved from the rock and their small crystals glittered like jewels beneath the beam of light. Kean stepped in front of Aideen and held one hand out to her.

"Slippery," he cautioned when she hesitated to take his hand, "and dark."

Palms sweaty, she took his hand. They began the rough ascent, their bodies pressed close together while the lap of waves against the cave's wall urged them on from below.

Chapter Five

The stairs widened at the top until Kean and Aideen were standing on a small landing. In front of them was a heavy oak door, its wood rotted from the cave's constant dampness. Kean pressed against it, the wood scraping over limestone tiles set in what appeared to be a cellar. The room was empty and, at its opposite end, there was another door leading out. This door was metal and modern. Its surface was smooth, no handle or slot for a key marred its shiny perfection. Above it, a fluorescent light flickered and set into the wall next to it was an electronic keypad. Kean's fingers danced over the numbers and Aideen heard the whining squeal of hydraulics as the door's locking mechanism was disengaged. Kean pushed against the door and it opened onto a small, dimly lit hallway. He reached out to his right and flipped a few light switches. Motioning Aideen to step into the hallway, he reset the door's hydraulic locks and then led Aideen to a galley-sized kitchen.

"Nothing perishable," he said and pulled canned soup from the cupboard. "But we'll have a full stomach to think on." He pointed to a white door at the end of the narrow kitchen. "There's a shower and toilet through there with a washer and dryer. I'll see what clothes I can dig up then start on making us some dinner."

Aideen entered the narrow washroom and examined its contents. As with the kitchen, there was a light coating of dust on the appliances and ceramic bathroom fixtures.

Towels were neatly stacked above the toilet and she took two down and breathed in their scent. Clean but stale. There were dryer sheets in a utility cupboard and she put the towels in the dryer for freshening then stripped her clothes and dumped them in the washer without starting it. Shampoo and a dust-coated bar of soap were in the shower and she turned the water on, letting the heat build. It had been days since she'd slept in a bed and every muscle registered its complaint. She stepped under the showerhead, stretching and turning until every sore muscle had received a good dose of pressure and heat. She lathered up, her hands slowly exploring her body, her thoughts drifting to Kean only to be ripped away with an image of Cenn. She'd never known a dream to be so vivid, so detailed. Nine months of detail she thought and ran her soapy hands over her stomach, imagining that it was still full as she carried Cenn's child.

The water turned cold and Aideen finished rinsing off. She stepped from the shower, pulled the towels from the dryer and then started the washer. The towel fell from her and she bent to pick it up. *Cenn will be able to get a shower around midnight*, she grinned, *if he's lucky*.

Her hand still reaching for the towel, Aideen froze. She felt her heartbeat accelerate at the same time her breathing slowed. Her stomach, empty, threatened to force her to the toilet in dry heaves. She leaned her forehead against the washing machine. The cool metal and soft vibration brought some of the color back to her cheeks. She stayed in that position, resting, her eyes unfocused, until Kean knocked at the door a few seconds later.

"Aideen, you okay?"

Christ, she breathed, *even the voice is as I dreamt it. Can you dream sound?*

"Aideen?" His voice was low, concerned, and she could tell he was speaking into the thin line where the door met the doorframe.

"Yeah," she answered hoarsely, her voice stuck in another time, talking to another man — one with the same voice and face. "Just give me a second." She stood and tucked the towel around her and rubbed absently at her cheeks before she opened the door. As she moved, she tried to convince herself that she had seen Kean at the estate sale. She must have seen him and heard him, and the memory of him, the beauty of his voice, the strong features equally at home on a warrior or cover model, must have become embedded in her mind.

Her mind set on asking him if he'd been at the estate sale, Aideen opened the door. Seeing the small bundle of clothes he held, she felt as if her spine had turned to stone. "No." She kept her denial short and flat but he held them out to her.

"There's nothing else, Aideen," he said. "And your street clothes will be washed and dried before an hour's passed—"

"I know what they are," she said, looking at the white shift and its red robe embroidered in gold.

Kean gave an irritated snort and pushed them closer to her. "What they are is irrelevant in this context." When she still refused, he softened his tone and tried cajoling her into taking them. "Since when," he asked, "does a woman find the finest silks and satin objectionable?"

Aideen tilted her head, her gaze narrowing as her temper flared even higher.

"Whatever," Kean said with a resigned sigh. He put the garments on top of the washer and turned away, pulling the bathroom door shut behind him. "You can sit in here until your clothes are washed and dried. I'm getting something to eat."

Aideen listened to Kean clunking around the kitchen, making no attempt to hide his irritation. He was mumbling and she rested against the door, his words reaching her in broken phrases. She realized he was arguing with himself about the proper amount of gratitude an abducted woman should show when brought a gown fit for a queen.

Not a queen, she corrected him in her mind. *But a high priestess.* She glanced down to find herself fingering the edge of the crimson robe. With the tip of her nail, she traced the golden outline of the figures that signified the feminine half of the godhead. Water, cups, wisdom, air, plants. These symbols, she knew, would be complemented on the high priest's robe by symbols of the masculine half. A ray of sunlight, a wild boar, a spear, a stag and a hawk. And was that other robe, she wondered, also here? She closed her eyes and imagined Kean wearing it. His image blended with her memory of Cenn and she felt a growing wetness between her legs.

"You'll be dead or in an insane asylum tomorrow, Aideen, girl," she said and lifted the white silk shift above her head. "Might as well have a hot supper tonight."

* * * * *

Kean wasn't in the kitchen when Aideen emerged a few seconds later. She stepped into the hallway and noticed a door slightly ajar with soft light spilling from the room. Barefoot, she crossed the cold limestone flooring and pushed the door until it was fully open. Kean was sitting at an oversized mahogany desk. A tureen was in the center of the desk with a place setting on either side. An uncorked bottle of wine waited to fill two glasses.

"You were expecting me?" she asked. The question came out harder than she meant and she took a tentative step into the room.

"No." He took the wine bottle and began to fill their glasses. He dipped his head so she couldn't read his face. "Just hoping you would change your mind."

"I'm hungry." Aideen sat down in the leather-cushioned chair opposite Kean. Arms folded, her hands tucked in at her sides, she watched him pour the wine and lift the tureen's lid to ladle still steaming canned stew into her bowl. She took a ravenous bite then raised her eyes to find him watching her. She gestured toward his empty bowl. "Aren't you going to eat?"

His gaze darted down to his bowl and he gave a little upward nod but didn't move to fill it. Instead, he looked at Aideen while she ate. His finger traced the rim of his wine glass and he took a slow sip. "I'm glad you came out of the bathroom sooner rather than later," he said before he finally spooned some of the soup into his bowl.

Aideen shrugged, not looking at him, and took a gulp of wine, its natural bitterness making her wince. Kean went to add more wine to her glass and she abruptly pulled it away from him. "I think a clear head goes better with a full stomach when it's time to be thinking," she said and slid her glass to the edge of the desk.

He cocked an eyebrow at her but didn't argue. He slid the bottle and his glass along the desk until they rested next to hers. Without the glass to occupy his hands, he began to toy with a grapefruit-sized globe of smoky quartz.

"Your crystal ball?" she asked sarcastically.

The side of his mouth lifted in a lazy smile. "Why don't *you* look inside it and tell me what you see, Aideen?"

Once he made the suggestion, Aideen found that she couldn't avoid looking at it. Deep within the quartz, a swirl of electricity followed Kean's caressing fingertip. She blinked and snatched the globe from its holder, turning it over in her hands, but the small storm had disappeared.

"I do find that it gives me answers I couldn't get elsewhere," he said and held his hand out.

Aideen dropped the globe into his open palm and saw the light begin its dance anew.

"Parlor tricks, mind games—" she started, Kean's narrowing gaze stopping the rest of the words before they could fall carelessly from her mouth.

"You forgot the mold," he said, his voice strained and tired.

"Don't ridicule me," she bit out.

"No, Aideen." He placed the globe back on its holder. "It is you who are ridiculing me, my beliefs. Your father's beliefs!" He leaned forward and pinned her with his cloudy gray gaze. "I do believe, Aideen, to the very core of my soul. As did your father. Just because you are incapable of holding a spiritual belief—"

"That's not true," she shot back.

"What then," he asked and gestured to the book-filled shelves that lined the wall behind him, "do you believe in?"

Aideen shifted in her seat, her eyes fixed on a small scar that ran down the desk's front leg. She chewed at the inside of her bottom lip, the iron taste of blood corrupting her tongue.

"Christ?" he inquired. "I've certainly heard you invoke his name enough times…"

"I see my father taught you sarcasm as well as witchcraft," Aideen said and pushed her chair away from the desk.

Kean came around the desk and caught her by the wrists before she could leave the room. "Aideen, please. I've been feeling my way blindly through this since your father died. That you and I had a role to play didn't mean that either of us could be trusted with the knowledge until the time came." He foundered and looked around the room desperate for something that would convince her despite her lifetime of disbelief. "Your education…your experiences were incomplete…"

Aideen tried to twist her hands free but he only pulled her closer to him. "Aideen, I need your energy…" He was touching her now, his chest brushing against hers so lightly she wouldn't have felt it had she not wanted him to touch her. He brought her hands behind her back, loosely trapping her against him. "The stone will answer your call, Aideen. It will listen to your voice…*they* will listen to your voice…"

"*They?*" she asked, her lips trembling against the strong curve of his jaw.

"The mother —"

"No!" she jerked her head back and tried to scramble from Kean's embrace. "You bloody fucking bastard," she yelled and slammed her bare foot against his shin.

His grip roughened and he turned, pinning her against the wall. "If Meyrick finds us and takes the stone...it will be a black rain of acid and ash covering the world," he warned. "You can't even imagine what it will be like."

Aideen closed her eyes and remembered the battle at Kenmare. The constant fog and the vague creatures that stayed always just beyond the borders of recognition. She could indeed imagine it and a small shudder passed over her.

"Aideen," Kean pressed, his tone gentling. "It's as much science as it is sorcery. Please..." He released her hands and stepped back, the barest semblance of calm falling over his features. "Just let me tell you what I know. Let me show you what I've seen, what you would have seen had you not turned your back on your father...on me...with that—boy."

"On you?" The question was a shocked whisper and she took a step toward him, reading but not understanding the source of the pain she saw in his eyes.

He reached out and caressed the edge of her robe. "On me," he confirmed and let the fabric drop against her breast. "You were to be my wife, Aideen."

Chapter Six

After dropping his little bombshell, Kean turned back to the desk. He retrieved the Bloodstone and diary from one of the drawers and placed them on the desktop. He took pen and paper from another drawer and translated the cover glyphs while Aideen prowled in front of the desk, her thoughts raging at her father's audacity. Kean ignored the increasingly heavier fall of her footsteps and opened the diary's cover. His gaze widened in surprise as he found the loose sheets of paper with her translations of the text.

"How much did you translate?" He leafed through the book and matched the pages with her notes.

Aideen stopped pacing and looked at him. Her nostrils flared at their edges when she answered. "All of it."

"In two nights?" He shook his head in disbelief and started verifying her notes.

A smirk surfaced at the corner of her mouth. Again, Cenn's image surfaced in a warm, sensuous swell. "I was — shall we say — driven to get it done."

Her voice, husky and laden with remembered desire, compelled Kean into looking up from the diary. He noted her flushed skin and the deep rise and fall of her breasts before his gaze became lost in the soft curves of her hips and thighs. He ran one hand across the rough stubble of his evening beard, his color high on his cheeks, and dipped his attention back to her translation.

"This doesn't say much," he said and placed her pages to the side.

"Not on its surface, no," Aideen agreed. She watched him as he flipped through the diary. Every few pages, his hand would casually brush against the Bloodstone. Each time, his immediate reaction was to lightly scratch the surface of his palm.

"You think the text is layered then?" He began counting off the glyphs for some hidden message.

"No," she said and he seemed taken aback by the confidence in her voice.

"There has to be more than this!" He closed the cover and rested his head in his hands for a moment before rubbing at his eyes.

"Why is that?" she asked. Her head tilted, she continued watching him, a new calm filling her. When he didn't answer, she took his left hand and traced a thin scar that ran across his palm in muted white anger. "Why does there *have* to be more?"

Kean removed his hand from her easy grip and rubbed more vigorously at the scar. "We've just been looking for it for so long," he answered flatly.

Aideen sat back down in the leather-cushioned chair. "This is the first time you've seen the diary...or the stone for that matter?"

Kean nodded and traced one of the cover's glyphs. "It was as if the two were keeping themselves hidden from us."

"Yet you knew of them?" she asked, confused. Never, despite all her familiarity with Irish antiquities, had she heard of the Bloodstone or so impossibly old a manuscript as the *Book of Cenn Cruach.*

"There is another diary," he explained.

At his words, Aideen felt the blood begin to drain from her face as some half-buried memory began to surface. "Another diary?"

"Etain's," he answered. "Their lives have been distorted into myths, but Etain's diary has been protected all these centuries, handed down from one generation to the next."

Echoes filled Aideen's head and she tried to shake them away. *...you are like a butterfly...I will call you Etain.* She shook her head again against the possibility that she really had heard those words spoken so long ago.

Aideen looked up to find Kean standing over her, one hand resting on her shoulder, concern darkening his features. "What's wrong, Aideen? Are you ill?"

She brushed his hand and worry away. "Would I have seen this diary?" she asked, hoping she had, indeed, caught some glimpse of it as a child.

Kean gave a hesitant shake of his head in reply. "No, not as young as you were when you left us."

Aideen felt fresh blood returning to her cheeks as her temper began to rise. "I did not leave anyone," she said tersely. "I was never willingly a member."

Kean shrugged and crossed to a locked cabinet. As with the rest of the house, the lock was keyless—a combination of eight numbers opened it. Once the cabinet was unlocked, he pulled out a retractable reading shelf and placed a loose-leaf binder on it.

"Photocopies," he explained and motioned for her to join him. Kean switched on a reading light in the cabinet and stepped back to allow her a closer look. "We thought, at first, that it must be layered, but nothing...then we thought Cenn's diary would provide a code key or itself be the answer..." His voice trailed off in an exhausted disappointment.

Aideen took a deep breath. Kean's scent, like morning dew on grass, filled her. She looked at him, and into him, for a brief second and then turned away. "The book, both books, have served their purpose," she said. He looked at her, confused but intensely curious. "It's gotten us to this point." She delivered her explanation with reluctance, still unwilling to retreat from her earlier position.

The fatigue so evident in Kean's face seconds before fell from him. "But for what purpose?" he asked.

Aideen ran a fingertip over her left palm and traced the thin white line that hadn't been there two days before. But for the hand it marred, it was a twin to the scar on Kean's right hand. She remembered the sensation of Etain's hand, her left hand, being cut in the joining ceremony with Cenn. Aideen shoved her hands deep in the robe's folds and shrugged.

"Tell me what you know outside of Etain's diary. Was there..." she faltered and drew another deep breath. "Was there a child?"

Kean arched one dark eyebrow, surprised at the question. "Yes...a direct ancestor of mine."

"And Etain raised the child?" She knew this wasn't the case but did not trust herself to ask what she really wanted to know—what had happened to the child, to her child.

He shook his head. "Nothing is known of Etain outside what she wrote in the diary...before she disappeared, she gathered together those who were closest to Cenn…the guards who had witnessed his death at his mentor's hands and his rebirth with the stone's magic…some of the women who had befriended Etain." He paused, pulling together the threads of his family history he had learned at his mother's knee. "It was this group of people who formed the temple and educated Etain's daughter."

"Daughter?" The question broke from Aideen in a strangled whisper.

"Girls all until I was born," he answered.

Kean motioned her back to the cabinet. He pulled a sheaf of computer printouts from a manila envelope. "The stone and the diary, we think, were stolen nine years ago when burial mounds in Kenmare were vandalized. Eventually, they fell into Michael Meyrick's hands — the book only recently."

Aideen pointed at the long column of numbers and tried to force a joke past her lips, tried to say anything that would stop the questions about Cenn and Etain's child that clamored in her mind. "You're getting all that from this?"

"Patience," he cautioned, the whisper of conspiracy in his voice stoking a small fire in the pit of Aideen's stomach. "Donald Meyrick had no use for his uncle's beliefs until he saw the stone. Donald," he said, the name quickly pushed from his tongue, "is a man of science — a physicist." At this, Kean tapped the printout. "Michael must have taunted him with the stone. Anyway, Donald had its properties secretly measured."

"And these are the results?"

Kean nodded. "We've always had members at the best museums and labs on the lookout for the unusual."

"So what got Donald so hot and bothered about the stone?" Aideen asked, although she'd experienced more than enough of the stone's power to understand why any scientist would be interested in it.

Kean pointed to the row of numbers on the far right, as if they would mean something to her. "It's seventeen times as dense as lead but only a quarter the weight," he said in response to her blank stare. "And it's similar to quartz in that it generates energy but at a magnitude that would suggest the tests were flawed."

"Suggest?"

"It hasn't been tested—it's a vibrational energy and requires an exact combination of pitch and key to release it."

"And once the energy is released?" Aideen asked, the answer resurfacing in her mind before she finished the question.

"Then the barriers to the dimensions science tells us exist fall away." His hands moved like a magician's pulling a bouquet of roses from thin air.

But, if the barriers fell, she knew, the bouquet would be black. She thought back to the confrontation in her store and the pale creature that had been only a few steps behind her and Kean as they fled. "Donald Meyrick's most recent actions don't seem like those of a scientist," she said, half to herself.

Kean stuffed the printout back into the envelope and closed the cabinet. "He's also a sadist of the highest magnitude. We believe he killed his uncle and an estate agent." He glanced back to the desk, a slight disbelief showing in his face at his continued possession of the Bloodstone. "It was only through some miracle of incompetence by his uncle's solicitor that Donald doesn't have the stone now."

Aideen collapsed into the chair and reached over to pick up the Bloodstone. Its dark red interior became illuminated at her touch and she drew it to her stomach. Light flared in the stone's center and Kean perched on the edge of the desk, watching her.

"And I'm supposedly Etain's ultimate heir?" she asked, despite knowing the answer far better than he did.

Kean cleared his throat before responding. "Yes."

She looked into his cloud-gray eyes and saw the stone's light burning in the black pupils. "And you are Cenn's?" He nodded and her gaze returned to the stone. That he was Cenn, she had more trouble believing. But Cenn had said they were bound forever — through eternity. *A pretty thought even if it seemed impossible.*

Kean leaned over her and touched the Bloodstone's top. Heat flowed from the stone, through her hands, up her arms, and into her stomach. She had a trancelike awareness of her nipples hardening, and heated desire, wet and hungry, coiled between her legs. Kean left the desk and knelt on the floor, both hands covering hers as she gripped the stone more tightly to her body. The gray eyes flashed a haunting black-speckled sapphire before he pushed the collar folds of her robe over her shoulders. The movement exposed her breasts, the nipples a hard pink that betrayed her excitement. Another pulse of power erupted from the stone and Aideen sank into Kean's embrace, the Bloodstone falling to the carpet.

Together, Aideen and Kean tumbled to the floor, his body cushioning her landing. His hands slipped through the center fold of the robe to play over her hips. She moaned into the hollow of his throat and gave him a hard nip. He bucked against her in pleasured surprise and grabbed her rounded cheeks. She reared up, her legs straddling his hips and her palms pressed flat against his chest. She leaned back, her center gliding over his clothed manhood. Aideen shrugged her way out of the robe and put her hands along the side of his narrowed waist. Kean's hands traveled in a stroke up her back. They fastened on her shoulders and dragged her down to his mouth for a heated kiss.

He rolled Aideen onto her back. She tugged at his shirt buttons while he feathered her face and neck with kisses. His hand slid between her legs and he thumbed her clit with sharp upward strokes that left her gasping in protest.

"I can't concentrate," she said and fumbled at the buttons. She had only managed to undo the top two. "I'll never get these undone if you don't—" Except for the fact that his hands, face and neck were unmarked, his tattoos shouldn't have surprised her. It was a detail, she realized, that she couldn't have concocted in her dream.

Kean looked down at where her hands had stopped moving. "They bother you?" he asked, undoing a third button before lifting the shirt over his head.

His chest was a matching canvas to Cenn's. Aideen reached up and ran a fingertip over the firedrake that curled just below his left nipple.

"Why is your dragon here?" she asked, her voice breaking from the flood of memories and emotions his body invoked.

Kean thumbed her partial tattoo in a soft caress before he answered. "My voice isn't equal to yours, Aideen." His hand left her collar and covered the hand she still held against his chest. "When it was time for me to receive my summoner's mark, it was decided I call my power up from my heart."

Letting go of her hand, he touched her collar again. "You raise your power from your voice." He gazed deep into her eyes for a second before repeating his question. "Do they bother you?"

Pushing away thoughts of her father's tattoos, Aideen ran her hand down Kean's chest. Between his navel and the belt line of his pants, knobby vines weaved their way into a Wizard's Star. She spread her fingers until each was touching the five points of the pentacle. He groaned at the firm press of each fingertip against his lower stomach.

Aideen ran her hand back up his stomach, stopping to tease one of his nipples. She clasped both hands around his neck and pulled him to her in a heated kiss.

Finding her body's response answer enough, Kean returned to teasing Aideen's clit. He slid a finger deep into her cunt and she released him with a hard growl as she pumped a wide arc in the air. Another blue-black flash of his eyes and he shook his head at her. Resting on his haunches, he spread her thighs and pulled her lower body onto his bent legs. Her ass rested against the base of his still covered cock and her cheeks contracted at its firm press. Aideen wrapped her legs around his waist, her cunt aching at the barrier between their flesh. With his thumbs, he parted her labial folds, the plump lips pinched against his forefingers as his thumbs rolled her pink nub.

Her flesh on fire, she ran her hands over her stomach and breasts and then clasped them to her face as she lifted her ass higher. Kean's thumbs traveled lower, exposing her rose red center, moist with her need for him. His pads played at the edge, traced maddening circles around the entrance to her cunt, dipping inside her only to retreat a heartbeat later. The same belief at his possession of the Bloodstone patterned his face as he looked down at Aideen's straining body. In a single, fluid motion he pushed her forward and stretched his legs out behind him. His face centered over her mons, he dove into her, his mouth attacking the sensitive outer lips before his tongue plunged into her. Her hands found the dark curls of his crown and she pulled him more tightly into her, her legs curving around his neck and shoulders as she rode the plunging tongue and questing lips to orgasm.

As her shudders slowed, Kean flipped Aideen onto her stomach. She heard the downward slide of his zipper then felt the thick penetration of his cock. The muscles of her vagina clamped down on the organ and she pushed her upper body higher, her ass locked in a furious rhythm of backward pumps. His hand slid under her stomach, steadied her at the same time he drew deeper into her. She reached out to the chair for support, a groan escaping her as his cock swelled inside her. The knowledge that she had been reduced to this frenzied state only made her wetter, made the walls of her cunt lock him to her as they both raced to climax. Kean shuddered against her, his breath hot on her neck as he gently rested his weight against her. She shattered against the chair in her own climax, her body trembling with exertion and ecstasy. Still inside her, he caressed her breasts, licked the length of her neck while his hands soothed her fiery skin. He reached down beside them, withdrawing from her, and kissed the back of her shoulders before draping the robe over them.

Chapter Seven

Kean lifted Aideen to the chair and finished securing the robe as carefully as if he were dressing a porcelain doll. He pulled a velvet bag from one of the desk's drawers and wrapped the Bloodstone in it before locking the stone and diary in the cabinet. Her mind a riot of sensations and memory, Aideen remained motionless until he cupped her elbow and led her back down the hall to the bathroom. He started the water running in the shower and leaned Aideen against the bathroom door while he stripped the robe from her and folded it.

Kean coaxed the still somnambulant Aideen into the shower and leaned her against the wall. Giving the showerhead a twist, he removed the nozzle and ran the warm water through her hair and over her shoulders, kissing her mouth and neck as his hands caressed the water over her skin. His soft touch drew Aideen back to the present. Kean saw her return in her eyes and gave a tentative smile before he re-hooked the shower nozzle and began to lather her body with a fragrant soap. Even as her heart shouted that she was betraying Cenn with this near carbon copy, her body responded.

He leaned back to soap her breasts and Aideen felt the tip of his erection firmly tapping against her navel. Her gaze traveled over his chest and muscled stomach, taking in more of the exquisite details she had failed to notice in the study. From his navel, the same blue-black ladder of hair traveled down to the base of his erection. The tip of his penis was a mottled purple that glistened from the soap's oils. The shaft's thickness equaled that of the head and Aideen curled her fingers, hand over hand, around its circumference. A heated sigh escaped her when her fingertips refused to meet.

She took the soap from Kean and began lathering his lower body, her hands caressing sudsy circles over his lean ass as his cock pressed more insistently against her stomach. Lightly, she dug her nails into his barely yielding flesh and stood on tiptoe to kiss him. She nipped at his top lip before thrusting her tongue into his mouth and exploring his upper palate with one long, withdrawing swipe. His thickly muscled cheeks contracted and he cupped her ass, lifted her higher. Aideen wrapped her arms around Kean's neck and spread her legs in invitation for him to lift her higher still.

"Perfection." Kean's word was a husky whisper as he slid into her and began to slowly pump himself deeper into her center.

Aideen laved the lobe of his ear, suckled at it in unison with his thrusts and her body's own contractions as her cunt milked his cock once again. "Yes," she gasped before her mouth smothered his. "Fill me, please."

Aideen used her legs to squeeze Kean closer to her, her tongue fucking his mouth in demanding thrusts as her climax claimed the last of her control. Kean pushed her back against the shower walls, his hands pinioning her shoulders against the tile. He dipped his head and his hungry mouth pulled, teased and sucked at her pink-tipped breasts while he pumped her to another climax. His cock contracted inside her and his seed reached into her womb, coating her with its heat and life. Still her body trembled and he wrapped an arm around her waist, and pressed his body against her while he turned the water off and opened the shower door. She collapsed against him. The weight of her relaxed body embedded him more deeply inside her and set off another tremor of orgasm in Aideen.

Kean walked through the house, nuzzling her neck as she rode waves of a climax she couldn't control. Kicking open a door, he pivoted and sat down on a bed, Aideen over him in the dominant position. Her body still burning, she looked down at him, her need stamped across her face. He reached up and gave her nipple a stroking pinch that had her flinging her head back and grinding her cunt down to the base of his cock.

"There's so much lost time to make up," Kean half groaned and grabbed Aideen's hips as he sought deeper depths. "Let me fill you again, Aideen."

Chapter Eight

Her sleep troubled by dreams of shadow warriors, their battle cries echoing inside her head, Aideen woke to find that she was alone in the bed. She touched the mattress where Kean had held her as she drifted into sleep. No trace of his body heat remained. Gathering the coverlet around her, she left the bedroom. Light peeked from beneath the study's door. She gave the door's wood paneling a soft rap with her knuckles and then pushed it open. He was sitting in front of the desk. Cenn's diary and the copy of Etain's were sitting on the desk, open. Aideen's notes, complete with samples of the glyphs in Cenn's diary, filled the space between the two books.

"Still looking for layers?" she asked. She moved around the desk to stand behind him, a hand on each of his shoulders. She leaned over to look at the writings and her chilled nipples kissed the warm skin of his bare back.

Kean shook his head, his stubble tickling Aideen's ear. His left hand crept up to hold hers. "No, not layers. Do you see this?" He pointed to a glyph in Etain's diary. She gave him a soft *yes* and rubbed her cold nose against his ear. "And here," he asked and pointed to Aideen's own notes.

"Same glyph," Aideen answered with the obvious response.

He pointed to a dozen more glyphs contained both in Etain's diary and Aideen's notes on Cenn's diary. "Not just the same glyphs, but written in the same hand,

Aideen." He turned her left hand until he could see her palm. "This hand, Aideen."

"I don't write with my left," she responded, her voice flat. She heard an irritated rush of air leave his body and she kissed his temple.

"You know what I mean." He traced the outline of her scar. "You weren't born with yours...like I was born with mine."

She shifted against him and tried to extract her hand from his insistent grip. "What are you getting at, Kean?"

"You've used the Bloodstone...really used it, Aideen. Haven't you?"

His words were a mix of hurt and amazement and she twisted her hand free and paced to the other side of the room. Wrapping the coverlet more tightly around her, she turned to face him. Half a dozen responses competed with one another until she was left with nothing to say.

"You used it," he said, his voice taking on a hard edge. "You aren't Etain reborn...you *are* Etain. Just admit it, damn it."

She shook her head, denying the truth of what he had said. "It isn't possible," she started in a rough stutter. "What I thought I saw —"

"Don't go on about the mold again," he warned. "You've been denying what you are, *who you are*, for over a decade."

Aideen gave a strangled laugh and crossed to stand in front of the desk. She flipped Etain's diary shut with a sharp flick of her wrist. "Why not?" she asked, her voice raw with accusation. "I really wasn't anyone until this weekend —"

Kean buried his face in his hands and his voice took on a gentling tone. "Aideen, I just need to understand the stone, to understand your connection with it…" He left the sentence unfinished as he raised his head to look at her. The stormy gray eyes threatened to spill rain and she had to avert her gaze from the raw pain she saw.

"Sunday, I didn't believe in reincarnation or time travel," she began. "I sold trinkets and artifacts to those who did believe—but I never did!"

Kean rose from his chair and came around the desk to kneel in front of her. He turned the banker's lamp until its light was tilted down at her stomach and then he pushed the coverlet away. His finger traced scars along the sides of her stomach nearly invisible to the eye, so faint were they that Aideen hadn't noticed the white lines of stretched flesh on the paler skin of her stomach.

"Etain had no beginning," Kean pressed. "And her end was a mystery—she vanished minutes after giving birth to Cenn's daughter."

"How can nine months fit into one night?"

Kean didn't answer, just placed his lips against one of the stretch marks. Aideen couldn't see his face but she felt the slide of a warm tear over her stomach. She had unwittingly betrayed him again by bearing another man's child, even if that child's existence was the key to his own. She knotted her fingers through his hair and bent down to kiss the crown of his head. She whispered her apology against the thick curls.

"No," he said and lifted his head to stare into her unblinking green gaze. "It has all happened as it had to happen. As you said, both diaries existed to get us to this point." He tilted his head to one side and studied her for a few seconds before continuing. "Did you love him?"

Aideen blinked once, a tear escaping to stain her pale cheek. "Yes."

"And he loved you," he said, not questioning his predecessor's feelings. He paused, his grip around her waist tightening. "And I love you. I've never known a moment of your existence when I didn't love you," he confessed. "Do you believe that we are the same, he and I?"

"I..." Aideen turned away, more tears spilling from her. She wanted to respond in kind but confusion strangled the words before she could speak them. She looked at the clock. Less than twenty-four hours had passed since she'd first met him. And if what they both believed were true, in the course of a night, she had fallen in love with Cenn, lost him, and been plucked from her newborn child with only a few physical traces of the course of events. Having loved Cenn so deeply, even for so short a time, was it really Kean she loved now? Could they really be the same?

Kean nudged her chin until she met his gaze. He saw the question in her eyes and ran the pad of his thumb over her lower lip in mute understanding. He pulled the coverlet's ends together and rose to gather the diaries. "We should get some more sleep."

Aideen nodded, still not trusting herself to speak. She waited for him at the study's door while he secured the cabinet and gathered his shirt and jacket from the floor. A weak chirping from his jacket startled him and he broke into a smile, pulling his cell phone from the inside pocket. He looked at the caller's ID and the smile morphed into a broad grin. "The cavalry, at last," he said and tossed Aideen a wink.

Not understanding what he meant, she listened intently, a growing unease pooling in her stomach as his smile faded to frown. She felt her own lips pressing into a flat line and Kean hooked her waist with one hand and pulled her to him. As he spoke to the caller, the side of his mouth pressed against her forehead in a comforting kiss.

"What is it?" she asked when he replaced the phone in his jacket pocket and started to put his shirt on.

"Meyrick's betting we're here," he said, once again retrieving the Bloodstone and Cenn's diary from the cabinet. He dropped the Bloodstone, still in its velvet bag, into a heavier bag that reminded Aideen of the lead apron her dentist placed over her stomach when taking x-rays.

"Good bet," she said, her voice smaller than she liked.

Kean managed an easy smile that reached his eyes and he nodded down the hall. "Get dressed, we're leaving before they get here."

She nodded but hesitated at the door. "What's that for?" She pointed at the second bag.

"Meyrick's developed all sorts of tools to pick up the stone's vibrational signal," he answered. "Unless one of his devices is rubbing up against us, this will hopefully block its signature."

With his hand, he motioned her to hurry while he continued collecting things from the room. Her stomach gave a little flip as she was going out the door, the flash of his pistol as he drew it from the desk momentarily catching her attention. "Quickly, Aideen," he cautioned and shoved the pistol into his waistband.

Aideen raced down the hallway to the small kitchen and bathroom where her clothes were still in the dryer. She slipped them on, relieved they were dry and hoping they'd stay that way. She was stepping into her shoes when he popped his head into the kitchen and motioned for her to follow him. Back in the bedroom, he opened a closet door and flipped a panel to reveal another electronic combination lock. Another door opened and he ushered her through.

"James Bond with a Jag," she half-sighed and was rewarded by a downward turn of his sensuous mouth.

"Only this is for real," he reminded her.

They were in a small room with a counter and top cupboards on one side. He reached into the cupboard and pulled out two backpacks. Next, he pulled out a rugged day tourist jacket and handed it to Aideen. Once she had it on, he put the Bloodstone in the bottom of one backpack along with half a stack of British pound notes and American dollars. This he handed to Aideen and then he wound her hair into a high pile and covered it with a bucket cap while she shouldered the pack. Next, he stripped his dress slacks off and donned a pair of jeans and tennis shoes, with a light windbreaker over his dress shirt that was just long enough to conceal the pistol. He stuck Cenn's diary in the second backpack, pulled out a flashlight, and then grabbed her elbow and led her through another door and down into a narrow passageway that descended underground.

"How long does this go on?" she asked. The space was a tight fit made tighter by the packs they were wearing.

"About two kilometers," he answered. "Comes up in the back of an alley about two blocks from the public ferry."

"When was the last time you went through here?" she asked. The walls were slick with moisture and so was the floor. Twice she reached out to clutch at Kean's backpack as she lost her foothold on the slippery rock.

"Mmm...six months ago?" he guessed, catching her and standing her upright with only a slight slowing of his pace.

"What if the walls have caved in?" she asked. The possibility squeezed at her and she clutched his backpack a third time.

"Unlikely, but we won't know 'til we reach the end."

Their voices bounced along the tunnel's walls and she asked her next question in a whisper. "We're taking the day ferry?"

"Mm-hmm," Kean answered just as softly. "I don't want to risk running into Meyrick's men alone on the open waters and they may close in more slowly if they see the Jag and boat and think we're still on the island somewhere."

"Where are we going from the ferry?"

When Kean cleared his throat but didn't answer, Aideen grabbed the slick walls for support and stopped. "I think I should know," she began, her voice growing louder as he continued moving through the tunnel. "And it keeps my mind off how pressing these walls are." She took a few steps forward and stopped again. She released her grip on the tunnel's rounded outcroppings and planted her hands on her hips. "But if you'd rather keep me in the dark on how you plan to thwart the baddies…we can always talk about how small your penis is."

She wouldn't have thought it possible with the tunnel's limited width, but Kean turned, backpack and all, in the passageway. He kept the flashlight's beam on her face as he returned to where she was standing. The sharp glare made her close her eyes and turn her head to the side. Her body gave a surprised jerk when his lips brushed the bit of her ear not covered by the bucket hat.

"Is it smaller than my predecessor's?" he asked and wrapped his free arm around her waist. "I *am* impressed, Aideen."

Aideen's breath, coming fast and hot, bounced off the tunnel wall and she turned to face him. Their mouths brushed against one another and, despite the tunnel's cool temperature, she started to sweat. "I just wanted an answer—" she protested before his mouth closed over hers.

Kean's hand dropped to her hip, his thumb digging into the softer flesh through the jeans. The kiss roughened and, through the layers of intervening denim, she could feel him grow hard, his cock swelling in protest at her insult.

Aideen melted into the kiss, the folds of her sex growing as wet and humid as the tunnel that surrounded them. She pressed her stomach against his shaft and gave a disgruntled groan when he broke away.

"Aw, Goddess, Aideen," he swore softly, his voice still thick with passion. "How am I supposed to get you and the stone to safety when all I want to do is…" Kean let his thought fall to the damp floor and backed a few paces away until he could turn a quick semicircle without hitting her with his backpack. He resumed walking, answering her earlier question as he did so. "I've an old beater stored in Rossaveal. At that point...it's about a ten kilometer drive to a *friend's* airfield."

"Flaherty?" she asked, remembering the old man in her father's temple who had often flown her and her father from Dublin to Rossaveal.

"The same," he answered. "From there, he'll get us into England without drawing the attention of any authorities."

"And then?" she asked. Kean abruptly stopped and Aideen ran into him, propelling him against something blocking the tunnel. Her chest contracting, heart pounding furiously, she reached past him to feel a solid piece of metal.

"End of the line," Kean said with evident relief. Cautiously, he opened the door and stepped into a room some two square meters in size. Thin slats of daylight filtered through dusty windows set near the high ceiling. He cocked an eyebrow in warning. "And the end of your questions...for now."

The door exiting the small room opened, as promised, onto a rundown alley. Garbage blocked the door and they had to push together before the door opened wide enough for them to squeeze through. Kean locked the door and kicked the bulk of the garbage back in place. He dragged in a lungful of air and then grimaced. "Which way is your nose telling you to go?" he joked.

Aideen pointed to the east end of the alley.

The grimace melted into a grin that left Aideen's knees wobbly. "You can smell the day tourists from here, can you?"

She gave the jacket she was wearing a disdainful sniff. The fabric's stale scent mixed with the sweat she'd worked up hiking through the humid tunnel. "I should fit right in, then," she offered in return.

Kean hooked his arm through hers and headed down the alley. "That's what I'm hoping for."

Two blocks later, they bought their tickets for the morning ferry's return trip to Rossaveal then found a breakfast stand serving scrambled eggs and sausages. They shoveled down the steaming eggs and meat before casually wandering through the shops and kiosks lining the street. They bought sunglasses at one kiosk and a disposable camera at another before the ferry's first warning bell sounded.

"That would be our signal," he said and turned his attention to the ferry.

For the first time since they'd stepped onto the lively street that morning, Aideen looked at the boat. *The Sea Monster*. The name's origin, her father had told her on one of their many trips, referenced the translation of Rossaveal's name — the sea-monster's peninsula. The thought had never filled her with the same pleasure it had produced in Gerald. Rather, she felt like Andromeda offered up on the rocks with no Perseus in sight. She looked up at Kean and wondered if she would have felt differently had she known about him then.

Kean caught her gaze and seeing only her apprehension, gave her a comforting smile and softly squeezed her shoulder. At the top of the boarding ramp, a middle-aged woman punched their tickets and waved them into the passage area.

"In or out?" Kean asked, nodding at the glass enclosure that would shield them against the worst of the wind and water spray.

She looked at the rough waters, a swirling gray that perfectly matched Kean's eyes. "In," she answered softly, a grateful warmth filling her when he slid an arm around her waist and led her inside.

Chapter Nine

As they picked a side bench remote from the ferry's other return-trip passengers, Aideen tried to quash the heavy sense of déjà vu enveloping her. Her father's pedantic monotones played in her mind. She would soon be old enough, he advised, to take a more pivotal role in the ceremonies, to prepare to lead them one day. She must learn, through meditation and prayer, to channel the goddess for the most sacred of the group's ceremonies. It was that, his last statement delivered in an uncharacteristic offhand way that had sent Aideen racing to the boat's side rail while Gerald remained seated, patiently waiting to resume their conversation. But she didn't let him continue with his little talk and he had foolishly thought he could wait out her opposition. But the docile child who followed her father's instructions with a trembling obedience was gone—cast out with a heaving stomach to sink beneath the dark waters of Rossaveal's harbor. Was the wraith of that child still waiting in Rossaveal to reclaim the sunlight and air? If she looked over the ship's rails, would Aideen see that child, white frocked and floating just beneath the water's surface, the pale blonde hair ringing her waterlogged face in a saintly nimbus?

Kean's hands on hers brought Aideen back to the present. Her eyes, kept open in memory, blinked once and filled but she didn't cry. She didn't want to. Her father was dead, the last years of his life spent in clandestine, arcane pursuits to which she'd never been privy. That he may not have been demanding too much of her was irrelevant. She could only remember how he had asked and how her refusal had erected a polite but unscalable barrier between them.

"You're thinking about your da, aren't you?" Kean reached to take her backpack. He nestled both packs between them and coaxed Aideen into resting her head on his shoulder. He tucked a lock of her blonde hair back into the bucket hat. "Gerald regretted pushing you away," he said, his thumb tracing the edge of her ear.

Aideen stiffened and she lifted her head from his shoulder.

"Now," he said, pressing her back down, "have you looked at it from his point of view?"

"I don't have to," Aideen bit out and raised her head again to look at Kean. "I wouldn't put my child in ceremonies, my mother certainly — "

Kean's eyebrows shot up questioningly, effectively shutting Aideen up. "Ah," he smiled and looked around at the scattered passengers. He spotted a young woman, rosary in hand, reading from a prayer book. His sharp gaze returned to Aideen. "You're not Catholic or Protestant, are you, Aideen?" he asked, although he knew she hadn't been raised as either.

He nodded at the girl. "But most everyone in Ireland is one or the other." Again, he gestured to the girl, who read from her prayer book blissfully unaware of all the attention she was receiving. "Do you begrudge her the rosary she's fingering?" Aideen's lips pressed together in reply. "Or the bit of wafer she holds in her mouth each week while she poses before the priest on bended knee?" Aideen shifted her weight away from him but he continued to press his point. "Or the communion dress she'll clothe her daughter in?"

"I get your point," Aideen responded at last, but Kean wasn't yet ready to relent.

"Maybe you do get my point," he said and leaned in to whisper against her ear. "But I don't think you get the *difference*, Aideen. Your father's religion was a secret one and secrecy carries with it a sense of shame, doesn't it, love?"

Aideen faced Kean. Tears brimmed in her eyes but her cheeks were flushed in anger. "My mother," Aideen began but Kean interrupted her again.

"Your mother conceived you during a temple ceremony, just as," he added, "three years earlier, my mother conceived me."

Aideen's skin began to itch as she remembered the feel of the silk shift she had taken off just a few hours before. Had her mother…

"No," she said. Her sharp tone drew the attention of the closest passenger and Kean gave a cautionary clearing of his throat.

"Aideen, I don't want my words to hurt you," Kean began. He kissed her cheek, his lips claiming a salty tear. She tried to pull away but he wrapped a restraining arm around her waist and another around her shoulder.

"I'm not feeling well," she protested.

He shook his head and kissed a second tear at the corner of her mouth. Her lips were trembling and he pressed his against them in a firm kiss. His hand stroked the back of her neck as he spoke. "You'll feel better if you accept the truth, Aideen. Your mother, Danae, was a high priestess in Danimir's temple."

Kean paused, his gaze scanning the choppy water and wall of mist that lay in the boat's path. "My mother was forty-seven when she conceived me," he continued. "Her voice already had peaked and was beginning its decline." He stopped stroking the back of her neck and ran his index finger over her throat. "And Danae's had reached its maturity. She became the new high priestess and was paired with your father as high priest because of his voice."

His gray eyes darkened to a smoldering black and his eyes traveled speculatively from Aideen's throat to her mouth. Her skin flushed a sharp rose and she turned to look at the other passengers, relieved to find them absorbed in their own business.

"Paired? Like some sort of religious breeding program?" She spit the words out but kept her voice low. She looked back at Kean, his composed gray gaze in place once again. "And your father?"

"A very famous Irish tenor persuaded to participate in the ceremony by the legendary Maola's beauty and a bit of opium-laced wine…"

Aideen lifted her brows in shock, her pink mouth forming a surprised "O". Kean tossed his head back and laughed. The laugh died when he looked back down and saw Aideen glaring at him.

"You're putting me on," she said. The corners of her mouth were tightly drawn down and a frown creased her forehead.

"I wouldn't joke about being a bastard," Kean said softly. "It was hell on my mother…and on me. Her wealth was the only thing that kept the matter cloaked in some level of social acceptability."

Aideen's irritation began to fade and she rubbed her hands together against the growing chill. The ferry's horn blew and Kean gestured to the fog that had built up around them. The mist brought with it memories of her time spent in Kenmare. She zipped her jacket up and leaned closer to Kean.

"I used to love the fog," she whispered against his chest.

"I never have." He pushed the bucket hat back up off her forehead and pressed his lips against her hair. His right hand rested loosely against his thigh but the fingers were clenched into a fist. "Scared the hell out of me when I was a lad."

He sighed and Aideen slipped her hand under his jacket and around his waist. His fingers unclenched and he moved the hand to her shoulder in a light embrace. "Now it just makes me uptight."

"Resonance," Aideen said, the weight of her body settling against the backpacks as she relaxed into him. "Cenn lived two of the worst years of his life surrounded by mist." She felt Kean's unsure shrug and she asked him how much longer until they reached Rossaveal.

"Fifteen minutes until we hit the harbor traffic, then it's up to chance," he answered. "Fog might mean more than the usual number of boats coming in."

"Probably safer for us, don't you think?" she asked. When he didn't answer, she looked up and he gave her a thin smile.

"At least for staying out of trouble, yeah," Kean answered but the smile didn't reach his eyes. He gave her forehead another kiss and then pulled her hat back down.

"Let's get closer to the door," he said and helped her into the backpack. "We don't want to be the first or last out."

They chose a spot close to where the young woman was still reading from her bible. The girl smiled at them, her bright eyes lingering over Kean a bit longer than Aideen would have liked. The sudden possessiveness irritated her and she tried to brush it away but the girl continued to sneak glances at Kean. He noticed the pink flush to Aideen's cheek and its cause. His hand brushed Aideen's knee and he leaned in, keeping his voice low.

"Jealous?" he whispered, his smile fading at her frosty silence. He glanced back at the girl, gracing her with an easy smile. "Look, Meyrick's men will be looking for a man and a woman." He tugged at Aideen's bucket cap. "You're not the easiest thing to disguise."

Aideen chewed at her lip, irritated at what he was about to propose.

"Why don't you go sit closer to the door," he nodded toward a heavyset, older man wearing a tattered sailor's coat and an old wool cap. "Go out about tenth or so but stay close enough to that old fellow."

Her nose twitched in annoyance and Kean gave a husky laugh, the sound buried deep in his throat. It was a laugh that reached out to stroke her nipples and her cheeks grew rosier. "I don't know where I'm going," she protested.

He leaned closer, his fingertips whispering over her denim-clad thigh. "Two blocks straight up the center street, there's a frock shop. Stop and do a little window shopping." She started to get up in mock anger but he pulled her down to whisper in her ear. "Don't look back when you get off the ferry." Feeling her hesitation, he gave her arm a tender squeeze. "I won't lose sight of you or be too far behind. I promise."

Relenting, Aideen extended her body to its full height, one hand resting against her hip as the other pointed at Kean in accusation. "I should have listened to my mother..." Letting out an angry squeak, she turned and stomped over to where the man was sitting. As she took a seat opposite him, she could hear the woman laughing beside Kean and the slide of her bag as she moved closer to him. Aideen let out an angry snort and the old man's gaze flicked over her with distant politeness. She gave another snort and settled against the backpack. Alone, it annoyed her that she couldn't feel the Bloodstone's presence despite its closeness to her. She wanted to open the pack and make sure the stone was still inside. She told herself that the stone's silence was proof that the special bag Kean had placed it in was working. Although she imagined the instruments Meyrick's men were using would be much more sophisticated than her newly attuned senses.

Across from her, the man started gathering up his things. He stuffed his newspaper in a worn saddlebag and closed his thermos before shoving it alongside the paper. He tightened the fit of his cap on his massive bald crown and began buttoning his coat. He caught Aideen watching him and gave her the briefest of smiles.

"I'm expecting a bit of a chill out on the dock," he said. He pointed at her jacket and shook his head. "Shouldn't have zippered up," he advised too late. "You're the warmest you're going to be right now."

She started to tell him she didn't have far to go and then realized he might be just polite enough to ask where she was going, so she nodded at him instead. She could hear the crew getting the ferry ready to dock. The heavy ropes, as thick as her waist, were cast onto a concrete pier that berthed the boat. Through the fog, she could see the ticket office, a bleak light breaking from it as passengers left the waiting area to line up for boarding. The passengers on the ferry began to line up as well, and Aideen tucked herself behind the old man.

They left the boat in a single line, the morning's weather subduing the usual bustle. She remembered Kean's warning not to look back and she somehow managed not to. The urge to know he was somewhere behind her slowed her down and she stumbled into one of the boarding passengers.

"Alright there, miss?" a young man asked.

"Yeah," she answered hastily and then, seeing his hearing aid, she repeated herself. He was staring at her and she still wasn't sure he had heard her, but a young mother was butting her pram against Aideen's legs in her hurry to get off the pier. Aideen gave the man a quick smile and moved on, the touch of his blue gaze still upon her.

A block away from the pier, she passed her hand along the back of her neck and tried to rub away the unsettling effect the man's glittering eyes had upon her. She was still rubbing at the spot when the old man she had attached herself to turned right at the first corner and she almost followed him. She pivoted back to her left and waited for the traffic to clear the crosswalk. She continued walking up the street, half expecting Kean to come up alongside her before she reached the dress shop at the second corner. But he didn't and she had to stand in front of the store's window feigning interest in a drab little daisy print. She doubted the store had very many customers and her suspicion was confirmed a few seconds later as the sales clerk came to the door.

"Lovely dress, isn't it?" the woman asked. "You could pop in, give it a wear."

"Uhm, no," Aideen answered. She shifted her weight, her body involuntarily turning back toward the pier. "I don't have the time." She half caught the woman's frown, her attention focused on not looking back. *Time*. How much had passed since she'd left the ferry?

"But the daisies would go lovely with all that pale hair you've got hiding under there." The woman reached out and pulled the bucket hat from Aideen's head.

Aideen gave a forward jump at the hat as her hair spilled around her shoulders. She snatched the hat up, her fingernails grazing the woman's skin. Backing up, she tried to give her hair a quick twirl and cover it but she bumped into something solid and unmoving. She started to turn but a strong hand caught her by the elbow and propelled her past the clerk and into the store.

"Don't you know that daisies are good luck?" Kean said and spun Aideen around and into a changing booth.

He tossed the hat over the booth's door and then turned to the clerk. Aideen wound her hair into a tight knot and shoved the hat back on. She waited just inside the booth's door and peeked through the slats. She could hear Kean sliding hangers on the racks and talking to the woman.

"But isn't she going to try them on?" the clerk protested when he handed her a bundle of clothes.

"Just ring them up. I know her size." His words were clipped, his voice brimming with irritation at the dangerous delay the clerk had caused. Kean opened the changing booth's door and glanced down at Aideen's shoes. "Six?"

"And a half," she answered.

He gave the hat a quick tug then walked over to a display of sandals. He quickly selected a red pair and a black pair and flashed them at the clerk before shoving them in the bag. Reaching into his jacket, he pulled out his wallet and thumbed two hundreds from it. "Keep the change for your troubles," he said, grabbing the bag and Aideen.

Kean and Aideen left the store and were immediately enveloped by the fog that had thickened during their impromptu shopping trip.

"It's thick as soup," Aideen cursed as a passerby bumped into her. She tightened her grip on Kean's arm. "Have you ever seen it so thick?" she asked.

"On a trip to California," he answered. "Pacific Grove. You?"

Only in Kenmare, she thought. She gave a quick, negative shake of her head. "No."

"Well, we've only one more block to go," he said and turned her down a small side street. "Of course, then we'll be driving in it instead of walking in it."

They walked the last block in silence. The sound of footsteps seemed to surround them but they could see only the brief flash of a dark coat or passing car. The street ended in a row of small warehouses, some no more than five meters in width with pull-down doors. Kean bent down in front of one such door, handing her the bag of newly purchased clothing before he did so. He selected a short, thick key from his chain and took the padlock off a slide bolt. He pushed the door up and the wet metal creaked its protest. On the other side, a lime green truck, rust holes eaten into its side panels, was parked. He spun around, a sheepish smile on his face.

"Not much to look at, but she'll —" He stopped, the color draining from his face.

With one arm, Kean shoved Aideen to the side while his other hand reached behind him for the pistol still tucked into his waistband. He didn't make it. A meaty fist smashed into his face, snapping his head backward. His body went limp, collapsing against the truck. The truck's keys clattered against the pavement and the assailant grabbed the collar of Kean's jacket and poised his hand to strike again. Seeing that his victim was unconscious, he pushed Kean over the truck's gate before slowly swiveling his head to look at Aideen. His thick lips were set in a cruel grin and he reached for her. She scrambled backwards and rolled over on her hands and feet to push herself up. Another man barred her escape.

"Where you going, pretty?"

Aideen looked up into the blue eyes of the young man she had bumped into when leaving the ferry. His eyes danced with a cold flame and there was the flash of black metal in his hand. Her stomach contracted, but it was only an electronic box and not a gun. He held his hand to the device in his ear and pointed at her backpack.

"In there." Rat-like, he looked back up the street and at the other warehouses. "Hurry."

Aideen was lifted into the air only to be unceremoniously dropped back to the ground when Blue Eyes' muscled accomplice unhooked the shoulder straps to her pack. He unzipped the bag, his lips smacking wetly against one another as he found the Bloodstone and lifted it into the air. Aideen felt the stone before she saw it. Her eyes followed its fiery arc as Muscles shoved the stone into his pocket. He scooped the bag of clothes up and tossed both bags into the back of the truck. Aideen heard the shift of Kean's body as he was rolled over and the man took the pistol. He pulled the slide back and pointed the gun at Aideen.

"You should see the hole this baby makes." The man's smile only made his lips thicker and his tongue snaked out to lick the top lip's inverted tip.

"Put that fucking thing away," Blue Eyes hissed and dragged Aideen into a standing position. "Boss says he needs her."

Aideen swayed, her head filled with the Bloodstone's insistent hum. She felt the stone's vibration in her throat and her body began to shake even as it swayed more heavily. Her arm stretched toward Muscles, her fingertips brushing the barrel of the gun. Her hand dropped to his belt and she pulled herself toward him...toward the stone. His mouth twisted in misunderstanding and he shifted the pistol to his other hand. He shoved her hand against his cock and rotated his hips.

"Is that what you're reaching for, cunt?"

Her body trembled, her mouth and throat contorting as the Bloodstone drummed its rhythm into her head. She gave a guttural shriek and Blue Eyes jerked her back.

"You're the bloody fucking cunt," he yelled at Muscles and clamped a hand over Aideen's mouth. "She wants the same thing Meyrick wants and it sure the fuck isn't your pencil dick."

Muscles' eyes narrowed and he bobbed the barrel of the gun at Blue Eyes. "You didn't have to get nasty about it," he growled. Sweat dotted his brow and he pulled at the fabric of his pants, his features paling. He started to pant. "God, it's hot. What is it?"

"Don't ask," Blue Eyes hissed. "Just finish the job on pretty boy before someone catches us!"

Muscles stumbled to the back of the truck. With an unsteady hand, he raised the pistol high, the barrel pointed down. Behind Aideen, Blue Eyes rose up on his toes to watch, his hand loose against Aideen's mouth. She bit down. His scream of pained surprise was joined by Aideen's voice, heavy with the Bloodstone's pulse. The note built, climbed higher. Her eyes watered with pain and the back window of the truck shattered. Behind her, Blue Eyes fell to the ground. Muscles was still conscious. He was down on one knee, his breathing labored, his face a bright red, coated in perspiration. The hand clutching the gun hung uselessly at his side. His hips were twitching and Aideen could smell his flesh as it burned from the Bloodstone's heat. She reached down with both hands, pulling the gun from his unprotesting fingers at the same time she freed the Bloodstone from his trousers.

She looked over the truck's gate at Kean's bloodied face. With the hand that held the stone, she felt for his pulse, relief racing through her at the faint but persistent throb. She leveled the gun at Muscles' head. His body was quiet now, his stare blank. She placed her foot against his chest and shoved him clear of the truck's path. She started to turn her attention back to Kean but Blue Eyes was rolling onto his side. His hands twitched along the folds of his jacket. At her feet were the keys and she snatched them up.

Aideen jerked the truck door open and jammed the oldest key on the chain into the ignition. It slid all the way in, the truck rumbling to life when she turned the key and pressed the gas pedal. She slammed on the brake pedal and clutch and put the truck in reverse, her brake foot hitting the accelerator once again as she let up on the clutch. The truck screamed into the street, cutting through the fog. Nearing the intersection, she slowed and swung the vehicle in a wide arc. Before she pulled onto the through street, she glanced through the shattered window at Kean. His body was still crumpled into a ball.

The Bloodstone rolled along the center of the truck's bench seat and she scooped it up. Power surged from the stone and showed her a clear path through the fog to Flaherty's landing field ten clicks from the center of town. She adjusted the rearview mirror until she could see Kean and then fought the gearshift into drive. The truck lurched forward, Kean's body sliding along the bed's length. Blinking back tears, she shifted gears, the truck picking up speed as she followed the flow of the Bloodstone's energy.

Her gaze flicked to the mirror, hope surging when she saw Kean's hand stretching out to clutch the ridged interior of the truck's bed. She pressed the accelerator and the display's speedometer needle pushed its way past one hundred kilometers per hour.

"Hold on, love," she whispered. "I'm not going to lose you again."

Chapter Ten

Flaherty was waiting for them when they reached the landing strip. He helped Aideen pull Kean from the truck but balked when she ordered him to help her load Kean onto the plane.

"Are you blind?" he protested and flailed his arms at the heavy mist that covered the airfield.

"It's clear another ten kilometers out," she assured him.

"Aideen, girl, you don't know that." He started to wipe at his brow with an oil-stained rag but she shoved the backpacks at him, almost knocking him off his feet with the force of her thrust.

"I do know it," she assured him. Her polite tone was in sharp contrast to the menace clouding her face.

"That won't help us when we hit a power line five clicks out," he said.

Wind whipped around her, pulling the bucket hat from her head and lifting her hair until it surrounded her like white fire. She turned abruptly and pulled Kean onto her back. She started dragging him to the plane while Flaherty stared, wide-eyed, at her. She felt the heavy weight of Kean's body lessen and she glanced back to find that Flaherty had grabbed him by the ankles. Together, they hoisted Kean through the door and placed him in the back cargo area of the plane's tail section.

"You better be right," Flaherty said and tossed the bags onto one of the passenger seats. He clambered into the pilot's seat and reached for the radio.

Aideen stopped his hand. "You don't have to believe me." She shoved the Bloodstone under his nose. "Believe this."

Flaherty swallowed hard, his eyes blinking rapidly. He gave a short nod and began flipping a series of switches on the engine panel. Aideen felt the low purr of the plane's engines and gave brief thanks that Flaherty had somehow managed to replace his four-seater prop plane with something more modern.

She placed her palm against the back of his neck and closed her eyes to allow him to see what the Bloodstone was showing her. Warmth spread through her arm, into her chilled fingertips and over Flaherty's skin. The fine layering of hair on the back of his neck bristled at the sudden electricity of her touch, but then he relaxed and leaned into her hand. He closed his eyes and pulled back on the plane's wheel. The plane climbed through the fog. Flying on faith, they both kept their eyes closed, concentrating on the images the Bloodstone brought them.

"You know where you're going?" Aideen asked a few minutes later when the plane broke from the fog into clear blue sky.

Flaherty patted his flight book. "Been ready since this morning."

Aideen grunted and began weaving her way back to the cargo area, the Bloodstone clutched to her chest. Kean was still motionless, his body secured by cargo nets rigged to form a hammock. Aideen loosened the nets and tested them against her added weight. Satisfied, she crawled in next to Kean. Holding the stone to his temple, she lightly ran her fingertips over his bloodied face. He let out a wet sigh that twisted through her chest.

"You'll find a first aid kit against the back." Flaherty's voice squeaked over the intercom.

Aideen looked above her, saw the kit's box and reached out while keeping the stone pressed against Kean. She thumbed the kit open and removed some disinfectant pads. She tried to think of something soothing to hum and settled for *Mockingbird* while she wiped the blood from Kean's face. His breathing came more freely, less liquid. As she wiped the last of the blood away, Kean opened his eyes. His gaze was clouded, unfocused, and she kissed his eyelids closed. She ran the stone over his forehead and along the back curve of his neck, trying not to remember how his head had snapped back from the massive blow Muscles had delivered.

"Don't you know another tune?" He was watching her, a half-smile warring with a grimace for supremacy.

"Give me a break," she growled and ran the stone down his spine and over his hips until it was nestled between their stomachs.

Kean stretched his neck slowly, testing the range of motion. He scanned the cargo area of the plane and then relaxed against Aideen. "How is it that we're alive and in the back of Flaherty's plane?" he asked.

Aideen felt a small arc of power sizzle across her stomach where the stone touched her skin. Kean's muscles contracted against the stone as the same energy flowed into him. A frown creasing his brow, he rested his hand on Aideen's hip and leaned into her. Lips pressed against her forehead, he sighed.

"It would be a powerful temptation for anyone," he said. His lips parted from her in a kiss and he tilted her chin up until their gazes met. "What are we to do with it?" he whispered the question, as if he trusted only her to hear or answer.

"Send it back," she answered.

"Where?"

She shrugged and picked up the Bloodstone. "It knows," she answered. "We just have to listen and figure out what it's telling us."

Aideen crawled out of the cargo net, taking the stone with her. She went through the curtains that separated the cargo area from the half dozen passenger seats and the open cockpit. Finding the backpack where Flaherty had dumped it, she put the stone back into its protective case, Kean's pistol on top.

"How long until we arrive?" she asked Flaherty.

"On the ground in forty-five," he answered. "Another fifteen or so getting parked after that."

She nodded and went back to the cargo area, the backpack slung over one shoulder.

"You look ready to drop," Kean said as he watched her store the bag in a side compartment.

"I haven't been napping the last hour," she teased. He put his arm out and forced the cargo net open while she crawled in next to him.

"Cold?" he asked and rubbed her arms. She nodded and he pulled her closer. Heat radiated from his groin and she found herself pressing her hips against him. "There'll be time enough for that in England," he said. "You need sleep." The first full smile since the attack played across his lips and he cupped her cheek, giving her a brief brotherly kiss.

"I've never done it in a plane," Aideen protested, eyes drooping with fatigue.

"I'll charter us a real one," he said and brushed his lips against hers.

Aideen snuggled closer to him and his grip relaxed as sleep claimed them both. Her dreams were liquid warm. A golden magma laced with fiery red embraced her. She pushed into the gelatinous heat. Wrapping a leg around him, she pulled Kean into the dream with her. Their clothes fell away and he dipped his mouth down to taste the rosebud tips of her breasts. Warm bodies swam around them. A woman's high, fine voice caressed them, pushed them closer to one another. The woman gestured across the bed of lava to where a man sculpted a divan of blue flame. *We would join you*, the woman said, sensually ushering them toward the divan.

Aideen turned to Kean but he was already reclining, wrapped in blue fire, his soul burning for her, urging her to hurry. His cock—thick, solid in its erection—bulged proudly against his stomach, eager to penetrate. Wet desire unleashed itself, its waves obliterating the awkwardness she felt at the presence of the other couple. She stepped into the flame, straddling Kean. The woman followed Aideen into the fire and placed a hand on each side of Aideen's head, cushioning Aideen between her full breasts. Aideen could feel the tickle of the woman's pubic hair against her bottom, even as she slid her own mound along the length of Kean's shaft. When she reached the tip, he raised it high enough for her to slide back down, its length buried inside her. Aideen arched her back and the woman moved with her, their flesh pressed so closely together that they seemed melded from the heat surrounding them. Kean sat up and captured Aideen's breasts. He squeezed them together, suckling first one, then the other peaked nipple. His tongue flicked at the rosy tips, while his finger and thumb explored the contours of her clit, twirling them mercilessly while she rode his shaft in near orgasm.

The woman's companion slid behind Kean. He reached around the mortal lovers to knead the woman's ass. Her moans joined Aideen's as the first burst of Aideen's orgasm exploded around Kean's cock. Aideen bucked, the press of the woman's mound against her back spurring her on to a second climax.

And then the woman and her lover were gone, the blue flames disappearing in a distressed wail. Body still shuddering with sensual fulfillment, Aideen opened her eyes. Her gaze met Kean's, which flicked from sleepy satisfaction to black obsidian in an instant.

"We're on the ground," he said. Worry edged his voice and he slid from the cargo net to the side compartment in which Aideen had stowed the backpack. He opened the compartment and turned to her, his face stretched in disbelief.

Empty! Aideen skittered out of the cargo net and pushed past the curtains. The front of the plane was empty and the side door was open, the steps laid down. She raced down the steps, Kean close behind. They were on a dirt landing strip that looked little more than a single lane road cut through an English field. Two hundred yards away, trees formed a solid line. Behind them, at the far end of the runway was a rundown shack and another line of trees.

"Flaherty—" Aideen began.

"Has been with the temple longer than I've been alive," Kean interrupted, disbelief choking the words from his throat.

Aideen squinted at the tree line, her stomach somersaulting with dread. She clutched Kean's arm and pointed. Emerging from the thin row of trees that served as a backdrop to the shack were two white sedans, an orange stripe running along the side of each and blue lights flashing in great swooping circles. She took a step back, ready to flee, but Kean held her steady.

"Give them your name and address and nothing else," Kean said and plastered on a friendly smile. "If they take us in, it will only be for a few hours as long as you tell them nothing else."

She squeezed his arm, her legs still telling her to run. He turned to her, his gray gaze intense. "Trust me, Aideen."

Aideen nodded her understanding and, to her amazement, her fear melted away. She watched Kean pull his cell phone from his jacket and dial a preset number. The pulse at his temple slowed to match the phone's ring at the other end of the call, each ring bringing the police a car length closer.

"Kean here." He snapped the words into the phone. "Some of your Wadebridge boys are about to take me and a friend in." Kean stopped short the person on the other side of the conversation. "Immediately—Claubine has orders to release the documents in two hours."

Kean disconnected the call and began punching more numbers in as the police pulled their vehicles to a stop three car lengths away. There were four of them and they exited their vehicles slowly, shielding themselves with the doors. The driver of the first car reached back into her car, one wary eye focused on Kean and Aideen. She pulled out a megaphone.

"Hands on your heads!" The megaphone took her already rough bark and made it eye watering in its volume at such a close distance. "Slowly!" she added as Aideen's hands jumped into the air. Kean moved more slowly, punching more numbers on his cell phone as he watched the fidgeting police officers.

"Drop the phone, sir!" the woman screeched. The woman's temper got the better of her when Kean smiled and ignored her command. She tossed the megaphone to the ground and was to the front of her patrol car before her partner caught her and pulled her back behind the safety of the car. The man was reed-thin with bright orange hair cropped close to his head, but the ease with which he pulled his stouter partner back behind the door testified to his wiry strength.

A cop from the second patrol car picked up the megaphone and repeated the command. Kean gave them an all-finished grin and dropped the cell phone to the ground. "Hands on your head!"

Kean complied, his face a bland expression of perplexed innocence.

"Turn around, the both of you!" the orange-haired cop shouted.

Kean and Aideen turned slowly, the rush of footsteps pounding behind them. The female cop reached Kean first and jerked his arms behind his back. Aideen's wrists were roughly encircled and her arms were twisted behind her while handcuffs were cinched into place.

"Hoy, Janet, leave off him and do the girl." It was Janet's partner who spoke, his voice deeper than his thin frame would suggest. Aideen had a second to read his name tag, P.C. Everett, before he bent down and plucked Kean's cell phone from the dirt landing strip. He pressed the power button and then swore softly a few seconds later when he realized the phone's password feature had been activated. "Think you're brilliant, do you?" the cop inquired. His cheeks glowed a ruddy copper and he waved the phone under Kean's nose.

Kean's cool gaze flicked over Everett's face but he didn't otherwise respond.

"Well, genius, you're not getting it back." Everett shoved the phone into his navy blue windbreaker. He nodded at his partner, who was finishing her pat-down of Aideen. "Got anything?" he asked.

Janet grunted and stepped away from Aideen.

"Check the plane then," Everett said with a jerk of his thumb. He studied Kean, quickly coming to the conclusion that he would more easily wring an explanation from granite. He turned to Aideen and smiled as he noted her flushed cheeks and averted eyes. "You look like too sweet a bird to be mixed up with this bloke."

Aideen felt her burning cheeks cool and she looked at the man. Something dangerous was coiled like a whip inside him. Her mossy green irises hardened to a blazing emerald as she tried to see beyond the human façade the cop wore.

"You don't want to play it that way, love," Everett warned and stepped to within a few centimeters of Aideen. Beside them, Kean stiffened, a low growl involuntarily rising up from his chest. Everett grinned and waved one of the other officers over. It was the cop who had picked up the megaphone. The hair under his cap was a thin gray and he looked like he'd spent every night of a very long career sleeping in his uniform.

Everett whipped his chin in Kean's direction. "Don't think this dog's cuffs are tight enough. Why don't you lock 'em up another notch or two for me."

The older cop cleared his throat, still not moving to carry out the order.

"Have you gone deaf all of a sudden?" the cop asked.

The man gave a nervous cough and hooked a hand over Aideen's cuffs. "Station just radioed in," he offered and began to lightly pull Aideen in the direction of his car. "We're to take them in now."

Everett grabbed Aideen's elbow and pulled her arm tight in a silent tug of war. "Fine, then. The bird rides with me."

Janet stepped from the plane, her face a sour twist of disappointment. Her irritation melted as her quick gaze took in the episode of subtle confrontation between her partner and the third cop.

"Station said they're to ride together," the older cop protested.

"Then they can both ride with me 'n Janet."

"Station—"

"Bloody hell with the station!" Everett screamed. Spit began to fleck at the corner of his mouth and he released Aideen's arm. "I told you not to call this in yet."

"Didn't. The *old man* called…said *I* was to bring them back to the station in *my* unit," the cop replied, confidence oozing back into his voice.

Everett's eyes were blazing a cold hate when his gaze returned to Kean. "Looks like you're not without friends in Wadebridge." His body remained tense, not yet ready to relent. He nodded at the fourth cop, who had been judiciously hanging back by the patrol cars. "Filch will ride with Janet."

"Hoy," Filch protested. "I'm not riding with Janet. She smells like she's on the rag all the time—acts like it, too." He turned to his partner, who was impassively staring at the side of the plane. "You tell the Pumpkin King, here—"

"None of that," Everett growled, his thin frame puffing up.

The light dusting of hair along the back of Aideen's neck stood on end as Everett pulled his lips back in a half-smiling snarl. She thought of the spindly-legged scarecrow that had danced across her father's garden. As Halloween approached, Gerald would switch out the cloth head with a carved pumpkin, candles glowing eerily in place of eyes. *Now, Aideen, nothing to be afraid of with ole punkinhead guarding the house.* Everett's gaze lighted on Aideen and his smile compressed into a thin line of rage.

"You don't think that's funny, do you, bird?" Everett asked. He stepped in front of Aideen, his body all but brushing against hers. Reaching out, he lifted a strand of her hair. "What kind of bird are you? Only birds hanging about Wadebridge this time of year are crows—but you're so blonde, you're nearly white." He twisted the lock of hair around his finger until the knuckle of his thumb rested against her cheek.

Everett looked past Aideen to someplace only he could see. His voice dropped lower. "Crows used to be white...before they were punished." He looked at her, shadows obscuring his irises. "Is that it, little bird? You're still all white because you haven't been properly punished?"

Kean's voice cut through the space that still divided Aideen and Everett's bodies. "You can uncuff us now."

"The hell?" Everett asked, his attention effectively diverted from Aideen. "Uncuff you, you say?" He looked to Janet to confirm that he hadn't misheard the request. She gave an indifferent shrug.

The older cop slid the key into Aideen's handcuffs, freeing her with a sharp click of the key and a momentary tightening of the cuffs before they fell away. Everett turned, gaping at the other man's audacity.

"You're breaking protocol," Everett threatened. "You damn well know prisoners can't ride—"

"Are we prisoners?" Kean leaned forward, reading the older cop's nametag as Filch took Janet's key and unlocked Kean's cuffs. "Officer Crumpler?"

"Supposed to give you a *friendly* escort back to the station house," Crumpler mumbled, his earlier confidence waning as Everett stepped behind Aideen to loom over him.

"I *was* being friendly," Everett joked, his face freezing into a good-natured mask. "Well then, by all means, let's provide our new friends with an escort back to the station house and the old man."

Everett moved to take Aideen by the elbow but Kean already stood beside her, his gray gaze unyielding. The corner of Everett's mouth twitched and his hand played around the lapel of his jacket. "You're not the only one with friends," Everett warned in an undertone. "Everyone's got a friend or two, even me."

Crumpler led them back to their patrol car, Everett following closer than their own shadows. Behind him, Filch, extolling the virtues of using douche, continued grousing at having to ride with Janet. The noise was an unwelcome distraction for Aideen, who was fighting with herself to keep from trembling at what she had seen in the Pumpkin King's shadowy gaze. Even after she climbed into the back seat of the patrol car and Kean wrapped a protective arm around her shoulders, she silently cursed the Bloodstone's lingering effects and hoped they weren't permanent. She had never seen a soul as ulcerous with lustful hate. And in the center of each sore, she had seen her own face reflected.

The interior of the car was silent except for the radio traffic. Crumpler called in to the station that he and Everett would be returning to the station with two guests. He placed an awkward emphasis on *Everett* and *guests* and his hand shook as he returned the mike to its cradle. He glanced in the rearview mirror and Aideen gave him a grateful smile for his earlier intervention.

"Out here to see the *stones*, are you?" Everett asked. Crumpler's gaze narrowed and Everett leaned his head back, laughing and slapping his knee. He turned in his seat, looking at Kean and Aideen for the first time since he got into the car. "We've quite a few famous standing...*stones*...here in Cornwall. Some of the best in England."

Aideen tensed at his knowing tone and wondered if he knew exactly who they were and why they were in England. Her gaze met Crumpler's in the mirror again and he gave her a confused frown. Out of view, Kean's thumb stroked the back of her shoulder blade and he shifted in his seat, his body pushed out and closer to Everett.

"Stones here are all for burying people," Kean observed. Everett nodded and offered a sharp smile. "Well, then," Kean finished, reaching out to casually rest his hand against the back of Everett's headrest, "that's more the sort of thing you'd be interested in." He offered his own hard, glittering smile. "But thanks for the suggestion."

"Hoy, city limits," Crumpler announced. His body, unnerved, sank against the car seat and Aideen was sure she heard the air rush from him in a relieved sigh.

A few blocks later, they pulled in front of the station house. Crumpler got out of the car and opened the door for Aideen. He tossed his keys to a young constable leaning against the hood of another patrol car.

"Put her away for me, Joe," Crumpler said and tilted his cap at the cop. He looked at Everett and his voice was uneasy when he spoke again. "You coming inside?"

Everett rubbed his hands down the front of his jacket, his expression fixed. He shook his head, slowly, as if he were still thinking his answer over. "Feeling lonely all of a sudden," he said and looked at Aideen. "Feel like reaching out to a friend or two, myself."

Ignoring Everett's blatant appraisal of Aideen's body, Kean steered her around the patrol car and toward the front steps of the station house. Crumpler walked behind her, his body shielding her from Everett's hungry eyes. Aideen wondered just what the scope of Everett's appetite was and her stomach tightened.

"Hey, bird!" Everett called out.

Kean's hand gently pressed against the small of Aideen's back, allowing her to slow but not stop. She fought the hypnotic quality of Everett's voice and kept her eyes locked on the door ahead of her. Even at a distance of thirty feet, she could hear every stop in Everett's rough laugh as he continued addressing her.

"I'll be seeing you again, bird!"

Chapter Eleven

The station house was bright, the light hurting their eyes after the slow ride beneath Cornwall's overcast sky. With Everett still outside, Crumpler walked straighter and he cut a quick line in front of Aideen and Kean. He led them past the intake sergeant's desk and into a bay of desks bordered by glass offices. He took them all the way across the room and abruptly halted in front of an office door. The shades were pulled down but shadows bounced against them as someone paced on the other side.

Crumpler looked at Aideen. She saw something of her father in his worried smile and she placed a reassuring hand on his arm. He patted it then knocked on the glass door.

"In." The succinct command was delivered with an equal economy of sound.

Crumpler turned the knob and pushed the door open. Kean entered the room first and Crumpler caught Aideen's sleeve, momentarily halting her. "Leave as soon as you can, miss."

She nodded but he didn't notice. He had said what he had to and, duty discharged, his features returned to a composed blandness. Crumpler released her sleeve, gave a smart half-bow to the man behind the desk, and turned sharply on his heels and marched back across the open bay.

Kean pulled Aideen the rest of the way into the room. She was surprised to see a second man in one corner. He turned, revealing his profile to her and she realized, a second before his identity hit her, he had been the one pacing in front of the drawn shade.

"Tea?" the man behind the desk inquired.

He was smooth-cheeked, young. Aideen's gaze flitted to the brass nameplate. Too young to hold his position and, yet, Aideen was sure this was the *old man* to whom Crumpler and Everett had referred. Her gaze returned to the second man in the room. She remembered his face from the countless Parliamentary pontifications on the most recent IRA cease-fire. He turned to the youthful inspector and flicked his hand in the direction of the door.

"Leave us."

With the police inspector gone, the man turned to Kean. "I'm finished with this — "

"I'll make the necessary calls when I get to London," Kean interrupted.

The man shook his head, the slightly jowled folds of his chin tightening as his jaw jutted forward. "Damned if you think you're getting a police escort to London."

"I just want to make sure we get out," Kean said. He pulled the window's shade to one side and stared out at the bay of desks. "You've got a dirty constable out there."

"Just one?" the man asked with a rough laugh.

A shiver ran along Aideen's spine and she wrapped her arms around herself, wondering what Kean was blackmailing this man with. Kean noticed how Aideen held herself and let the shade drop back against the window. With a dismissive shrug at the other man, he opened the door and held it for Aideen while she stepped from the office and into the bay.

Everett was leaning against a desk, his legs blocking the aisle. She froze. Heat from the anger at her fear did nothing to un-root her. She couldn't bring herself to step over his legs and felt ridiculous at the idea of going around one of the other desks. He would only take that as a sign of weakness. He wasn't even wary or respectful of force. Standing there, she had time enough to wonder what had so pummeled him that he had acquired an immunity against the threat of violence. Or had he always possessed it? Her gaze met his and she knew that the latter was the better answer. Her earlier thought that his soul was ulcerous had been wrong and the thing she had glimpsed inside him no more than shadows bouncing around an empty shell.

"Everett, our guests have tarried long enough." It was the inspector's voice, laced with irritation that made Everett curl his legs back into his body.

Aideen passed between the inspector and Everett, Kean close behind her, his gaze locked on the Pumpkin King. He stopped in front of Everett and extended his hand, palm up. Everett's mouth twitched but he reached into his jacket and pulled Kean's cell phone from it.

"Slipped my mind," he offered. "Wouldn't want you and the songbird stuck alongside the road with no way to call for assistance."

Aideen's gaze jumped to Everett. Her breathing shallowed and her heartbeat slowed to match its pace. *He knew, but how?* Kean put his hand in the center of her back and urged her forward, not giving her time to contemplate the source of Everett's knowledge. When they were outside the station house, he flagged down a cab.

They slid into the back seat and Kean tapped the driver on the shoulder. "Car rental," he said. The cab pulled away from the curb and Kean relaxed against the ripped vinyl seat. He turned the phone over in his hands and then opened the battery panel. He reached inside the small hollow, scraping with his nail until he pried a small black dot loose.

"He didn't waste any time," Kean murmured and shoved the tracking device between the seat's cushions.

"How did he know?" Aideen asked. For a moment, she had relaxed, thinking they were pulling farther away from Everett. Now it looked like he intended to travel with them.

"Flaherty must've called after he ran off," Kean answered. His face folded into a perplexed frown. "But why send someone back when Flaherty had the Bloodstone?"

Aideen turned to look out the window. The glass was cold and she scooted toward the center of the seat, her back relaxing against Kean's expansive chest. He wrapped his arms around her and pulled her closer.

"It freaked you out when he called you *songbird*," Kean remembered. He kissed her temple and gave her a little nudge but she wouldn't respond. "They came back for you, didn't they?"

"Don't you know already?" Aideen asked.

"I thought Mey... I thought he had built a sort of tuning fork for it, or was doing so," Kean answered, his hug tightening. "I know our parents were selected because of their voices..." he started and then faltered. Aideen turned until she could look at him, her gaze expectant and urging him to continue. "But I thought it was for the ceremonies...for channeling the goddess."

"Maybe that, but more than that, too," she said.

Kean released Aideen and pressed her back against the seat. His hand and lips trembled as he cupped her face and kissed her. It was the first time since they'd met that he felt vulnerable to her and she wrapped her arms around him. "What is it?" she asked.

"I was just thinking that the better course of action may have been running away," he answered flatly, his self-composure partially regained.

"No," she said, shaking her head at him. "Don't second-guess yourself." She looked over his shoulder and caught the cabbie's gaze. She frowned and nudged Kean away from her. "We almost there?" she asked the cabbie.

"Two blocks up," the cabbie answered and returned his attention to the traffic ahead of them.

Aideen and Kean didn't talk for the rest of the ride. Her hand rested in his lap, half enclosed by his and they leaned against one another. She felt herself nodding off and jerked upright as the cab pulled into the rental agency's parking lot.

"You still haven't had much rest," Kean observed as he helped her from the back seat. "I'll drive the first bit," he offered before turning to the driver. He pulled out his wallet and thumbed through the £100 notes. He pulled two out, stopping short of handing them to the driver. "I need someone to deliver an envelope to Newquay," he said and folded the notes in half.

"Cost you more than that," the driver started. Kean shrugged and put the notes back in his wallet and pulled out a £20. "Hold on, don't be hasty," the driver protested.

"How big is this package you want delivered? Maybe we can work something out."

"As I said, I need an *envelope* delivered to Newquay." Kean's expression was cloaked with bored impatience and he started to put his billfold away.

"Hold on," the driver bounced in his seat and looked over his shoulder before leaning closer to where Kean stood. "Ain't nothing illegal in the envelope?"

"No," Kean answered. "Just a message that I can't entrust to conventional means."

"Alright," the driver relented. "Two hundred quid *plus* the fare for this ride."

"Fair enough, wait here." Kean motioned Aideen into the small rental office. Its interior was empty of customers and only one clerk sat behind the tall counter, her nose buried between the pages of a horror book. Kean began speaking to her before she acknowledged their entrance and she had to race to catch up with his requests. "A sedan for London, one way, one driver." He pulled his license out and placed it in front of her then reached over the counter for one of their envelopes.

The clerk started to protest but he cut her short with a snap of his fingers and a sharp jab in the direction of the agency's printer.

"Get me a clean sheet of paper," he said and scribbled out the agency's name on the envelope. Below the scratched out return address, he put two glyphs and then wrote a Newquay address in the center of the envelope. "Paper," he repeated his command.

The girl looked at Aideen but Aideen only shrugged and motioned for her to get the paper. The clerk moved like molasses on a midwinter day as she got up from the stool and crossed the half meter to the printer. She pulled a sheet from the feeder tray and repositioned herself on her stool before she relinquished her hold on the paper.

"Keep working on the rental," he said and scribbled a note on the paper. He folded the sheet and stuffed it in the envelope. He sealed the envelope then handed Aideen his bankcard before going back out to the cabbie.

"Is the home address valid?" the clerk asked. Her face was screwed tight in a sour grimace and she rolled her eyes when Aideen offered her another helpless shrug. "Well, I need to know."

Aideen's cheeks flushed a bright rose. "Just go on to the next part." She snapped the words out, her tone peevish at the thought that there still was so much she didn't know about Kean.

"Phone?" the girl asked.

"Just skip the bloody personal information until he gets back," Aideen bit out. *Good Lord!* she groaned internally, *I don't even know his phone number.*

She looked out the window at the lot and saw the cab pull onto the street, the driver offering Kean a backward wave. Kean nodded and turned, a satisfied smile on his face. The smile paled when he saw the waspish red that tinged Aideen's cheeks.

"Well," he said and rubbed his hands together. "Where are we?"

The clerk looked up, a blank expression on her face. "Wadebridge, sir…"

Kean stifled a sigh and pulled the rental application from the girl's unprotesting fingers. "I meant, how far along are we with this?"

"She needs your personal information," Aideen offered, her words clipped short in irritation. "You know, home address, phone, that sort of thing."

"Ah," he said and began filling in the form's boxes. He kept his attention focused on the paper in front of him but couldn't avoid the slow burn of her gaze. After a few seconds, he looked up at Aideen. "What?"

She nodded at the lot outside. "Why'd you send him to Newquay?"

Kean pulled his cell phone from his jacket and tapped the battery cover. "Hopefully, his little trip will buy us an hour or two."

Aideen grunted and tried to smooth the pout from her mouth. She walked over to the window that overlooked the available cars. She'd started out yesterday in a Jag and then battled the lime green truck all the way to Flaherty's landing strip. Directly in front of her was a sapphire BMW 7 series with heavily tinted windows. She tapped the glass with one long nail, drawing both Kean and the clerk's attention. "We want that one," she said, a trace of a smile forming on her lips.

The girl looked at Kean and he nodded his approval.

"You've got the bankcard still?" he asked Aideen. She extended her arm and dropped the card in his outstretched hand.

"When can we eat?" she asked. They hadn't eaten anything since before they boarded the ferry and her stomach was moving beyond quietly protesting. "I'm famished."

He glanced over the wall map behind the counter and frowned. "Bodmin, maybe…not here, that's for sure."

"There's vending in the garage area," the girl offered and jerked her thumb in the direction of the door leading out to the area behind the rental office. Her interest in the strangers was overcoming her initial irritation with Kean's gruff orders and she offered him a tentative smile. "I can make change for you."

"That would be brilliant," Kean said and handed her a £10 note. The girl handed him ten £1 coins and he gave them to Aideen.

She wrinkled her nose playfully. "Aren't you hungry?" she asked as she brushed past him.

Kean caught Aideen and pulled her close enough to whisper in her ear. "I'm sure I'll find something to satisfy me once we're on the road."

The clerk's curious gaze was fixed on them and Aideen blushed, pushing against Kean's body until he released her with a wistful growl. He watched the soft sway of Aideen's ass as she crossed to the door and disappeared from his sight. Then he turned back to the clerk and signed the charge slip before pocketing the BMW's keys.

"Honeymoon?" the girl asked with a knowing grin.

"Actually, we're on an extended first date." He chuckled as the girl's jaw dropped down and she stared at him in gaping disbelief.

Chapter Twelve

Satisfying their immediate hunger with corn chips and soft drinks from the vending machine, they waited until Exeter to stop for food and petrol. Most of the distance passed in silence, Kean's gaze frequently returning to the rearview and side mirrors to make sure they weren't being followed.

"But Flaherty would know we were going to London, wouldn't he?" Aideen asked as she wolfed down a hamburger and vanilla shake.

"Yes," Kean agreed, pinching one of the chips from her plate and dipping it in her shake before he popped it into his mouth. "But he can't be sure we won't change our plans, now that we don't have the stone."

She chewed over her next sentence carefully before she let the words slip casually from her mouth. "You told the minister that a Claubine would release documents if he didn't have you out of jail in two hours…"

An embarrassed red highlighted his cheeks and he avoided her gaze.

"Oh," she said, correcting his assumption. "I don't care that you were blackmailing him… I mean, for the most part I don't care…if he has a mistress or something…sod him…if he's diddling his nephew or selling nuclear launch codes, that's another thing." Her chest constricted around her heart as Kean hesitated to acknowledge her point. But his face was guileless when he nodded his agreement.

"What I meant," she continued in a hurry, "was that you didn't really contact Claubine before you called him. Why? Were you worried she might have joined Meyrick's ranks by now?"

A shadow passed over his features but he wouldn't give voice to any suspicions as to Claubine's loyalties. "I sent a text message to several temple members while Janet was bellowing at us," he said after another minute's hesitation. "I thought it best to deliver the threat first."

"But you couldn't expect to have gotten him so quickly," she pressed. "What if an assistant answered?"

"Not that number," he said and waved her argument away. "Besides, didn't you say no second-guessing?"

"I didn't say that *I* couldn't second-guess you," she protested but nudged his foot under the table in concession. She picked up a chip and experimentally swirled it in her shake before biting into it. The cold from the ice cream coated her tongue, followed by the heat of the salted, fried sliver of potato. The mix of sweet and salty, of cold and hot, swelled in her mouth and she closed her eyes like a well-fed cat. Opening her eyes, she dipped another chip into her shake. "Who is Claubine?" she asked, forcing a certain disinterest into her question. But her body couldn't hide her underlying tension as she waited for him to answer.

Kean reached across the table and squeezed Aideen's hand. "Don't worry, she's one of the temple aunts, as old as—"

"You're certainly full of yourself," Aideen said and pulled her hand away. Her body, relaxing against the seat, gave her away and Kean laughed.

"I'd rather have you full of me," he teased in a sotto voce and chuckled at the instant flushing of her cheeks.

Aideen clasped her hands together and placed them in her lap. She forced her brows to knit together in a frown and then tried to stare Kean down. But he wasn't interested in a staring contest and he blinked first, dropping his gaze to the soft swell of her breasts. Aideen unclasped her hands and planted them on her hips. "I'm wearing this god-awful jacket you dressed me in this morning," she started, her cheeks growing redder as he focused his attention on her hips. "There's nothing for you to play at seeing!" she finished and started clearing the wrappers and cups from the table.

"I've got my memory, haven't I?" he asked and hooked her by the waist as she rose from her seat. He rested his forehead against her hip and kissed the covering of fabric. "Hopefully, I'll get a refresher soon."

The curve of Kean's mouth dropped from a wistful longing to a pensive frown. Aideen pulled at his lip to keep him from biting it. "What's wrong?"

Her tone left him no room to dissimilate but he still tried. "Nothing," he lied and stood to help her with the tray and paper cups. She stared him down and he relented with a heavy sigh. "Psychic now, are you?" he asked. Aideen looked away, not answering him and tossed the paper cups in the store's trash bin. Kean pinched the sleeve of her jacket and stopped her from moving further from him. "Well?"

"With you," she started, still unwilling to meet his sharp gaze. "It's like something that's right on the tip of my tongue." Her hands moved in the air, trying to shape her words into something that made sense. "I know how you're feeling — or, more like I feel the vibrational patterns of your emotion. But not its source. That's teetering on the edge of understanding and when I reach out to pull it back onto the ledge, it's gone."

"And other people?" he asked, looking around the room.

"I don't think they're feeling their emotions strongly enough." She wildly shook one hand in irritation at her inability to explain it. "They aren't vibrating with it."

Kean grabbed her restless hands and held them in his own. "And Everett?"

He could feel her hands turning ice cold. He looked up and blinked against the near bloodlessness of her face. "Shh," he said and pulled her close, needing to chase away the cold pallor that embraced her.

Aideen's teeth chattered as she answered. "It wasn't so much feeling — he was empty. Like a shell for something else. Smoke and mirrors. And each mirror held a woman's face that slowly lost its form until I was looking at myself a dozen times."

Aideen shuddered against him and he held her more tightly. One or two of the more curious diners at the restaurant watched them and Aideen slowly pushed Kean away. She rubbed her hands down her arms and brushed off the memory of Everett. "You're not getting out of it that easy," she said, reminding him of her earlier question. "What is bothering you?"

Kean nodded toward the rental car and she followed him from the restaurant. Inside the car, she fastened her seatbelt before turning to him expectantly. "Not in town," he said. "I'll miss a light and we'll wind up in the backseat of another patrol car."

Aideen waited patiently until Exeter was fading in the car's rearview mirror before she repeated her question. She could feel the tension in his body, knew he didn't want her to ask.

"Lots of things," he answered and switched lanes for no other reason than to have the excuse of concentrating on the road ahead.

"I know that," she answered peevishly. "But you look at me and something comes to mind and it's there, hovering, waiting for you to say it...almost where I can hear it." She snapped her fingers in the air. "Then it's gone, pushed back down." When he didn't answer, she turned toward her side of the car. "For Christ's sake, Kean. Have a little pity on me. The sensation is driving me mad."

A warm fire started to burn in her stomach and she turned back to him, her eyes wide in disbelief. "Is that it?" she laughed. "You want something on the side of the road before we hit London?"

"No," Kean growled then hesitated to reconsider. "I mean...that's not what's bothering me. But if you want to stop—"

"I want to know what's bothering you about me!" Aideen interrupted.

"Do you appreciate how much danger you're in, Aideen?" he asked.

"Yes." She could see that he wasn't stalling but carefully laying the foundation for something he had to ask her.

"More so than anyone else..." he pressed. "The whole world is fucked if Meyrick uses the Bloodstone. But you...he needs you to use it."

"You think he'll try to kidnap me," she said, her voice flat at the possibility. She turned the idea over and wondered how much worse the next would-be kidnapper could be. Aideen shrugged and immediately regretted her nonchalance when she saw the sharp wince it provoked in Kean.

"Yes, Meyrick will try to kidnap you," he answered. "That puts people around you in danger and, even if we can stop him from reaching you...he still has the stone."

"And, if he finds a way to use it..." she started.

"The whole world is fucked," he repeated.

"But that isn't what's knocking around inside your head so loudly I can feel it."

Kean changed lanes again, this time to avoid a weaving lorry. His fingers tapped an impatient beat on the car's steering wheel. "On the plane, before we woke up, I was dreaming," he stopped, at a loss to describe the dream.

Aideen felt the sharp jab of sensual heat fill her groin as Kean thought of the dream that wasn't a dream. "You and me," she filled in the words for him. "Surrounded by fire."

"And we weren't alone." He abruptly pulled over to the side of the road, passing cars honking wildly and offering them obscene gestures. His cheeks colored and he refused to meet Aideen's gaze as he spoke. "I've seen them before...far off, never venturing near—never gracing the ceremony with their full presence."

Aideen felt another stab of heat. This time, the blade penetrated her chest and she stiffened against its assault. "Are you saying..." she began. Her hands fluttered through the air and she wanted to roughly tap his forehead and force him to look at her. "Are you saying that you've participated in a temple sex ceremony?" She put one hand on the dashboard to still it and the other on the center console.

Kean was biting at his lower lip, his entire face flushed a bright red. When he answered at last, his voice was a low rumble of warning. "Yes, Aideen, I have." He raised his head, meeting her narrow-eyed gaze. "You can't say that you're jealous?"

Aideen realized she had started to chew her own lip and pulled her face into a placid mask. If she was jealous, she sure as hell wasn't going to tell him! In fact, until he offered more facts about his own life, she wasn't going to tell him so much as whether the sky was blue or gray.

"Aideen, you were living your life," Kean explained. "I was trying to live mine." His voice held no hint of conciliation. They were facts, his unwavering gaze explained. Facts she would have to live with, just as he had to live with the fact she'd known other men before him.

"Just how much living have you done?" she asked quietly.

"What do you mean?" The hard edge around his mouth softened and he placed a hand on her knee.

"Kids...a wife...things like that." Aideen shrugged as if the answer wouldn't matter but her whole body was poised on the verge of shattering into a million pieces.

Aideen had time to note the rapid dilation of his pupils before he cupped her face and crushed her lips with a relieved kiss. The kiss deepened and she tilted her head back, letting his tongue slip past her lips to explore the contours of her mouth. His tongue teased her upper palate before withdrawing. His teeth drew on her lower lip and then his tongue invaded her again, sweeping against her, demanding she respond.

She pushed him away, her breathing reduced to hard pants. "You haven't answered me," she protested and held him at bay before his mouth could reclaim hers and drive all questions, all thoughts, from her mind.

"No, Aideen," he said, his voice a solemn vow. "No wife or children. No attachments whatsoever." He looked away, locked in silent battle as he tried to still his voice and shaking hands. "I was raised to love you, Aideen. How could I love another?"

She blinked, tears spilling down her cheeks as she took his face between her hands and dusted it with kisses. "I never knew," she said and stroked his hair. Her body struggled against the seatbelt as she tried to wrap herself around him, to comfort him with her entire being. "I never knew," she repeated. "I never loved."

She felt a sharp flare of pain rise up in him and she pulled back, stared into his guarded gray eyes. *Cenn.* It was a lie, even if it wasn't purposeful. She had loved. And the pain of it was written across his face.

Aideen dropped her hands to her lap and fell back against her seat. She stared out the front windshield, unable to recall or explain what she had said. All she could manage while he waited for her to say something, anything, was a simple, "I didn't know."

"No, you didn't," Kean agreed. He put the car in gear and watched the rearview mirror until he could pull back onto the road.

Chapter Thirteen

Kean waited until they were outside London, pulling into Riegate off the A-27, before he finally made the request weighing so heavily on his mind. He caught her while she was straining to catch glimpses of the manor houses they were passing.

"I've been thinking," he started in an offhand manner. Aideen turned, eyeing him sharply as she sensed a change in his energy pattern. He cleared his throat and ran the pad of his palm across the top of the steering wheel. "I've been thinking that an invocation ceremony would give us the guidance we need. Both to find the Bloodstone and keep you safe from Meyrick."

"Even if I wanted to—which I don't," she said forcefully. "I haven't prepared or trained for *that* kind of ceremony."

His jaw worked from side-to-side and he took a deep breath before responding. "Aideen, you managed to travel through time." He voiced the protest softly but the glance he shot her was unyielding. "And you've assisted in hundreds of your father's ceremonies. Of course you're prepared!"

"*Assisting* doesn't include being stretched out on an altar," she started. Her voice dissolved into bitter acid. "Unless you're telling me that's all you need me to do!"

They arrived at a gated estate and the guard waved them in. Kean's mouth puckered and she thought for a second he was going to withdraw his request. Instead, he stopped in the middle of the drive. The house, if something that large could be defined by such a short word, was still half a kilometer or more ahead of them. Engine idling, he turned to her.

"Aideen, you're not refusing merely because your role would be primarily receptive." He reached out to brush her cheek with the tip of his finger but she jerked her head back.

"No mystery there." She folded her arms across her chest and exhaled through pursed lips. "More like I don't care to have sex in front of a bunch of people," she said, her voice squeaking as she finished.

"You wouldn't be—" Kean began and held his hand up as Aideen sharply inhaled, ready to provide him with a lungful of disbelief. "You become part of the outer circle— looking in at the goddess and her consort."

Unconvinced, Aideen arched one blonde brow. "That's how it was for you?" she asked.

Kean frowned, his sensuous lips pulling down at the corners, and Aideen had to look away.

"It was more like walking up a down elevator, forever getting no more than a glimpse of her robe's hem…" He threw his hands up in the air and put the car into gear. "But we've already seen them, Aideen!"

"When we were only a meter from the Bloodstone," she reminded him.

Kean shook his head and pulled the car onto the paved circle in front of the estate house. "You still feel its vibrations."

"That's not any guarantee—" she started but he abruptly fixed his gray gaze on her. The normally dark irises paled and fissures of white heat snaked through them.

"It was never with you, Aideen," he said. "All those times, it should have been and it never was. It *will* work this time."

Aideen looked through the windshield at the old woman walking down the granite steps to greet them, her arms joyfully held outward. "Maybe we should discuss this when we don't have company," Aideen said and gave a slight tilt of her chin in the woman's direction.

Kean and Aideen exited the car together and the old woman embraced Kean before turning to Aideen. The thin lines of her silver eyebrows rose in a delicate curve and she stood with arms slightly akimbo, as if she wanted to embrace Aideen as well but worried the gesture would be unwelcome.

"Aideen!" she said with a smile on her faded pink lips. "So much like your mother." Nothing in the woman's face or voice was familiar and Aideen stood at the side of the car, mutely observing her. The old woman's smile dropped at the corners and she offered an exculpatory shrug. "Well, let's get your bags inside and get you settled in."

"No bags, Claubine," Kean explained and started up the steps with the woman. "Things have been a bit of a blur the last two days—no time to pack." He glanced over his shoulder, relieved to see that Aideen still wasn't standing stubbornly alongside the car or—worse yet—walking back to the gate.

"Well, there's plenty here that will fit you both," Claubine responded. "And I'll send Vera out for the more personal items we can't round up."

Kean put his arm around Claubine's shoulder and lightly kissed her cheek. "I think our immediate comforts can be satisfied with a bath, food, robes and," he said, stifling a yawn, "a nap while we wait for Julius to arrive."

A middle-aged woman stood in the foyer watching them as they entered the estate house. Dark brown hair, mixed with an iron gray that matched her neatly pressed suit, coiled in a bun. Her mouth was a slash of crimson that showed a sliver of pearl when she smiled.

"Vera," Claubine said and extended her arm in Aideen's direction. "This is Miss Godwin, Gerald's daughter. She'll be staying with us indefinitely."

Aideen chafed at Claubine's use of *indefinitely* and halted her progress across the foyer. Kean caught her hesitation and raised one brow in annoyance. Then he saw her fragile expression and his irritation evaporated. He moved across the marble floor until he was standing next to her. Had he not spent the last two days in such intense contact with her, he wouldn't have noticed her almost imperceptible recoil when he placed his arm around her shoulder.

Claubine turned, seeing only a lovers' embrace, and smiled. "Will you be sharing a room?" she inquired softly. Claubine's smile grew nervous as Aideen gave a quick, negative shake of her head. "Two rooms, then, Vera."

Aideen felt Kean tense beside her but he remained quiet while they followed Vera up the curving staircase. Halfway down the hall of the second floor, Vera stopped in front of a set of double doors. Drawing a heavy keychain from the folds of her suit, she unlocked the doors and pushed them open. She pointed at the nightstand beside the canopied bed. Next to the lamp was a key to the room on a velvet pull-tab.

"You can use this room," Vera said and stepped into the center of the room. She gestured at a closed door. "Bathroom's in there. No one's in the opposite side, just yet, but we're expecting more guests, so lock it when…" her hands fluttered and Aideen cut the woman's discomfort short.

"I will."

Vera gave a perfunctory nod and stepped back toward the hallway. "Kean, you'll have your regular suite." She turned as if expecting him to follow but he remained standing inside Aideen's room.

"Thank you, Vera," Kean said, his gaze fixed on Aideen. "Just unlock it for me, if you will."

Another swift nod and Claubine's personal secretary was gone.

"Aideen," Kean said, reaching out to keep her from shrinking away from him. She stiffened against him and he clamped down on the urge to tighten his grip. He dropped his hands to his sides and marched to the double doors, closing and locking the two of them in the room. "Let's start with how foolish it is requesting a separate room."

Aideen's mouth twisted into an angry pucker and her hands found her hips. "Foolish? Just deal with the fact that I don't want to share a room with you, Kean." She turned, casting a baleful glare over her shoulder as she approached the balcony doors. "Or a bed, for that matter."

"I'll sleep on the floor," he offered, his tone businesslike in its indifference. "But you're vulnerable on your own. The gate's just for show and the security system wouldn't stand up against professionals. And Meyrick's men may be mad dogs, but they're most definitely professionals, too."

Kean sat on the edge of the bed and waited for her to respond. She stood at the balcony doors, one hand holding a curtain back while she looked out at the lawn where Claubine was overseeing preparations for an outdoor dinner. Aideen counted the number of place settings. Twenty!

"And I regret pressing you on an invocation ceremony," he said. Cold calculation poured from him and she looked back to where he sat on the bed, feet planted wide apart as he watched her. "I won't request that you participate in the ceremony again," he continued. "It was asking too much and I'm sorry."

She played over his words and flat expression. From the balcony doors, she turned to face him. Her hands hung limp at her sides. "Are you implying the ceremony will still be held?"

Kean's flat gaze held hers. He took a light breath, gathering the words he knew would hurt her. "I think every avenue of action must be pursued to keep you safe and to locate the Bloodstone."

"And you're going to...participate?" she faltered over the end of her question and retreated back to looking out the window. Fresh arrangements of white calla lilies were being placed on the tables. Claubine bent over one of the centerpieces and waved the flowers' fragrance closer to her as she inhaled.

"That is my position within the temple, Aideen." He slipped his shoes off and padded across the carpet toward the bathroom. "I'll run you some bathwater," he suggested. "You'll feel more yourself afterwards."

Aideen heard the water running in the tub and glanced at the half-open bathroom door. Kean was bent over the water, sprinkling bath salts. She started across the room, her steps tentative as she neared the double doors that would take her to the hallway and out of the house.

The water stopped running and Kean's voice drifted to where she stood, her hand resting on the doorknob. "Aideen?" She didn't answer and he released a remorseful sigh. He stood and walked back into the bedroom, his gaze unerringly going to where she stood ready to flee.

"You're not leaving the estate, Aideen." He ran his hand, still wet from running the bathwater, absently over the front of his shirt. "You don't have to take a bath, or sleep, or talk to anyone…but you're not leaving."

Aideen nodded slowly, in mock understanding. "I'd forgotten."

"What?" he asked, body tense in anticipation of her answer.

"That I'd been kidnapped…by you."

He was across the room in three quick strides, his hand pressed against the doors' centerline. "Aideen, I wish—" he began but then he broke the thought with a sharp shake of his head. "No, that's not true. I don't wish I could just let you walk out of here." He brought his other hand up, an arm on either side of her, her back pressed against the door.

Aideen tried to block his emotions from her mind but they were too parallel to her own to be denied. She looked at the floor, trying to conceal the consent lingering in her eyes. Kean pressed closer to her. He bent down, his lips whispering across her mouth.

"I lost you once." He forced her to look up at him.

Kean weaved his fingers through the length of her blonde hair and cupped the back of her head. He pulled her closer to him until their bodies were pressed against one another. Aideen felt a bridge of need arching between them, its power overwhelming her senses as he tilted her head further back, her lips parting at the gentle strain on the muscles of her neck.

"I'm not going to lose you again, Aideen."

His mouth covered hers while one hand slid over her shoulder to cup a breast. Aideen melted into his touch and strained against him, rising up on her toes to feel the delicious glide of his cock against her. His other hand moved to caress the curve of her ass and grind her closer still. He bent, his hand pressing against the back of her knee until she wrapped both arms around him and allowed him to carry her into the bathroom. The tub was a third full, its water steaming. Kean stood Aideen on her feet and pulled her top off. He reached behind her, his mouth nuzzling her breasts as he found the clasps and unhooked her bra. He paused to suckle one nipple, his hands moving to the front of her jeans and unzipping them.

Kean sank to his knees, his tongue darting into her navel before his head dipped lower, following the downward sweep of her jeans as she stepped from them. He pressed his lips against her mound, the fabric of her panties a feeble barrier against his heat. He caressed her hips, one hand pulling at the elastic band while the other slipped between her thighs. His fingers found her center, steaming like the air around them, and he stroked the inside walls of her pussy.

Aideen clung to him, her body rocking as his tongue found her clit. She leaned back, pressing her cunt against his mouth, wanting his touch, his kisses to continue forever. "I want you inside me," she groaned and tried to force him to stand.

Kean caught her hands and encircled her wrists behind her back. His tongue explored the surface of her clit, laved the warm folds of her labia. His upper lip massaged the pink button while his tongue stroked the spongy entrance to her vagina. Kean released Aideen's hands and pulled her into a sitting position on the edge of the tub. She swung her legs over his shoulders and leaned back over the tub's open expanse. Gripping the opposite rim of the tub, Aideen locked one leg over the other, her ass hovering on the thin line of porcelain as she met his thrusting tongue. A hot flush spread across her breasts as the first wave of climax crashed against her. She released a low moan and said his name.

"I want you inside me," she pleaded, her body pulsing against his probing tongue.

Kean ran his hands under her back and helped Aideen into an upright position. She was at eyelevel with his jean-clad cock and her fingers raced to release the top button. She flipped the zipper pull up and separated the jean flaps. The tip of his cock was breaching the top of his silk boxers and she nibbled at the head. She tasted the salt of his pre-cum as it beaded and she dipped her tongue into the small slit.

"Aideen, I can't," he said, his voice choked as he gently pushed her away.

She looked at his cock, swollen in its readiness to penetrate. "I think you can," she said, her lips seeking the glistening tip.

"I'm sorry," he said and pulled away. His hands fumbled with the zipper and he refused to meet Aideen's gaze. "I shouldn't have let it get this far…not before the ceremony."

Aideen sat naked on the edge of the tub. She felt played and she searched his face for some hint that he was trying to manipulate her. But when he finally did look into her eyes, she saw only his pain. He went down on his knees again. His head in her lap, he wrapped his arms around her waist. His body trembled against hers and she smoothed his hair.

"I don't want to meet those people out there," she said softly, still stroking his head.

He shook his head against her lap. Not fully understanding, he tried to reassure her. "You don't have to. We'll have our meals in here and Julius can stay with you when…" His breathing hitched and he let the sentence go unfinished.

"No," she said and forced his head from her lap. She cupped his face, the pads of her thumb caressing his cheeks as she made him look at her. "I don't want to know them…the people who'll be watching us. I don't want to know their names, or who they are or where they're from, before or…after. Promise me."

Slowly Kean understood what Aideen was saying and he nodded. He blinked, hot tears spilling onto the strong cheekbones. She dipped her head, her tongue snaking out to catch a tear before kissing the next one away.

Chapter Fourteen

Kean's suite within Claubine's estate house was comprised of a bedroom, bath and study. Entry into the bedroom from inside the house was through the study's double doors. Those study doors were partially open as Aideen sat on Kean's bed and flipped through the TV channels. She kept the volume low, not only because Kean had to consult with a stream of worried visitors in the study but also because Aideen could feel his anxiety level spike if he couldn't hear her. Those levels spiked even higher if he couldn't lean forward occasionally from where he was talking with someone and catch a glimpse of her foot or some other visible sign she was still in the room instead of slung over the back of one of Meyrick's thugs.

Among the many channels, Aideen was most interested in the news broadcasts. After the first few hours, she realized she was hoping to catch some hint of the Bloodstone on the news—as if it would leave a trail of signs to aid her in finding it. Worse yet was the possibility that Meyrick's attempt to use the Bloodstone might make its way on to the news in the form of a dragon or some other fanciful creature sailing from a cloud. She knew that by the time anything showed up on the news, it would be too late, but the urge to channel surf was unconquerable.

And she certainly couldn't join Kean in the study. The curious looks of the visitors and the naked hope that flashed across their faces were unbearable. And what had they to be hopeful for? Even if the ceremony worked, there was little chance Meyrick would keep the Bloodstone in one location. And, if he did, she couldn't see anyone from the temple storming in to retrieve the damn thing. Kean was alone in his spy-like abilities. *Hell*, she thought and ran through five more channels, from what she had seen through the crack in the door and yesterday's lawn supper, the temple's membership had been reduced to a few rich senior citizens who had nothing better to do.

Aideen heard the brush of the door against the carpeting and looked up to find Kean watching her. She switched the TV off and smiled at him. "Safe for now. No sign on the telly that the world will end anytime soon."

Kean stepped into the room and pulled the study's doors shut behind him. He sat on the center edge of the bed, his back to her, half looking at her, half looking away as he spoke. "Claubine will be up in a few minutes."

Aideen's gaze darted to the clock. 10 p.m. already! She felt nausea swirling in her stomach.

Kean reached out and covered her hand with his. "You don't have to," he repeated.

"So nice of you to be ready to fuck someone else," she answered dryly and switched the TV back on.

Kean's hand returned to his lap to dangle uselessly between his legs. After a few seconds, he stood and returned to the study. Aideen watched his retreating back from the corner of her eye. Damn, she wished he would cave in. The ceremony wasn't going to work and he was blackmailing her, even if he didn't mean to.

Aideen was still furiously flipping through the channels when Claubine and Vera came into the bedroom five minutes later. Aideen stiffened at the sight of Vera, but the woman was there only to collect a few of the things

Kean would need for the ceremony. Vera quickly bundled the robe and chasuble and left the room, her spine ramrod straight. On her way out, she brushed past Julius, who closed the door, leaving Aideen and Claubine alone.

"She's going to dress him?" Aideen inquired with a false lightness.

Claubine nodded and handed Aideen two vials and a bar of rough, scented soap. She pointed to the larger vial. "Rub that all over before you shower and be careful not to slip. And that," she said and motioned to the second vial, "put in your robe pocket for the ceremony."

"What's its purpose?" Aideen asked.

A wry cackle erupted from Claubine. "Lubrication, dear, pure and simple," she explained. "No matter how much you want him before or after the ceremony...your body's bound to get stage fright."

Her curiosity satisfied, Aideen's attention drifted back to Kean's preparations. "If I weren't here—" she began but Claubine chopped a dismissive hand in the air.

"It's not like that, at least not between them," Claubine answered. "Maybe after a time...your parents certainly took their time warming up to one another." She caught Aideen's sharp glance but shrugged and continued. "Simple truth. But Kean wasn't meant for Vera, nor she for him. Probably why the goddess never visited them."

Aideen thought about the woman she was replacing in tonight's ceremony. Dry, like black sand, with a viper's eyes. And a pale tongue that flicked the air when she was deep in thought. Aideen shuddered as she walked into the bathroom to shower and the image fell away. She uncapped the larger vial and began rubbing the oil over her, the piney scent of lilac rising from her body. Her mind drifted back to the bathroom of her small shop in Dublin and how she had performed a similar ritual to prepare for the journey to Cenn. Those preparations hadn't been a cold chore like the one now. She closed her eyes and let her fingers play over her nipples but they remained unresponsive. *Christ*, she thought, it wasn't as if she didn't want Kean. Just not in front of a masked group, half of which would probably retreat to some spare room after the ceremony to masturbate.

Finished with the lilac oil, she stepped into the tub and turned the showerhead on. The soap was another concoction of flowers, their fibers scouring away the lilac oil she had just coated herself in. Lilac oil slickened the tub's floor and Aideen finished rinsing off, careful to heed Claubine's warning. She towel-dried her hair and let the water on her skin evaporate. The robe was similar to the one she had borrowed on Inish Oirr. Its color was the same deep red with gold embroidery. She slipped the second vial into the small inside pocket and opened the door for Claubine's inspection.

Claubine had a brush in hand and after walking a slow circle around Aideen, she began to smooth the tangles from Aideen's damp hair. "If you forget anything," she said. "Just look at me."

Aideen nodded. Weak-kneed, she felt too shaky to try to say anything. She looked at the clock. 11:15 p.m. The initial pageantry was timed to end a few minutes before midnight, at which point she and Kean would, she thought derisively, drop robe.

Claubine put the brush down and hooked Aideen's arm. "Time to go, child."

Julius was waiting for them in the study and he took Aideen from the old woman. He held his arm slightly away from his body, his palm facing upward. Aideen covered his hand with her own, his touch a cold relief. He led her down the hallway to the staircase. Even before they left the study, Aideen could hear the low hum of the women who waited on the staircase. Their voices filled her until she began to vibrate with their rhythm. Her heartbeat slowed and she moved down the staircase as if she were swimming in deep waters.

From the staircase, Julius led her into what had once been a grand ballroom. Its crystal chandelier, massive in size, still hung from the ceiling. Candles interlaced the faceted stones, their joined brilliance dancing across the room. Behind Julius and Aideen, the women followed and took their place beside a male. The men, too, were softly chanting, their deeper voices lengthening the rhythm. Across the ballroom floor, Kean was moving toward her, similarly led by Vera. They met in the center where an altar of semi-rigid cushions and soft pillows had been constructed. Aideen knelt before the altar, her left hand still resting lightly atop Julius's upturned palm. Her right hand, the little vial in front of it, she put palm upward on a cushion, where Kean covered it.

The chanting stopped and Kean's voice filled the ballroom with its rich baritone. "I am a ray of sunlight."

Aideen answered in her pure soprano. "I am the greenest of plants."

"I am a salmon in the river," he countered. His hand grew warm atop hers and she felt the heat spread up her arm.

"I am the river that cuts through the plain," she answered and offered in return. "I am the wind that blows across the sea."

"I am the hawk on the cliff at the edge of your sea." His voice grew richer, its volume pressing against Aideen and making her lightheaded. "I am the stag of seven battles."

On her left, Julius pulled his hand from hers and moved behind her to strip the robe from her body. She broke contact with Kean for a second and both of their robes fell to the floor.

"I am the wave of the deep," she said, her voice edged in naked power. "I am the word of knowledge, the lure beyond the ends of the earth."

Kean's breathing grew erratic and she could hear the pulse of his blood in his voice. His bare hip brushed her waist and she leaned against him, her own breath breaking into ragged pants. Both of his hands found her hips and he slid her onto the altar bed. He opened the vial, the scent of lilies filling the air. He took a fingertip of oil and touched it to her left nipple. He repeated the motion with her other breast, her nipples sharp stones. A third dip of the vial, heavier than the other two, and he caressed her clit before sliding his slickened fingers into her canal. "I am a wild boar, I am the point of a spear," he said.

"I am the wound," she said, her legs spreading in invitation.

"I can shift my shape like a god," he finished, his rod poised at the moist entrance of her sex.

Aideen lifted her hips, the tip of his cock easing into her as she spoke the final words of the invocation. "I am the goddess incarnate."

Kean entered her, driving the length of his shaft into her in one swift motion. She felt her cells exploding, another presence leaking in to fill the void. Red shaded her vision, her sight blurring until the man hovering above her, pumping her body while he serenaded her with unearthly notes of exquisite beauty, was no longer recognizable as Kean.

Aideen turned her gaze inward, searching for herself and finding another. Her own voice took on an ethereal quality as she embraced the newcomer.

Thank you, daughter, the woman smiled. She danced in flame, her body slick with sweat. The fire took form, rising like a snake to insert itself in the woman. She arched her back and strong arms reached around her waist to steady her. Legs shot up, powerful thighs melding to a firm ass and broad back. The woman wrapped her legs around her lover's waist and softly breathed his name. *Myr.*

Aideen looked past the veil of passion to see Kean above her, his body locked in the lovers' rhythm as his cocked swelled to fill her, to push against her quivering muscles that contracted around his thickness in a delighted torment. She lifted her ass off the cushions and pumped him more deeply into her.

*Yes…*the woman sighed. *Harder, daughter. Make him fill us completely.*

Her lover laughed and pinched a nipple. *Careful, Danu, you would not have us break the girl.*

Aideen growled and wrapped her legs around Kean's waist. Her arms encircled his neck and she molded her body to his. He groaned against the onslaught of her tight, short thrusts that milked his cock until his seed spilled from him and filled her like molten rock, burning its essence into her soul.

Aideen released Kean and collapsed against the cushions. But the woman wasn't finished. *Again, daughter!* Flames licked her breasts, their hot tongues teasing her nipples. She felt herself being rolled over. Kean's thumbs found the entrance to her cunt. He massaged the slick folds, coaxing them to relax and allow him to reenter. Another hard stroke and his cock was buried inside her, the slap of his balls toying with her clit. Aideen began to writhe with the woman's ecstasy. Kean grabbed Aideen by the hips, ramming his cock into her, hot semen again erupting from him to fill her channel and run in pearl drops down her thigh.

Kean's weight pushing her down, Aideen collapsed against the mattress once again, her breasts flattened. Still, the woman would not relent. She wanted more. Too many lifetimes, in a place where time was nothing and everything, had she and her lover waited for the perfect communion, the perfect couple. Too long had they merely graced the periphery of these ceremonies. *More, much more,* she demanded of Aideen. *Every orifice teased, every ounce of flesh enflamed with passion.*

Would you have news of the Bloodstone? the woman coaxed. Aideen nodded and the woman covered Aideen's mouth with her own, her tongue slipping into Aideen to stroke the back of her throat. Aideen wiggled against Kean, who was already pulling her body back up. She was in front of him on her hands and knees, her body still panting for more, her ass rubbing against his still erect cock. She felt the warm glide of the lily oil over her puckered flesh as the pad of Kean's thumb explored her nether hole. She moaned, another orgasm sending her body into a paroxysm. The scent of the oil reminded her of the calla lilies that had adorned Claubine's dinner table and the thought of that sensual flower, its petals cupped like a woman's pussy, the stamen an engorged clit, left Aideen clenching the pillows, her ass bouncing against the probing thumb.

"Fuck me," she growled, her voice vibrating with Danu's need.

Kean dripped more of the lily oil across the constricted opening. His finger eased past the tight circle of muscle, preparing her for the much thicker penetration of his cock. As he slowly finger-fucked her ass, adding a second digit to the first, he pressed his stomach flat on the mattress. His head was even with Aideen's cunt and he pressed his mouth against the pulsating slit. His tongue entered her, probing with the same speed and intensity with which he fingered the velvet channel of her ass.

Aideen clamped down on his fingers and tongue, every trembling muscle focused on the climax that rumbled through her body. Kean withdrew from her and she reached behind, spreading her ass cheeks again. "Fuck me," she ordered. "Now!"

At her heated invitation, Kean pressed the bulbous tip of his cock against the tight hole that winked above the center of her sex. As he pushed into her, her body pushed back, the muscles narrowing in anticipation of the imminent invasion. Aideen released a frustrated grunt and ground against him, forcing the head of his cock into her. Her muscles sealed around him as the mushroomed tip breached her. Kean tried to take her in slow strokes, tried to ease the full length of his swollen shaft into Aideen, but neither she nor Danu would accept such tender affection.

Aideen lunged backward, drawing the full length of Kean's cock into her in one hard stroke.

She squeezed tight, pinching his cock in place and began slowly gyrating her hips. Kean moaned and leaned against her, one hand sliding under her belly to pull at her clit, stroking the enflamed button to a sharp edge. Aideen relaxed her hold on Kean's shaft marginally, just enough for him to start a rapid withdrawal before ramming his cock back into her. She coiled and uncoiled around him in sharp flutters as he drove in and out of her, the hard slap of his balls beating against the entrance to her cunt. Aideen began to shake, another orgasm building deep inside her as Danu whispered secrets in her ear, told her of the time before time and the sacred center that was everywhere and nowhere. The first wave of her climax hit and Aideen let out a single note—sharp, pure—before she fainted.

Chapter Fifteen

Aideen woke in Kean's arms. They were back in his rooms, their bodies wrapped in cream-colored terrycloth robes. Someone had washed them, the scent of lily and their passions wiped clean. Kean was watching her when she opened her eyes, his own gaze masked. She touched his mouth, trying to melt the thin line of despair it formed.

"I know what she told you," Kean said, his voice laden with regret.

Aideen thought of the many things Danu had revealed to her. She sifted through the bits of information, looking for the piece that was causing him pain. Her fingers fastened around something and she held it up.

"You have to see beyond this," she said without acknowledging the source of his desolation.

"You can't go to him," he pressed. "It's too dangerous."

"It's the only way to get the Bloodstone from him."

Kean shook his head and raised his body over hers. "He'll use you and then kill you!"

She considered the idea and threw it to the side. "No," she promised. "His greed and arrogance will destroy him."

"And what about those around him?" he asked. "All the Everetts and two-bit thugs?"

"But the stone will be out of reach," she answered. She put her palms on his chest to soothe him but he brushed them away.

"I don't give a bloody fuck about the stone, Aideen," Kean said.

Aideen pushed him away and stared up at the ceiling. The ceiling was no less ornate than the rest of the room. Decorative wood molding formed a rectangle in the center. Inside the rectangle was an image she knew well, two swans linked by a gold chain—Oenghus, son of the Dagda, and Ibormeith, his dream lover. She turned her head to Kean, caught his obdurate gaze, and returned to inspecting Claubine's ceiling. The gold chain that linked her to Kean weighed as if it had been hammered from lead.

"Stop being so conceited," she said at last.

"Conceit has nothing to do with it," he argued but she held up a hand.

"Stop thinking you can keep me safe and save the world at the same time." Kean started to protest but she shoved her hand higher. "I played the little part you were happy to have me play, to hell if you don't like the results. You wanted her guidance—you've got it!"

"Fine—but you're not going alone," Kean said. His body was stiff, transmitting his unwillingness to entertain any objection she might have.

"Meyrick has a reason to keep me relatively unharmed…anyone else—particularly someone who shot him in the leg—can't expect such courtesies."

"And yet I'm going," he said as if the matter were settled.

Aideen rolled onto her side, her green gaze blazing. "Damn it, Kean, stop using my feelings for you to control my actions!"

"Your feelings for me?" he asked, the bitterness in his laugh unconcealed. "Aideen, I'm not letting the woman I love surrender herself to Donald Meyrick and his criminally insane posse."

Tears welled in Aideen's eyes and Kean's hard features softened for an instant, but no longer than that. "You're not leaving the estate, hell, not even this room, without me," he said. "Besides, you're not getting a bit of help from me otherwise and you've no idea where to start."

Aideen folded her arms over her chest, more in defeat than defiance. Kean wedged one hand under her arm, his hand cupping her breast through the terrycloth. His words still stung with the dividing line he'd drawn between her feelings for him and what his heart held for her. Was it too late to tell him she loved him?

"Stop pouting," he coaxed. "And tell me what else you know."

"You mean other than your being the most arrogant man I've ever met?"

"You sound as if that wasn't one of the things you like about me." Kean smiled, his wicked grin whipped around Aideen and pulled her toward him. She shifted the smallest bit in his direction. Kean interpreted her movement as an invitation and his hand moved to her hip. He reeled her in until her stomach pressed against his groin.

"Because it isn't," she said. Her tone lacked conviction and she buried her head against his chest.

Kean chuckled and slipped his hand between the folds of her robe. His hand caressed the curve of her bottom and stilled, cupping her gently to him. "Alright, I'm an ass," he confessed. "But tell me something I don't know, something about the stone."

Aideen frowned, the corner of her mouth brushing his hardened nipple. She felt a wistful contraction below and she closed her eyes, trying to focus on what Danu had whispered to her. She took a frustrated breath and then started, her mind stumbling around for words that would give meaning to what she had seen.

"The stone is a part of where they are," she hesitated, testing the accuracy of what she had said. She shook her head. "It's a part of what they are."

"What are they?" Kean asked. His body was filled with a relaxed interest and his thumb lightly stroked her tailbone.

She rolled the word around on her tongue before she released it. "Calabi." She looked up at him to see if the word had meaning. It didn't. "What they are is where they are, too." The frown lines along her forehead deepened and Kean pressed his lips against them.

"But where is Calabi?" he prodded.

Aideen thought of the flower Danu had shown her—a fire lily, its petals closing in on it. "It's the center dimension." As soon as she said it, she saw the lily's petals unfurling in a red blaze. Her face gained certainty and she nodded. "And it serves as a balance for everything around it—like a gyroscope or the earth's core."

Kean thought of the Bloodstone's fiery red brilliance and the volcanic dream demesne Danu and Myr inhabited. "So the Bloodstone is like cooled magma?" he ventured.

"Kind of...but it shouldn't be here...it creates an imbalance." She remembered the way the stone pulled at her whenever it was nearby. "The other dimensions try to wrap around it, too. The curtain between dimensions tears and things leak out." She gave a shudder and Kean stopped the gentle teasing of her bottom and wrapped his arms around her. Her shudder turned to shaking. "It has to go back."

"You said before that the stone knows the way?" he asked.

"Yes, I just need to get to it and release its energy."

Someone knocked at the double doors that led to the study. Kean stiffened and sat up, his body shielding Aideen. "Yes?"

"Claubine thought you might be hungry." Vera waited impatiently on the other side.

If Aideen closed her eyes, she could see the woman tapping her right foot, her mouth puckered in anger. Undetected, Aideen reached into Vera's mind. Vera seethed with perceived betrayal and plans for revenge.

Kean rose and opened the door. He moved to take the tray from Vera but she brushed past him and placed it on the bed, her gaze glossing over Aideen's robed body. Leaving the room, she ignored Kean's softly voiced thanks.

Well, there's our Judas, Aideen thought and lifted the tray so that Kean could sit on the bed. She watched him pop a strawberry in his mouth, his thoughts too focused on the problem at hand to notice the fruit's ripe sweetness. A fat drop of juice glistened at the center of his bottom lip and Aideen leaned forward. She sucked the juice from his mouth and offered him a second taste with the tip of her tongue. His body's reaction was immediate but he shook the temptation away.

"How are we to get you to Meyrick?" he asked. He picked the fullest strawberry from the bowl and pressed it against Aideen's lips. His gaze heated as he watched her open her mouth, her pink tongue sliding under the fruit to pull it into the moist cavern.

Aideen looked at the door Vera had so recently marched through. "Someone is already taking care of that."

Kean's gaze followed Aideen's. The line of his jaw hardened and he stood. Aideen caught his wrist. The hand was balled into a fist. Kean tried to shrug her hand away but Aideen held tight. He looked down at her. His lips were bloodless from being pressed too thin and his eyes were shining from Vera's treachery.

"She has no right," he started. "No claim —"

"She loves you," Aideen corrected him. "Even if you don't love her, that is claim enough."

A shadow passed over his features and his anger collapsed under the simplicity of her statement. The look on his face told Aideen he understood Vera's feelings all too well. Aideen captured his other wrist and knelt on the bed in front of him. Their bodies almost touched, only the distance of a word separating them. She had rebuffed his earlier declaration of love in the house on Inish Oirr and had danced around her love for him just this hour. Surely, he would think it forced if she said it now.

"I would walk through fire for you," Aideen said, releasing his wrists and laying her palms and head against his broad chest.

His laugh was hard edged. He captured her chin and looked at her, gray gaze meeting green. "We've walked through fire together," he reminded her. "It's the shadows that worry me."

"We'll build our own fires if we find ourselves in shadow." She reached up and curled one arm around his neck, lightly stroking the fine taper of hair. "We've done it before."

Kean released her chin. Standing as straight as a beam of steel, hands at his sides, he searched Aideen's face for some hint of what she was feeling. "With what tinder?" he asked, a trace of hope softening his tone.

"Love, Kean," she answered and clasped both hands behind his neck. "I love you, and there is no balance in losing you twice to Fate."

Chapter Sixteen

The tray, most of the meal it had been laid with still intact, was on the bed and Kean reached behind Aideen to remove it. With the tray on the floor, he pushed Aideen onto the bed. Her blonde hair fanned around her in waves and he caught a lock and brushed it against his lips before peeling back her robe. Pale bruises dotted the white skin of her hips and he matched his fingertips to the spots. She arched against his touch, the pink flower of her sex sending up its receptive aroma.

Kean kneeled in front of the bed. His hands moved from her hips to brush the warm petals. He parted them, his erection thrusting forward at the sight of the nectar that already coated the folds of the inner petals. He dipped his tongue into the centermost fold. The sweetness of her taste wrenched through his hungry soul and he probed deeper. His hands caught the bend between Aideen's thighs and hips and he held her firm to still the waves passing through her body. She called his name, wet heat blurring her pronunciation until there was no longer a distinction between the love she had lost and the one she now claimed.

"You know me now?" he asked.

Aideen looked at him, seeing the raw need for an answer mixed with an unconditional acceptance of whatever she might say. Tears pooled in her eyes, gentling the heat that threatened to burn her alive. Her voice tremulous, she nodded and pulled him closer. "Yes, my love, I know you."

With her body quieted under his command, Kean found that he missed the soft gyrations. His tongue a wet rod, he laved the inside walls of her pussy and she bucked against him. He licked a slow line to her clit, his mouth fastening on the small button while his hands reached up to pinch her nipples. Aideen reached past his arms and hooked her hands behind her knees. She pulled her knees to her chest, her cunt fully revealed to him. His appetite leapt, magnified, and he climbed onto the mattress, his form prostrate before her as his lips and tongue worked her clit.

Kean's hands pressed at the back of her thighs, pumping her against his mouth. She grabbed her legs more tightly, hugged them to her chest as the walls of her pussy contracted in anticipation of his touch. He groaned at her enthusiasm, his appreciation a gust of hot air against her sex. Kean slid three fingers inside her, stretching her with an exquisite fullness that had her moaning for his cock. His hand played along her interior, her body tightening against him while his mouth stacked pleasure on top of pleasure until she collapsed against the bed in climax.

As she shuddered beneath him, he rose up on his knees. His fingers, slick with Aideen's satisfaction, teased the swollen clit until cum, a warm thread of liquid, shot from her. His free hand squeezed the base of his cock, trying to prevent his own orgasm as she released her legs and invitingly pushed her full breasts together.

"I want to taste you," she said, squirming beneath the continued onslaught of his touch.

He shook his head but his gaze remained fixed on her half-parted lips. "I could come just looking at you," he moaned. His hand slid to the tip of his cock where pre-cum formed small pearls.

Aideen licked her lips and pushed her tits higher. She closed her eyes, nipples pinched between thumb and forefinger and moaned. She repeated her demand. "I want to taste you." Another slide of her tongue moistened her blood-flushed lips.

Kean moved over her body, his shaft gliding along her stomach. She opened her eyes as she felt his tip reach the press of her breasts. He pushed through the pliant flesh, her mouth widening to gently receive the offered delicacy. Her saliva lubricated his shaft and he pulled back for another stroke. Her lips pulled him in again and held him while her tongue swirled around the tip. Kean's breathing was ragged, every muscle in his body straining. She released him for another stroke, her own excitement pushing against her. She began to move beneath him, adding to his strokes, her tongue following his shaft as it pushed forward from her breasts and then retreated.

"I'm going to come, Aideen," he warned, the words broken into sharp pants.

Her mouth captured his cock, her hands darting from her breasts to cup his testicles. The brush of her skin against the sensitive pubic hairs made him shudder and he arched his back, thrusting his hips forward and flinging his head back. Aideen urged him deeper, her cheeks hollowing as she forced the remaining half of his length into her. Aideen looked up, saw that he was biting his lip. A bright red tear of blood pearled beneath the sharp canine.

She sucked at his cock more urgently, trying to beat down the control he was exercising. The flat of her tongue pressed against the inside curve of his shaft and she delivered hard strokes to the thick vein that throbbed with his approaching climax. Keeping the pressure on his shaft, the entry to her throat hugging the engorged tip of his cock, she relaxed her cheeks and rapidly puffed the air in her sealed mouth.

Kean, undone, groaned and bucked against her, the first spurt of cream forcing its way down her throat. The sharp tang of his semen washed across her palate and her lips constricted to milk another spurt from him. Even as he tried to withdraw, she held him tight to her, her finger snaking along the smooth skin of his perineum to tease his tight hole with shallow thrusts. Ensnared by her probing finger and greedy mouth, he bore down, riding her hand. His hands found her hair and he wound his fingers tight through the long tresses until she had sucked the last of his climax from him. When at last they released one another, he collapsed against the bed, his body twitching at the lightest touch.

Aideen rolled on top of him. Her lips covered his, her tongue, still thick with cum, invaded his mouth. Their juices mingled and the taste pebbled her nipples in a delighted thrill. She rubbed her pubic hair against his shaft and he jerked against her.

"Mercy," he moaned when Aideen finally broke the kiss.

Aideen squirmed over his lower body and wedged the tip of his shaft against her clit. "No mercy," she taunted and contracted her muscles against his semi-rigid length. "You started it," she reminded him.

Kean reached up, quickly pushing at her elbows so that they collapsed. With a quick turn, he had her pinned beneath him. Despite Kean's protests, his member already began to thicken with renewed desire. He gave her lips a sharp erotic nip then sat up. Her normally pale skin was flushed a gentle rose. Her breathing continued fast and hard, her mouth an open invitation. He fingered its full curve. When she closed her eyes in contentment, his chest swelled with tender emotion.

"I'm going to take a shower." He bent down and kissed each closed eyelid. "You can join me."

Aideen opened her eyes and he saw something lurking behind the green gaze. He studied her expression for a moment before fixing on that something's identity. Purpose.

"What is it?" he asked.

"Just a little business to take care of," she said. The words were crisp, the sensuality of her voice held in check. "I'll join you when I'm done," she promised. "Wait for me."

Kean nodded and rose from the bed. His robe was on the floor and he stepped over it on his way to the bathroom. Aideen wrapped hers around herself and lay against the pillow. She closed her eyes and let her thoughts wander from the room and down the hall. It took her only a few seconds to find Vera, to stroke the bare nape of her neck and coax her to the study's outer door.

The shower was already running when Vera knocked on the door but Aideen was waiting for the sound, saw Vera raise her hand to knock before the sharp rap reached her ears. Loosely tying the robe around her, Aideen got up and answered the door.

"Oh, Vera, what is it you need?" Her voice was sleepy innocence and she padded back into the bedroom before the woman could answer her.

"The tray," Vera answered. Distantly polite, she nevertheless managed to fill the room with a cold menace. "I thought you might be finished with it."

Aideen glanced down at the tray, its contents virtually uneaten. She pounced onto the bed, her breasts half spilling from the robe. Oozing sexual insolence, she stretched before answering. "I'm afraid we didn't eat much." She ran a casual hand across her breast in memory. "Taking care of other appetites, you could say."

Vera bent down to pick up the tray and Aideen put a hand on her shoulder. The woman froze, staying so motionless that Aideen thought Vera would shatter if she gave a tentative poke.

"Vera, there are stables here, aren't there?" Kean had given Aideen a verbal map of the grounds, pointing out what was visible from their balcony.

"Yes, but Lady Claubine doesn't keep horses anymore."

Aideen dropped her voice suggestively. "I'm not interested in horses," she said and smiled at the older woman. "I was hoping for someplace secluded." She looked at the clock. It was late in the day. Meyrick would undoubtedly need a little more time to plan his next move once Vera tipped him off.

"Someplace where Kean and I could be alone, without fear of being interrupted by the constant stream of visitors," she suggested.

Vera straightened up, her sharp gaze detecting all the little signs that Aideen had just been thoroughly loved.

The wild hair, damp at the temples. A dry film of sweat on her neck and partially revealed breasts. The pungent aroma of Kean's semen. "Nothing can be done tonight," Vera advised.

"In the morning, then?" Aideen asked, her tone wheedling with a false urgency. "When the dew is still on the grass. I love that time of the day."

Vera nodded slowly. The tray began to shake from her tight grip.

"You could take a sort of picnic breakfast out there ahead of us?" Aideen clapped her hands in delight when Vera nodded again. "Champagne and strawberries!"

"I think that can be arranged."

Aideen jumped from the bed and wrapped her arms around Vera's shoulders, the tray awkwardly dividing them. "That would be so perfect!" She placed her cheek against Vera's, her mind probing for some confirmation of the woman's intent. What she saw made her blood run cold. A man's form hiding at the edge of a tree line where the estate's stone wall ended. He stepped forward, the dawn's light spreading into an orange halo around his close-cut hair.

Everett! Aideen took a step back from Vera and shoved her hands into the robe's pockets. Even then, she didn't think she could hide the shake that infected her and she turned toward the bathroom door, releasing Vera with a backward glance and a forced smile. "Late for water play," she offered and disappeared behind the bathroom door.

Chapter Seventeen

"You can't take a gun," Aideen advised Kean as he puttered around the room waiting for dawn to stroke her rosy fingers across the horizon.

"No knife, no gun," he groused. "Do I get to take my hands? Should I leave my teeth and nails behind, so we're totally defenseless?"

"They'll only take them away from you," she said and picked at the hem of her shirt. "And it's hardly what you'd take to a romantic tryst."

Kean caught her fingering the fabric and pushed her hands away. "Don't play with it, you're probably giving Julius fits right now." Kean checked the stitching to make sure the tracking dot was still in place. Satisfied with the dot's placement, he released her shirt, his hand reflexively going to his collar where another dot was embedded.

Shoving his hands in his pockets, he sat down next to her on the bed. "I wonder who Meyrick will have dug up for the job."

"Better not to think about it," Aideen answered.

Kean caught her evasive tone. He turned to her, his hand leaving his pocket to keep her from looking away. "You know who he's sending? How...who?"

"I know who Vera's met with..."

"It's not those Rossaveal thugs, is it? I owe that over-muscled bastard a sledgehammer to those sausages he calls lips," Kean said.

Aideen closed her eyes. Her lower lip began to tremble and Kean released her chin.

"It's not that Wadebridge freak—Police Constable Pumpkin King?" When she didn't answer, he stood up to pace the room. Stopping in front of her, he hit his open palm with his fist. "I told you this was a bad idea!" Irritated by her silence, he grabbed her shoulders and shook her once. "Damn it, Aideen, *she* can't have told you to turn yourself over to Everett."

He let go of her shoulders and she looked up, her gaze distant. She felt the brush of a tree branch and its leaves against her shoulder. Breath misted the air. "He's here already," she told Kean, her voice reaching him from the end of a long tunnel. "Watching to see if it's safe for him to enter the stables."

Kean covered the distance to the dresser in two strides. Reaching into his drawer, he pulled the handgun back out. "She didn't mean for you to go...only to bring him here," Kean said, more to himself than the glassy-eyed Aideen. "I'll fetch that crazy bastard and bring him back for an interrogation."

Kean's words reached Aideen where she hovered looking down on the Pumpkin King. "No!" She shook her head violently and stumbled up from the bed. "If he sees you coming alone, he'll kill you. And then he'll turn his rage loose on this house...Claubine...Julius...me."

Kean paused, his hand on the door. He stared down at the gun, felt its uselessness. He switched the safety back on and placed it on top of the dresser, his fingertips still lingering over its metal finish. "He's not going to risk taking both of us."

"He will," Aideen said. Her face held a feverish expression, small beads of perspiration dotting her upper lip and forehead. "I'll make him."

Kean started to ask her what she meant but a mask had fallen over her face. She leaned back against the pillows and closed her eyes. Her lips moved, no sound coming from them. Every few seconds, her breathing stopped, as if she were hiding and afraid of discovery. Then she would exhale, her expression moving forward a few more steps.

* * * * *

Aideen floated in the air above the Pumpkin King. He was crouched in an empty horse stall. The cruel line of his lips caressed the barrel of his gun in a shallow act of fellatio. It wasn't his favorite toy but he found that people fought less when you pointed a gun at them. He couldn't decide whether it was the surety of the bullet that made people docile or the knife's promise of slow damage that put the fight in their fists. Not that it mattered. He had brought a bag full of toys along for his little songbird.

The Pumpkin King's tongue dipped into the gun's barrel. The taste of powder from last night's practice tingled against his tongue. He looked at his watch before peering through the stall's slats. A square of four rotting hay bales had been pushed into the center, a checkered cloth laid across them with a basket of strawberries and other fruit placed beside chilled champagne. That cold bitch Vera had set the scene before he reached the stables this morning. She was gone before he arrived. *Wisely so*, he thought, rubbing the barrel of the gun along the front seam of his pants. She would have provided a sufficient diversion while he waited for the little songbird to arrive.

His gaze returned to the bucket of ice with its champagne and two glasses. At least he would have someone on which to satisfy his bloodlust this morning. A little something to take the edge off and keep him from moving too fast with Aideen.

He shook his head and raised the barrel of the gun to scratch at his chin. No, killing her guard dog might not be a good idea. She'd fight him after that. He'd seen the silly cunt's devotion to the man in Wadebridge. The gun returned to his lap, the slow rub of metal over denim a meditative pleasure as the Pumpkin King decided how he was going to manage getting both bird and birddog back to his van.

* * * * *

Back in Kean's rooms, Aideen opened her eyes. Kean was standing near the bed, watching her. She reached out and squeezed his hand, relieved when the tension in him began to uncoil. Still holding his hand, she glanced at the balcony doors.

"It's getting light, we should go now."

Kean nodded and picked up a lawn blanket from the edge of the bed. He draped the blanket over one arm and helped Aideen into a light jacket. Cupping her face, he drew her to him for a final kiss. Her lips were ice cold and he covered them with his mouth until they warmed beneath his attentions. "Are you sure about this?" he asked one last time.

"Yes, I am." The color had drained from her face but her voice was firm. "I love you." She saw his heart breaking when he smiled, his throat too tight with emotion to respond in kind.

They moved quietly through the house. In a delivery truck a kilometer and a half away, Julius sat watching two small dots move through the corridor and down the grand staircase before slipping onto the back patio. They skirted the tree line, pretending they were sneaking off for a morning tryst. The early dawn air was frigid. They walked pressed together, sharing their warmth. Neither spoke— Kean's attention focused on the stables ahead while Aideen peered down inside the Pumpkin King's mind.

Everett had left off deciding how to get them both back to his van and was fantasizing the look on Aideen's face when he showed her the contents of his bag of toys. His sharp pants echoed inside her head and she laced her fingers through Kean's as they reached the stable doors.

Aideen forced a giggle past her lips and stopped Kean before he could push the door open. She waited, locked in an awkward kiss, while Everett brought his breathing back under control and leveled his pistol at the doors.

"Ooh," Aideen cooed once they were inside the stables. "Strawberries!" She kept her attention fixed on the impromptu table. She could feel both men tensing, their muscles ready to spring.

Grabbing a strawberry, she bit the tip off and held the juice end against Kean's mouth. "Taste," she ordered.

He let her smear his lips with the red liquid and lick it away. Even with Everett hovering nearby, his body began to respond and he slipped an arm around her waist. Aideen pressed against him and moaned, the sound a thin caricature of passion.

"We can eat later," she suggested and took the blanket from him. She placed the blanket over a collapsed haystack and then crawled onto it, her arms reaching out to draw Kean to her. His body was tense as he leaned into her embrace. Aideen reached out with her mind to massage Kean's worries before Everett realized his presence had not gone undetected. At the same time, she monitored Everett's thoughts.

She need not have worried about Everett noticing Kean's emotional state. The Pumpkin King's attention was riveted to her. Perspiration beaded along her brow as she tried to step lightly through Everett's head. Being inside him was nauseating. She could feel his erection as if it were her own, feel the drops of sweat that trickled down his thighs. He looked at her, not as she was but as he anticipated having her—face up in a shallow grave. Stripped naked, her eyes were glassy with death, her mouth pried open with rubber stops to keep her lifeless jaws from clamping down as he fucked her mouth— spooning her body as he took chunks of flesh from her thighs and labia. His hollow cry of *feed me* piercing the abandoned woods.

"You're shivering," Kean said. The distance in her eyes unnerved him. She looked at him, her pupils dilating in a heartbeat.

"Then warm me," she said softly and hoped Everett didn't hear the shake in her voice.

Aideen wrapped her arms around Kean's neck and locked him to her in a kiss. She heard the soft rustle of the stall's gate across the dirt floor, felt Kean stiffen in anticipation of Everett announcing his presence. Both lovers froze as Everett placed his revolver against the base of Kean's neck.

"Well, Lord of the Manor," Everett said. "Where are your friends now?"

Slowly, Kean turned his head to look at the intruder. His brows lifted as he feigned mild surprise. "Constable, aren't you out of your jurisdiction?"

Everett's grip on the trigger tightened. Aideen whispered in his mind, reminded him of his earlier resolution. Everett shook his head, his hand slapping the air around him at some imaginary fly. He offered Kean a thin grin of malice and emphasized his point with a nudge to the back of Kean's neck with the tip of the gun's barrel. "I've got extra-jurisdictional power now."

Kean managed his own thin-lipped smile. "Surely you're deluded...what was it that fat cop called you? Pumpkinhead?"

Aideen gave Kean's shoulder a warning squeeze. The gesture didn't go unnoticed. Putting the barrel against her wrist, Everett pushed her hands away from Kean.

Not here, not here, not here! Aideen pushed the words into the air. Everett's finger eased off the trigger.

"Better watch it, birddog," he warned Kean. "I haven't made up my mind whether I'm going to let you live."

"Your mind?" Kean's laugh was harsh. His lips peeled back in a growl. "Haven't made up your mind? I thought someone else did that for you, Pumpkinhead."

Everett hesitated, his finger caressing the trigger as Aideen's silent plea for calm feather-stroked the line of his nose. Everett's nose twitched and he tried to remember why he didn't want to kill the birddog immediately. Something about the girl. He looked at Aideen for some clue. Her face was a mix of worry and fear. Her eyes were kind of flat, too, he noticed. Not the emerald fire that had flashed at him in Wadebridge. Something about keeping the girl docile. *Right, that's it.*

"Hoy, I think killing you now would be a kindness," Everett said. "All the pretty tortures I have planned for songbird... I'll have you both screaming in stereo." He nudged the back of Kean's head again. "You 'cause there's nothing you'll be able to do about it."

Everett pulled out a pair of handcuffs. "Hands behind your back, handsome," he ordered. When Kean didn't move, Everett slid the barrel of the gun from Kean's neck and placed it beneath Aideen's eye.

"Aideen?" Kean's eyes were pleading with her to stop the charade, telling her it wasn't too late to turn the tables on Everett and take her safely back to the house.

Put them on, she urged. *It will be okay.*

Kean put his hands behind his back, his stomach lurching at the sharp click of the handcuffs as they closed around his wrists and locked. Everett booted Kean onto the straw and pulled another pair of cuffs from his jacket.

Everett moved the gun from below Aideen's eye to her mouth. He pushed the barrel tip past her lips until the metal pressed against her unyielding teeth. He slid the barrel horizontally across her mouth, the weapon, a poor extension of his cock, exploring the texture of her lips. The skin around his balls, already stretched from his erection, grew tighter still. "On your knees, songbird."

Aideen complied and Everett moved behind her. He kept the gun in her mouth and the cold metal pulled her lips in a lopsided, despairing grin. Putting the cuffs around her wrists, he held his body close to her. She could feel his erection pressing against her backside. His ragged breathing rattled in her ear. It smelled of the charnel house and the image he had held of his eating from her labia rose unbidden in Aideen's mind.

Grabbing hold of the cuffs' chain, Everett pulled Aideen to her feet. He waved the gun in Kean's direction. "Get up, birddog." When both his prisoners were standing, Everett pointed at the side of the barn that intruded on the tree line. "Some loose planks over there, then straight into the trees and my van." With the barrel of the gun, he forced Aideen's chin in the air. "You even look like you're thinking about running, and she's dead."

With the gun no longer pointed at Kean, Aideen felt some of the tension ease from her body. But she couldn't release all her tension—Everett's creeping, moist odors and hot breath guaranteed a certain terror-filled alertness despite the calm façade she kept in place for Kean's benefit.

"Such a willing little songbird," Everett whispered in Aideen's ear as he opened the back of his van and shoved Kean face first onto its floor. "I almost think you want to come with me."

He ran a hand down the front of her shirt, pausing for an instant at her fear-pricked nipple. Again, Aideen was aware of the growing tightness that hugged his balls. A tightness that threatened to release a hot burst of semen at the slightest sensation. Kean, regaining his balance, saw Everett's caress and charged toward him but Everett was too quick and brought the van door slamming against Kean's head.

Stay down! Aideen commanded as Kean shook the cobwebs and dancing stars from his head and prepared to charge again. *Damn it, Kean, stay down!*

Understanding flickered in Kean's eyes and he collapsed to the van's floor, his growl turning to a pained groan. Seeing Kean flat on his back, Everett tucked his gun into his belt and lifted Aideen into the van. She stumbled, falling against the thick mesh fencing that separated the cargo area from the driver's seat. There was, she noticed, no passenger seat, just an oversized gym bag on the floor where the seat had been removed. And the windows were a dark tint—no one would be able to see in. She took a tentative sniff of the van's interior and swallowed the need to vomit. More than one person had died in the back of this van. The whole vehicle was saturated with the smell of their frightened sweat, dried vomit and, a metallic taste coating her tongue and sinus passages, their blood.

Aideen leaned against the side of the van, her hip pressed against Kean's shoulder. He pulled his body up until he was even with her. In front of them, Everett opened the driver's side door, sunlight spilling in and making them blink. He caught the press of Kean's lips against Aideen's temple and his mouth curled in a smirk.

"You'll be feeding at her breast by the end of the day, birddog, just to keep your worthless ass alive," Everett warned. He punched the key into the ignition and checked his watch before shifting the van into drive. Catching Aideen's gaze in the rearview mirror, he offered a wet kiss and rolling tongue. Reaching down to the bag on the floorboard, he patted it. "And there's still plenty of time to have fun with you, too, pet."

Chapter Eighteen

Aideen could feel Everett's agitation stirring inside his gut. It was still early morning, perhaps no more than forty-five minutes having elapsed since he had forced them into the van. But he checked his watch every few minutes. She could hear the time ticking down in his head. She tried to soothe him. *Time enough. Shhh. Plenty of time.* His need, refusing to define itself in Aideen's mind, drummed her soft voice out of his thoughts. *Not enough time,* he said, refuting her gentle coaxing. *No time to play...have to play.*

The hand he wore his watch on, when he wasn't raising it to check the time, stayed planted in his lap, pressing down on his cock. *Not yet...mustn't get wet. Put it in the ground first. Soft dirt down its throat.* Pressing harder, the need almost overwhelming. Quick glance at the watch. Meyrick waiting for the bird. *Fuck it...put it in the ground and then we can play.*

The van jerked to the left. Car tires squealed behind them, horns blaring. Aideen's pulse beat a fast, faltering rhythm against the cuffs. Everett couldn't hear her now. Too many voices fought for his attention. She saw an older woman, matronly, a prudish mouth pinched tight in constant disapproval. The same woman appeared again, this time through a keyhole. Leaning over a tub, water running, her pussy winked, the lips pursed in denial. *Mustn't get wet!* The voice screamed at him as he scrambled back against a wall, cum on his school clothes, his hand coated with the thick cream of pubescent desire.

Girls walked by, eyes flicking over him, talking behind their hands and laughing. Always laughing. In the shower after a match, gaze fixated on Ronnie Carrington's limp cock, his own cock growing rigid. The rage in Ronnie and the other boys' eyes. A foot in his stomach and Ronnie's cock, soft no more, buried in his ass, the ring of boys calling him a faggot. Cum spilling from him, from his ass, from his own cock. *Mustn't get wet, mustn't get wet, mustn't get wet!* The voice chided him over and over.

Bile rising in her throat, her skin feverish, Aideen pressed her face against the cool mesh that separated prisoner from jailor. *Let him listen*, she pleaded. *Just a little longer, make him hear me.*

Aideen raised her head at the sound of rocks crunching beneath the van's tires. Everett slammed on the brakes. The sudden stop catapulted Kean into Aideen, crushing her between wire and flesh. In an instant, Everett was out of the van, flinging open the back door and dragging Aideen by the feet.

Kean flung his legs around her waist. "Let go of her, you bastard!" Kean shouted, trying to hold on to Aideen and dodge Everett's wild punches. "Meyrick will kill you if you touch her!"

"Drop the histrionics, lover," Everett snarled, his fist connecting at last with Kean's face.

Aideen felt Kean's leggy grip on her loosen for a second and she pushed free.

"Aideen, no!" Kean yelled as Everett pulled her onto the rocky dirt road and slammed the door shut.

Kean's anguish at her willing departure rumbled through him and she tried to soothe him. Her own fear and the growing disquiet in Everett's head made it hard to reach Kean and she stopped struggling for some purchase in the slippery insides of the Pumpkin King's shell. She concentrated on Kean, on stilling the rage and hurt within. Body limp, Everett half-carrying, half-dragging her into the trees, she willed Kean to listen to her.

I am the wave of the deep.

"Aideen!" he yelled her name again and again, his voice growing hoarse and cracked, receding as the trees closed around her. He would not listen.

More forcefully, despite her ebbing strength. *I am the word of knowledge, the lure beyond the ends of the earth.*

She could hear him in her head now, still yelling her name, kicking viciously against the unyielding door. She started again. *I am the wave of the deep.*

He relented at last and collapsed onto the van's floor as his mind shaped the words. *I am a wild boar, I am the point of a spear.*

She exhaled, her breath misting in the stand of trees but warm across his eyelids where he lay in the van. *I am the wound.*

I can shift my shape like a god.

Aideen felt Everett flinging her down and she landed in freshly turned dirt. *I am the goddess incarnate*, she reminded Kean, reaching out to stroke him one last time before shutting him out completely.

Everett was standing over her, his legs spread wide as he straddled a shallow grave. He was angry, but the din of the voices was ebbing. One-by-one, he blocked them out until it was just him and Aideen. Pumpkin King and his Songbird. He got down on his hands and knees and lowered his body until his weight rested on her. She was trembling. He could feel it everywhere but, most of all, he could feel the hum of her body in his cock.

He had to stop the hum, stop it before it made him wet. Already, drops were forming, threatening to turn into a putrid stream. He grabbed a handful of dirt and pushed it into her mouth. Her gaze widened but she didn't fight him and the shaking stopped. Flakes of sod peppered the skin around her mouth and he brushed them away with his lips, the stench of dead flesh overpowering her until she gagged on the dirt.

Everett smiled, bits of old meat showing between his teeth. He rubbed against her body, stopping when the wetness threatened, starting again when the bursting sensation ebbed. He needed his cock down her throat, but he couldn't. The birddog had been right, Meyrick would kill him if he damaged her voice and there was, he knew, no hiding from Meyrick. Still, he could scare her. And maybe taste her…taste her fear. The thought broadened his grin and he raised himself onto his hands and knees again. He turned a semicircle and scooted backwards until he could smell her sex.

The songbird was wearing jeans and he reached into his pocket and retrieved a pocketknife. He hated jeans. Only dykes wore them. But she wasn't a dyke. She was fucking the birddog. Everett sniffed the denim at the crotch, his teeth scraping the center seam. He pressed his own crotch against Aideen's face, grinding it against the side of her face when she turned from him. Her pussy was wet, he could smell it. Fear did that to them, all the little birds were wet by the time he put them to bed. He rubbed himself against her. His mouth pressed harder against her jeans.

Everett opened the pocketknife and placed the blade at the crossed seams that marked her cunt with an X. She squirmed, her terror building and the blade slipped, cutting her thigh. *Damn it!* Meyrick's voice thundered a warning at him. *Bring the girl intact!*

His tongue darted out to test the wound's depth. Shallow, like the grave she rested in. He probed deeper, forcing the cut wider. He could hear her starting to gag on the dirt that filled her mouth, her chest barely moving. Most were near comatose from fear by now and he suddenly envied her stamina. He growled, wanting more from her. Mindful of Meyrick's warning, he unbuttoned her jeans. She tried to twist to her side but he brought his full weight down on her. Unzipping her jeans, his hips pumped against her skullcap.

Everett pushed her panties down into her jeans until he saw the bright triangle of fur between her legs. He slipped a finger down, the fabric pulled tight by her protesting body. *Wet*, he sighed and brought his finger back to his mouth. He sucked his finger and sighed. Liquid fear. The best. He buried his nose against the furry mound, inhaling her perfume. His hand crept to his pants and he cupped his balls, bucking against his palm until he came.

His breathing was ragged as he crawled back into a position where he could see her face. She had been crying. He hadn't noticed. He licked the trail down her cheeks the tears had left. Straightening up to zip and button her jeans, he treated himself to another finger full of her fear. After he licked his finger dry, he reached into his pants. His semen was drying, starching the fabric of his pants, but he was wet enough. He brought his fingertips, moist, to her lips, smeared his juice on her mouth and then licked it away.

"Just a taste," Everett murmured. He was ready to come again. She could make him come again, this one. Make him come until worms were crawling out her eyes. "You're the best," he assured her. "You really are."

Chapter Nineteen

Kean heard Aideen whisper the final phrase of the ceremony in his ear and then she vanished. He kept his eyes closed and tried to reach her. His body trembled with the effort but she locked him out. He repeated her last words—a prayer, a talisman. *Let it be so*, he prayed at the same time he cursed Danu. When he was finished cursing the goddess, he continued on with Gerald and his mother. Then Julius and Claubine. No one he knew was immune. Even Aideen, the source of his despair, was berated for her willingness to be a sacrificial lamb. She who had spent a lifetime running from her father's beliefs was now ready to die for them. Harmony in there, someone would say— someone pretending to be wise but understanding nothing.

He was lost in this thought when Everett opened the van's back door and tossed a limp Aideen inside. Kean snaked his way along the van's floor until he was next to her. She coughed lightly, her breath carrying the smell of fresh dirt with it. Dirt and something else. His stomach lurched but, when her eyes fluttered open, he managed to bite back the need to vomit.

Everett climbed into the front of the van, whistling. He checked his watch and chuckled. "Plenty of time." He put the van in reverse and backed up to the trees before pointing the vehicle in the direction of the main road once again. "Even time enough to stop off for a bite to eat, don't you think?" Only silence answered him and he laughed again, his chatter euphoric, unending.

"I mean, I really worked up an appetite back there," he said. He rapped his knuckles against the wire fencing that separated front from back. "You know what I mean, birddog, huh? She makes a man hungry."

Kean eased Aideen's exhausted form against the side of the van and cradled her as best he could with his arms locked behind his back. He pressed his cheek against her ear, hoping to block out Everett's mounting insinuations. He wanted to bathe her, to unbind her hands and lower her into a warm tub. To caress her battered body with a soapy sponge and kiss away the memory of the tears he could tell she had cried while alone in the woods with Everett. He felt her go limp again and her sudden relaxation clogged his throat. He nudged her, felt the light exhalation of her warm breath. His own breathing started again. She had passed out and the realization was a double relief. Asleep, she could no longer hear Everett's sick praise.

"Sleeping?" Everett queried from the front of the van. When Kean didn't answer, Everett jerked the steering wheel to the left, jostling his cargo. "What happened to your bark, birddog? Didn't leave it back there in the trees, did we? We could go back, take another look, the songbird and me."

"Odd you calling me a birddog when it's you answering your master's summons." Kean's voice was a low rumble of menace that raised the hairs on the back of Everett's neck.

"You'll be answering his call soon enough, birddog," Everett jeered and smoothed the hairs back down on his neck. The van turned and pulled to a stop. Everett rolled down his window and there was the sound of an electronic code key being entered followed by the deep hydraulic whine of heavy gates sliding open. "Real soon," he warned cheerily.

The drive the van traveled over was smoother than the public road and they seemed to float to their final destination. The van's interior grew dimmer and Kean realized they were inside a garage. He guessed they were on the other side of London but couldn't be sure. He thought of the small tracking devices contained in their clothing and hoped Julius had been able to follow the signal. But if he had, then why was there no reprieve in the woods? Surely, Julius wouldn't have allowed Aideen to undergo such horrors? He looked down at her face, the slim, distant beam of an electric light caressing her cheekbone and pale blonde hair. She was the only one he trusted now, but he couldn't trust her to keep herself safe or not to sacrifice herself for his well-being.

"Time to get out, birddog," Everett called from the front as the van's back door was opened and two of Meyrick's steroid-laden thugs pulled Aideen out.

The larger of the two, his craggy features uncompromising, cradled her limp body in his arms. He jerked his head at Kean, the motion commanding him to get out of the van and follow. Kean crawled from the back of the van, Everett and the second thug at his heels as they entered an elevator. The elevator rose one floor and opened onto a blindingly white room. Ceramic tiles, four feet wide, covered the walls, floor and ceiling. Every few feet, a clear sheet of glass housed a white fluorescent light that burned the retinas of anyone careless enough to glance up. At the end of the room, sitting on a metal throne, a set of doublewide white doors at his back was

Meyrick. His hair was as white as the room and he would have seemed bald without the high-backed seat and the red robe he wore. In his hand, he held a scepter cast from the same metal and, in its center, was the Bloodstone.

Kean would have laughed at the man's lurid preparations if the thug holding Aideen hadn't placed her on her feet and given her cheek a gentle slap. She opened her eyes, swaying, her expression disoriented. Kean inched closer to her. Her body brushed against his, finding support and then she saw it—the Bloodstone. She stood straighter and Kean could feel her energy returning in the stone's presence.

Meyrick's flat gaze flicked over them before turning to Everett. "Why are there two?" he asked. "I only need the woman. You knew that."

Everett's face screwed into a puzzled frown while he groped for the answer. He looked at Aideen and his reason for keeping the birddog alive came back to him. "To keep the songbird quiet," he said.

Meyrick looked around the tiled room and bared his teeth in a crypt keeper's grin. "Well, there's no need to keep her quiet now," he replied. He cast a long look at Everett, noted the solid outline of the Pumpkin King's erection, the sweat stains on the shirt's armpits and the hard-starched front of his pants. "And killing him should ease some of your…tension."

"I didn't think you were that stupid," Aideen said softly. Her gaze centered somewhere behind Meyrick, focused on a secret knowledge he didn't share.

Meyrick laughed and leaned back against his metal throne. "I'm sure I'll find this amusing."

"Kean is your only chance of living." Her voice had a distant quality to it, the tone disturbingly matter-of-fact.

Meyrick shifted in his seat and ran a hand over the Bloodstone. His gaze narrowed as he inspected Aideen. She was trembling, he realized, but not with fear. Power streamed between her and the Bloodstone, its flow bidirectional, such that neither was the source nor the recipient. He could feel the handle of the scepter warming, threatening to burn his hand. He tightened his grip on the scepter. *Very well,* he thought. *Let it melt metal to bone. It will still be mine.*

"He's already killed two of my men—those incompetents I sent to Rossaveal." His left hand involuntarily brushed the thigh Kean had shot. "Doesn't sound like someone I should keep alive."

"He didn't kill those men in Rossaveal. I did."

Calm, polite, unblinking. The woman unnerved him. He wanted to kill her then and there, and her lover, but couldn't risk any more near catastrophes. Already, the papers were picking up on the underground tremors rippling through London. And he had lost a technician to something unspeakable. He shuddered at the memory of the young man wrapped in the gray, decaying grip of some vaguely humanoid creature that had crept from the mist they'd managed to conjure in the lab. Metal shards served as the creature's teeth and needles for its nails. Flesh sloughed off from the creature as the lab's refined air hit it. Fat and muscle peeled away to reveal a skeleton, not of bone or even metal but wriggling, wormlike things— parasites bloated with the creature's life juices.

Aideen picked the images from his head. She had no time for him to decide whether he would let her and Kean live. "Shall I show you how?" she interrupted and sucked in a lungful of air.

"Stop her!" Meyrick shrieked.

The same man that had woken her tapped her at the base of her skull, a sharp, skillful hit that folded her to the floor.

* * * * *

Aideen opened her eyes. Her cheek was pressed against the cold tile and she was staring at Everett's dirt-caked boots. Her gaze followed the line of tile to Meyrick's throne. Kean was at his feet, a collar around his throat. From the collar, a chain led to a manacle secured around Meyrick's wrist. She glanced up at Meyrick's face, the smile far colder than the tile pressed against her cheek. She looked back to Kean. His face was bloodied, one cheek swollen but his gaze was alert. Battered but unbeaten. Aideen's chest swelled in relief and some of her energy reached out to caress him. He straightened noticeably, his features softening and his mouth shaping a word. She nodded, stopping him, and pushed herself into a sitting position.

The room swirled around her and she mentally clutched at the latent power that floated through the air. The swirling stopped and she looked up at Meyrick again, her vision clear.

"I'm not sure what it is you're proposing, Miss Godwin," he said and jerked Kean's chain. "So why don't you stop wasting my time and tell me."

She looked at the large square tiles that covered the distance between her and Meyrick and she smiled. "A game...one of strategy." She looked at Kean and the pained grimace he wore. "You've already taken my knight."

"So, I'm well ahead." Meyrick seemed pleased and he loosened his grip on the chain.

Aideen merely shrugged. "One would think."

"What were you last week?" Meyrick's voice was a coarse laugh, heavy with insolence, as he asked his question. "A shopkeeper!" He shook his head and his body bounced in amusement. "And yet you think you can play *and win* against me!"

Again, she unnerved him with her simple response. "Yes."

"And whose move is it?" Meyrick asked. Aideen nodded at him and he rose, pulling Kean along with him. The double doors opened as he moved before them, some hidden sensor triggered by his proximity.

Aideen suppressed a small gasp as she saw what lay on the other side. On a platform stood a structure straight from the movies. It looked, she thought, like a time machine but without any moving parts. It was dodecahedral, each of its twelve faces a pentagon. Each pentagon was made of interlocking triangles that alternated between metal and cut crystal. The metal was polished to a high shine that reflected the room's contents.

Meyrick turned to Aideen, his grip tightening on Kean's chain. "We're very close to the endgame, aren't we Miss Godwin?"

"Yes." She let her gaze travel over the structure in admiration, hoping to stroke his ego enough that he would divulge some nugget of useful information. "What is it?"

"A resonance chamber," he answered.

Aideen stepped closer, her eyes just picking up thin filaments of fiber optic strands that led from the floor, ceiling and walls to Meyrick's chamber of glass and metal. She guessed the strands served some sort of sensing and recording purpose. He meant to make her obsolete.

"And why do you need me?" she asked.

"I figured out well before anyone else what your purpose was," he said and reached out to caress one of the chamber's metal plates. "Even your father went to his grave not knowing exactly what you were."

She pointed at the strands. "And what are those?" She stalled for time while she thought through her final strategy. The image of Myr and Danu, awash in pleasure in that center dimension, filled her head. She looked at Kean. It would hardly be a fate to lament.

"Detectors."

"To record me?" She tried to sound disingenuous but it didn't matter if he saw through her. Whether he thought her truthful or conniving, he would always think he was outplaying her. That had always been his downfall—from one life to the next.

"Yes, to record you." Meyrick tilted his head at her. "What is it you see, Miss Godwin?"

She hitched her shoulders and gave him one of many honest answers available. "An egomaniac."

His mouth twitched and he put the end of the scepter through one of the links to Kean's chain. He twisted it, the lever increasing his strength several fold.

"You still haven't explained why you need me," Aideen reminded him.

Meyrick slipped the scepter from the link and tapped his nose with the tip of the stone. He swept his arm in the direction of the chamber. "Everett," he whipped the name out, its force a cold slap to the Pumpkin King's face. "What is it you call Miss Godwin?"

"Songbird." Everett's hand snaked out to stroke a strand of Aideen's hair. He was as impatient as the players for the game to be over. Wanting her was unbearable, as was the attention she lavished on Meyrick. He glanced at the phantom that held the songbird's attention, anger welling up inside him at the realization that, his answer given, he was forgotten once again.

"Well, songbird," Meyrick said and gestured for a technician to remove one of the pentagons. "What I want is for you to step into your cage and sing."

She shook her head. "It'll do you no good."

He looked around at his technicians, every one of them a male, and rolled his eyes. Some responded with uneasy smiles, others laughed outright at her presumption.

"Why is that?" Meyrick asked after his amusement subsided.

"The stone itself is a resonance factor," she said. His sudden frown told her he hadn't considered the idea and that, once considered, he understood it to be true. "The stone has to be with me in the chamber." Meyrick shook his head, discounting the idea. But Aideen pressed on. "If you want both of your new toys to work, you'll have to step into the chamber with me."

He thought her proposition over slowly. He turned it over and rejected it, only to turn it over and examine it anew. "It's a trap. You'll use it against me."

"If I use it against you," she said, her gaze lighting on Kean, "I use it against anyone close to you."

"No," he said and backed away. Kean, sensing Meyrick's hesitation, stood firm, his resistance compelling Meyrick to return to his original position. "We'll try it my way and then see—"

Aideen, her fingers at the bottom edge of her shirt, stopped Meyrick with the sharp rip of her hem. She held the small tracking dot up in the air. "Take your time," she suggested. "What little you have left."

"Just fucking do it," Everett prodded his one-time mentor. "She's not going to do anything to hurt him and then it won't matter whether an army breaks in," he promised. "You'll have an army of your own." *And, oh, what an army*, Everett thought, remembering the murder of one of Meyrick's white-smocked lab boys. An army of creatures fit for a king. A real king. Not some pretender the likes of Meyrick. He looked at Aideen, the feather of an idea stroking the inside of his head. Everett reached out and grabbed Aideen by the elbow.

Meyrick saw the movement and the mutinous look Everett wore. "Control yourself," he commanded. "Or you'll find yourself rotting away in a jail cell!" Reluctance leadening his limbs, Everett let go. But the final threat to Meyrick's authority was too much for him. Meyrick stepped into the chamber, Kean dragged behind him. "Come," he said to Aideen, only a thin layer of power coating the order.

Chapter Twenty

Aideen watched the lab technician reseal the opening after she stepped into the chamber. The fit of their three bodies was tight. Kean's hip was pressed against hers, lending her strength, while the cold touch of Meyrick's flesh threatened to steal her soul. Around the chamber was an audience of brain and brawn, each eager for the impending show. One of the technicians finished adjusting the slides on a control panel and gave Meyrick a thumbs-up signal.

"I need to touch the stone," Aideen said and reached toward the scepter. Meyrick tensed but didn't voice his objection. Her fingertips touched the Bloodstone, its energy an erratic pulse at first. Then the pattern came to her. She closed her eyes and saw the notes written in red against the black backdrop of her eyelids. She took a deep breath and began to sing the notes. On the fourth repetition, she heard Meyrick's pleased gasp of wonder. The song etched forever on her brain, she dared to open her eyes.

Gossamer creatures floated above the men's heads. They had no permanent shape, floating into contact with one another, lending a bit of their diaphanous flesh to one, borrowing some from another — aerial jellyfish. One of the lab technicians was standing on a stool trying to capture one of the creatures. Aideen lowered her pitch and they dissolved. Red membranes appeared along the floor. She could tell by the expressions of those outside the chamber that a horrible smell filled the room. She smiled, her pitch growing sharper and the membranes began to pop, black liquid spilling from them.

"How low can you go?" Meyrick chuckled beside her as one of his thugs leaned over and retched on a lab tech's white coat.

On the tenth repetition, Aideen brought her voice down as low as she could while keeping the notes intact. Gray mist filled the room. Next to her, Meyrick stiffened.

"No, bring your voice back up," he warned.

Aideen smiled but her pitch remained the same. Something snaked along the floor, parting the mist. She knew these horrors. From his wide-eyed gaze, she guessed Meyrick, too, had gotten a taste of what lurked in the mist. The mist thickened, pressed itself against the chamber. Something wet hit one of the clear panels and slid down its side. Her gaze flicked to that side of the chamber and she almost faltered. It was a bloody hand, still connected to its owner, several fingers bitten off at the joints.

"Bring your voice back up!" Meyrick demanded. But he had nothing to barter with. His men were outside and, from the look of things, not faring very well as the experiment progressed.

Slowly, she brought her voice up a notch. The mist iced in the air and fell to the floor like ground glass. Surrounding the chamber were several bodies, mauled. Meyrick's men were all dead, dying, or hiding under a lab table. Except for Everett. Blood coated his face and one eye hung limp against his cheek, secured only by a filament of tissue. But he was still standing, not cowering. Her voice faltered as her gaze crept lower down his body. He was bleeding from his crotch, a dark stain spreading. His hand groped, fascinated by the wetness. When he discovered the emasculation, he smiled and began to pump his fingers into the wound, his face a contrast of blood and ecstasy.

Aideen's throat constricted, her voice rising higher. A drop of blood dripped from Kean's nose and she could hear Meyrick's pained breathing. The air around the chamber began to glow red and those still alive began to writhe on the floor, with Everett once again being the sole exception. He continued pumping his fingers in and out of the wound while his clothes burst into flames. Then his flesh began to burn. He sniffed the air, realized the odor was his own, and threw his head back in a wild laugh that Aideen could only see and not hear. On the floor, Meyrick's entourage crumbled to black ash. Only then, did Everett follow, his laugh extinguished in an explosion of flame.

The red atmosphere thickened and began to eddy around the chamber. Its spinning made her dizzy and she tried to focus her gaze on Kean. The drop of blood had become a small stream that fell from his chin onto the bottom pentagon of the chamber, but he still was standing. Meyrick, having no connection to the rhythm of the Bloodstone's song, was further gone. Blood trickled from every orifice. The growing pool of blood on the chamber's floor began to swirl, its direction opposite that of the whirlpool of red outside. Aideen could hear the metal frame of the chamber begin to creak but she couldn't relax her voice. The stone wouldn't let her.

And then she saw that the Bloodstone itself was softening, its shape kept intact by its own rapid spinning. They were going to die. The idea hit her in her chest. It took her breath away and her voice broke. In the silence, Meyrick dropped to his knees, a bloodless husk. Aideen's hand shot out and grabbed the chain that still linked Meyrick to Kean. The metal began to glow red, the light spreading up her arm. The center chain link broke from the heat and Meyrick fell the rest of the way to the chamber's floor, his scepter clattering beside him.

Aideen looked at Kean. He was bathed in a soft crimson light. She followed the length of her arm and saw that the same glow infected her body. Liquid fire shot into the chamber as the last of the metal frame gave way and Meyrick disappeared, absorbed by the center, the dark corruption of his soul balancing the Bloodstone's purity.

Don't let go of the chain. Aideen looked at Kean but he hadn't thought the words. The speaker's identity became clear as she felt the warm push of breasts against her back. They were here, swimming alongside Kean and Aideen, keeping them safe as the center sought balance. Her grip on the chain, her lifeline to Kean, tightened.

A low hum built in the air around her. Beyond Kean's shoulder, she could see Myr's form slowly taking shape. *Sing, children*, Danu commanded. Aideen opened her mouth to comply and warm liquid flowed in, filling her throat. She looked at Kean. His throat expanded as it filled with the center's wet flame. Behind her, Danu was singing low. Aideen tried to push the liquid out, to draw breath and join Danu's song. Her body shook, buzzed with the dissolution of her flesh. Before the heat reached her brain and wiped all thought from it, she had an instant's recognition of the lullaby with which Danu was singing them to their final rest.

Chapter Twenty-One

Heat cooled to mere warmth that, in its turn, ebbed to a faint chill that insinuated itself against her skin. Aideen opened her eyes, a wide ribbon of stars winking down at her. She started to sit up and felt the sharp rubble of broken concrete gouging at her jeans and sweater. She lifted a hand, her fingers locked in a numb claw, and heard the clink of metal as the chain slipped from her hands and fell against the concrete.

Her eyes adjusted to the night surrounding her and her memory slowly began to unfold, offering tantalizing glimpses of the day just passed. Her body still reluctant to cooperate, her throat cemented with dust and dried blood, she patted the rubble around her and found the chain she had dropped. She rolled over and took the chain in both hands. She inched her way along it, careful not to pull on the chain. At last, she reached the dark crown of hair.

Aideen worked the muscles of her throat until she was able to croak his name. Only crickets answered her. She crawled until she could lay alongside him and placed her head on his chest. His body was cold but she felt the soft rise and fall of his chest, heard the dust-clogged rattle of his breathing. She thought someone called her name but she couldn't answer. It had taken everything she had just to say his name. Her hands found Kean's and his fingers curled in response. She wanted to sleep, to lie next to him, sharing his warmth and offering her own. But the voice was insistent, demanding that she answer.

Light joined the insistent call and her lids fluttered open only to snap shut in pain as the beam of a flashlight pierced her skull.

"Here!" The voice was excited—a man's pitch shooting high and then cracking. "Over here, both of them." Someone hushed him, told him to turn his flashlight off but he didn't listen. "Hurry!"

The man bent down beside Aideen, his knees cracking at the effort. He brushed her hair back from her face and slipped his hand under her chin to feel for a pulse. He whispered his thanks to the stars and leaned across Aideen to check Kean.

"Barely, boy." The man's voice was thick with emotion that obscured his identity. "Hold on...you're not about to leave me with a bunch of wailing women to look after."

"Are they alive?" It was Claubine, voice trembling but recognizable, who asked the question.

"Just," the man answered. "Get those men up here!"

Aideen heard the click, click, click of a flashlight, felt its bright tattoo.

"To hell with being quiet," the man barked. "We've got worse things to worry about than the police." The man lifted Aideen's arm and she snatched it back to Kean's chest, curling her fingers into his clothing. "Aideen, let go so we can carry you down to the van."

Her fingers curled tighter. She couldn't remember why but she knew she didn't want to be carried to any van.

"Damn it, woman," the man gently chided and pulled at her arm. "Let go."

"Shh...leave off her, Julius," Claubine ordered. Something light and feathery stroked the back of Aideen's hand. "We can't carry the two of you together, dear."

Claubine continued her gentle stroking until Aideen released Kean. There was the sound of more feet stumbling across the collapsed building and someone lifted her. She slipped in and out of consciousness. She was laid flat while hands clinically explored her body and searched out all the cuts and bruises. A sharp prick of a needle woke her but she kept her eyes closed and the hum of a motor lulled her back to sleep. People talked around her, their words unintelligible. Aideen sorted through their voices, but the one she searched for was silent. She rummaged around her mind but he wasn't there—just echoes.

The next time Aideen woke, she convinced her eyes to open to a thin slit. Something heavy lay across her chest and legs and she forced the thin slit of vision downward until she could make out the white-on-white pattern of a comforter. She picked out the slim line of a lily and realized she was back in Claubine's estate house. She reached along the mattress and her hand brushed Kean's hip. Sleeping, he sighed heavily, his breath warming her cheek. She rolled to her side, every muscle protesting, and fully opened her eyes. There was a small goose egg, bruised purple and half hidden behind his hairline, just above his right temple. The skin around his left eye was ringed black but already fading to a brownish yellow. A cut puffed his upper lip. She eased forward and kissed the tip of his nose. His right eye opened and he managed a groggy smile.

"Why'd you do that?" he asked.

"It looked like the only spot on you that doesn't hurt," she answered.

Kean lifted an arm and pulled her to him. "But won't kissing them make all the hurt parts feel better?"

"You're joking, right?" Her voice was light, the worries and fears of the last week washed away. London could be smoldering right now, a city of ashes, but the worst of it was behind them.

He answered with a drowsy shake of his head. His hand slid down to cup her ass, molding her body to him. She pressed her lips to his throat. His even breathing matched her own and she closed her eyes. Kean melted into her. His pulse beat beneath her lips. With a sigh, she let sleep claim her once again. There was an endless amount of time left for loving him now that the heat and the rhythm were their own.

Enjoy this excerpt from

Adonis 5000

© Copyright Ann Vremont 2004

All Rights Reserved, Ellora's Cave Publishing, Inc.

Arlissa entered the research complex at 6:02 a.m. the following morning. The hem on the cyan skirt that fell mid-calf was ripped, and one stocking bore a run and a grease smear down its side. Dropping her gym bag on the x-ray machine's conveyor belt, she caught the morning guard, Jimmy, examining her disheveled state while he ran her security card through the reader.

"Flat tire," she explained. Her voice was tight, like the knot between her shoulder blades, and she tried to soften her statement with a smile. "I think I need a different jack."

The guard nodded and handed her card back to her. "I was beginning to worry, it's not like you to arrive later than five thirty."

The knot tightened, forcing her shoulders back in a pinched spasm. She started to sling her gym bag over her right shoulder and then shifted it to her left. "It was a particularly unaccommodating jack."

"Well, you call the gatehouse next time," he offered, and began to search the night janitor's trash buggy. "I'll send one of the guards down to change it for you."

Arlissa smiled her thanks and started down the long main corridor, but he called her back.

"One thing, Dr. Spence." He wore a sheepish, almost guilty, look on his face.

"Yes, Jimmy?"

"I went ahead and let your visitors in, Mr. Cayce—"

Arlissa didn't wait for Jimmy to finish his sentence. Her crisp walk broke into a graceful run. The pain centered in her back traveled down to squeeze at her hip as her running shoes bounced around in the gym bag. Her heart constricted as she saw that the door to the lab was open. Thoughts of who had conned their way into her lab ran through her head—*Mason? He was furious that she had gotten the grant. Dautrich? That sneaky bastard always seemed to be up to something.*

The flash of light in her face as she stepped into the lab told her the intruder was far worse than she had anticipated.

"Oh, Clark, get another picture of Dr. Spence," Faye Keller the marketing director for Cayce Industries cooed as she took the gym bag from Arlissa's shoulder and tucked a loose strand of Arlissa's hair into the tight bun at the base of her neck. "This time when she doesn't look so untidy."

Arlissa, stunned, stood like a deer caught in a trucker's headlights, as a second photo was taken. The flash jolted her back to reality and she snatched the camera from the photographer's hands.

"What in the hell do you think you're doing here, Faye?" Arlissa asked. Her fingers curled around the camera's lens and the photographer's gaze widened.

"Hey, lady, that's a $3,000 camera!" he yelled, and made a grab for it.

Arlissa spun out of his reach, plopped the camera down on a rolling cart and shoved the cart through the door to the lab. "It's about to be a $3,000 pile of rubbish if you don't catch that cart," she said.

The photographer pushed past her, swearing. Arlissa brushed her palms against one another and turned to Faye. *One down, one to go.*

"Again, Faye, what are you doing in my..." Arlissa stopped, the question stalling mid-air as she noticed the Five Thousand on the gurney behind Faye. Instead of being safely tucked away in the room's built-in security vault, it was clothed in a blue policeman's uniform, with the jacket flung open to reveal the un-shirted chest. "Please tell me you didn't..." Her throat swelled in anger, left her unable to finish her sentence. She gripped Faye by the elbow and steered her toward the lab door.

"But Mr. Cayce—" Faye protested. Her free arm was across her chest and she gestured wildly at the table.

"I don't care what that idiot Cayce says, this is my lab!" Arlissa yelled, and pushed Faye over the threshold. She seized the edge of the door and sent it swinging closed until the astonished face of Faye Keller disappeared behind a loud slam.

Arlissa locked the door before quickly crossing over to the gurney. Her gaze swept over the Five Thousand, stopping abruptly when she came to its chest.

"Dammit, Cody," she groaned under her breath. She had left him working on the skin last night. As she had prepared to leave for the night, after long hours spent crunching numbers, she had told him to make it realistic. Pulling the jacket sides together, she buttoned the top button. On the second button, she felt the soft whisper of hair along the edge of her palm and her hand started to shake. With the third button, she stopped and placed her hands flat against the unit's hard stomach. The unexpected warmth of the machine caused an equally warm dampness to spread between her thighs. Her nipples peaked and a slight shudder passed over her body. "Not this realistic," she moaned appreciatively.

"Do you really think I'm an idiot, Lissa?"

Arlissa jumped back. Her hip caught the instrument cart beside the gurney, sent it and its contents crashing to the floor. "Mr. Cayce!"

"Do you?" The chocolate-brown gaze held her, demanded that she answer him.

"Mr. Cayce, I thought you let marketing in here for a photo shoot of the Five Thousand," Arlissa explained. Her hands, seeking the comfort of the lab coat that still hung on a hook by the door, brushed against the front panel of her skirt. She turned and quickly pulled the white coat over her. The stroke of the heavy cotton against her already hardened nipples elicited an agonized gasp of pleasure from her. "That *would* have been idiotic," she finished, and slipped her hands into the lab coat's pockets.

"He's my toy, too, Lissa." Cayce swung his legs over the edge of the gurney and sat up. He looked down at the buttons, saw that she had mismatched them, and slowly undid them. He stepped onto the floor, his toes pointing toward the ceiling as the bare soles touched the cool tile. "If I want to bring marketing in to play with him, I can."

"It's not a toy," Arlissa snapped, and tried to keep her eyes on his face.

"If he isn't a toy," Cayce teased, "then how do you explain your attachment to him." Yesterday's edge was back to Cayce's otherwise smooth voice. He took a step toward her and then another until less than a foot of air separated them. "Dautrich says you're too fond of your toys, Lissa. Is that true?"

About the author:

Ann Vremont is a mother, wife, licensed attorney, technical writer, high school dropout and former Russian linguist for Army SigInt. She's called Bingo for a living, waitressed at a strip club, scooped ice cream and conducted political surveys—including for the wrong party. She maintains that, if she hadn't dropped out of high school, she would probably be a mineralogist or a geophysicist—lifelong interests reflected in her first book with Ellora's Cave, *Calabi Chronicles: Bloodstone*. Ann further maintains that if she had never met her husband of fifteen-plus years or had their son when she did, she would probably be making her living illegally—or, if unsuccessful, sitting in jail. She has a large collection of minerals and a growing collection of lighthouses. Having been born and partially raised in Arizona, the mineral collection doesn't surprise her, but she's still puzzling the source of her lighthouse fetish.

Ann welcomes mail from readers. You can write to her c/o Ellora's Cave Publishing at 1337 Commerce Drive, Suite 13, Stow OH 44224.

Why an electronic book?

We live in the Information Age—an exciting time in the history of human civilization in which technology rules supreme and continues to progress in leaps and bounds every minute of every hour of every day. For a multitude of reasons, more and more avid literary fans are opting to purchase e-books instead of paperbacks. The question to those not yet initiated to the world of electronic reading is simply: *why?*

1. *Price.* An electronic title at Ellora's Cave Publishing runs anywhere from 40-75% less than the cover price of the <u>exact same title</u> in paperback format. Why? Cold mathematics. It is less expensive to publish an e-book than it is to publish a paperback, so the savings are passed along to the consumer.

2. *Space.* Running out of room to house your paperback books? That is one worry you will never have with electronic novels. For a low one-time cost, you can purchase a handheld computer designed specifically for e-reading purposes. Many e-readers are larger than the average handheld, giving you plenty of screen room. Better yet, hundreds of titles can be stored within your new library—a single microchip. (Please note that Ellora's Cave does not endorse any specific brands. You can check our website at www.ellorascave.com for customer recommendations we make available to new consumers.)

3. *Mobility.* Because your new library now consists of only a microchip, your entire cache of books can be taken with you wherever you go.

4. *Personal preferences are accounted for.* Are the words you are currently reading too small? Too large? Too...**ANNOYING**? Paperback books cannot be modified according to personal preferences, but e-books can.

5. *Innovation.* The way you read a book is not the only advancement the Information Age has gifted the literary community with. There is also the factor of what you can read. Ellora's Cave Publishing will be introducing a new line of interactive titles that are available in e-book format only.

6. *Instant gratification.* Is it the middle of the night and all the bookstores are closed? Are you tired of waiting days—sometimes weeks—for online and offline bookstores to ship the novels you bought? Ellora's Cave Publishing sells instantaneous downloads 24 hours a day, 7 days a week, 365 days a year. Our e-book delivery system is 100% automated, meaning your order is filled as soon as you pay for it.

Those are a few of the top reasons why electronic novels are displacing paperbacks for many an avid reader. As always, Ellora's Cave Publishing welcomes your questions and comments. We invite you to email us at service@ellorascave.com or write to us directly at: 1337 Commerce Drive, Suite 13, Stow OH 44224.

Discover for yourself why readers can't get enough of the multiple award-winning publisher Ellora's Cave. Whether you prefer e-books or paperbacks, be sure to visit EC on the web at www.ellorascave.com for an erotic reading experience that will leave you breathless.

WWW.ELLORASCAVE.COM

Printed in the United States
28180LVS00010B/7-36